THE HOUSE ON THE CLIFF

Actor Gwydion Morgan's dramatic appearance at Jessica Mayhew's psychotherapy practice coincides with a turbulent time in her own life. Gwydion, son of the famous Evan Morgan, is good-looking and talented but mentally fragile, tormented by an intriguing phobia. Jessica is determined to trace the cause of his distress. So when his mother phones to say he is suicidal, Jessica decides to make a house call. In her quest to help her client, Jessica finds herself becoming embroiled in the Morgans' poisonous family dynamic and then there is also the growing attraction of her new client...

THE HOUSE ON THE CLIFF

THE HOUSE ON THE CLIFF

by

Charlotte Williams

Magna Large Print Books
Long Preston, North Yorkshire,
BD23 4ND, England.

British Library Cataloguing in Publication Data.

Williams, Charlotte
    The house on the cliff.

    A catalogue record of this book is
    available from the British Library

    ISBN 978-0-7505-3932-6

First published in Great Britain 2013 by Macmillan

Copyright © Charlotte Williams 2013

Cover illustration © Robert Jones by arrangement with
Arcangel Images

Published in Large Print 2014 by arrangement with
Pan Macmillan Publishers Ltd.

Magna Large Print is an imprint of Library Magna Books Ltd.

Printed and bound in Great Britain by
T.J. (International) Ltd., Cornwall, PL28 8RW

For Henry and Natàlia

ACKNOWLEDGEMENTS

Many people have helped guide this book through to publication. Special thanks go to Helen Williams, who offered advice from the start; to Margaret Halton, who helped knock the manuscript into shape; to Peter Straus for finding it a home; and to Trisha Jackson for her sound and sympathetic editorial judgement.

Thanks to Natasha Harding and all at Pan Macmillan for their work on the book.

Thanks also to Izabela Jurewicz for her advice on technical aspects of the text, and to Carol Jones and David Rees for reading early versions of it.

I am grateful to my mother Susan for many helpful discussions about the book; and to John for his continued support in every way.

I would like to acknowledge the award of a writer's bursary from Literature Wales for the purpose of writing this book.

PROLOGUE

You used to watch her, didn't you? Watch her like a hawk, her every move. Well, people did, of course. She was a pretty little thing. Pink cheeks and a sky-blue sweater, fair curls, short shorts, and those long, tanned legs with the square, bony knees, like a child's. Those thighs with not a dimple on them, and the soft, silky peach fuzz of hair along the inside of her shin. Only just out of childhood she was – you could see it in the way she couldn't keep still, watching TV, reading, sitting there on the sofa, her legs all gangly, wriggling about, twiddling her hair, and then noticing that you were looking and straightening up, putting her feet back on the floor, folding her arms across her chest, hiding her breasts, self-conscious all of a sudden.

And the way she laughed, like a peal of bells – bells you only hear in fairy stories, tinker bells, snow bells, jingling on a sleigh... Oh, what fun it is to ride... It was good to hear that in the house, cutting through the gloom, slicing it as if it were jelly, clouded aspic, with all of us inside it. Calling us, she was, reminding us how happy we could be, too, could have been, might still be, if only...

She was always on the point of laughing, you could see, her words wobbling on the edge of it, slipping out on her pink tongue like a kitten's, her breath sweet and warm as a saucer of milk. They don't do that when they grow up, do they, girls – answer every ques-

15

tion with a wriggle and a giggle. A blessing, in a way, that she stayed like that forever, high and happy, happy and high, and half dizzy on the edge of her life, looking down at the water, plucking up the courage to dive in. That she never woke up tired, with no one beside her, and lay alone, her limbs slack, with a pain in her gut, an empty, sour, missing pain, looking out through the rain on the window at the trees outside, branches hunched and hunkered up against a winter sky, and wondered how so many years could have gone by just like that, crept up on you so quick, so cunning, each one a player in a long summer evening shadows lengthening game of statues, tiptoeing up close every time you looked back, close, close, and closer, until at last one of them stepped forward, and tapped you on the shoulder...

Oh, come on now, stop that. You're not going to croak yet. Don't get maudlin. The past is the past. It stays where you left it, far behind. You turn a corner one day, and you can't see it any more. It's gone. There's nothing left of it, nothing. No one else knows, do they? It was only you and her, so now, if you choose not to remember ... well, then, that's the end of it. God's left the quad, and he's not coming back.

Of course, she only had herself to blame. She knew perfectly well what she was up to. You told her she'd no right to mess around with people like that. Flaunt herself, take whatever she wanted, whenever she wanted. It just wasn't fair. You only did what you had to do. Put a stop to it, there and then.

And you didn't feel sorry afterwards, and you don't now, you still don't, you won't ever, because, at the end of the day, she bloody well deserved it. Sitting there twiddling and wriggling and giggling, as if

16

butter wouldn't melt.

Silly little bitch. It was her own fault. Her own stupid fault. Not mine...

1

It was a sunny Monday in September. The day started out like any other: Bob away on business, Nella and Rose quarrelling over breakfast, both silent in the car as I drove them to school. I dropped them off at the gates and watched them walk down the road, keeping a firm distance from each other, Rose neat in her navy anorak, hair tied back, Nella shambling along in her ripped jeans, nodding her head to her iPod. I wondered whether Rose was slightly too well turned out perhaps, a little too eager to please. And Nella the other extreme, rather too scruffy, too insouciant. I sighed involuntarily as I watched them go.

I hope they're all right, I thought, as they disappeared around the corner out of sight, one after the other. I felt that familiar tug of love, or fear, or whatever it is, that always hits me when my children walk away from me, out into the world; and then I leaned forward, switched on the radio, and headed off to work.

There was a traffic jam all the way along Cathedral Road, and while I was waiting I tilted the rear-view mirror towards me, examining my appearance. I hadn't slept well the night before, and there were bags under my eyes to prove it. I

17

took a lipstick out of my pocket and rubbed some of it onto my cheeks. I hoped it would distract attention from the bags. It did, but not in a good way. I was wondering whether to wipe it off again when the driver in the car behind began to bang on his horn, so I tilted the mirror back up and put my foot on the accelerator, resisting the temptation to flick him a V-sign as I went.

On the way in to the office I bought myself a takeaway cup of coffee from the local deli. I parked the car at the back of the building where I work, and went round to the front door. I stopped on the way up to my office to say hello to Branwen, the receptionist, and we had a detailed discussion about the possibility of rain that day. Then I climbed the stairs to the second floor, unlocked the door and let myself in.

As ever, the room was calm, pale, welcoming. The sun was filtering through the leaves of the trees outside the window, casting a shifting play of shadows over the ceiling, and there was a gentle hum of traffic from the street below. Everything in the room was in perfect order, my books lined up straight on the shelves, my Ben Nicholson-style relief resting serenely on the wall opposite. The two armchairs in the corner were positioned exactly right – not too close for comfort, not too far for intimate revelations – and the couch by the window, with its muted green upholstery, looked inviting, rather than intimidating.

I went over to my desk, switched on my computer and, while it buzzed and flickered, began to look through my post. There was nothing much of interest among the bills and junk mail, just a

18

couple of invitations to conferences that I was unlikely to go to, one in Leipzig and one in Stockholm. At the bottom of the pile I came to a small brown envelope with my name and address written out on it in neat capitals. I opened it, wondering what it could be. There was no letter inside, just a photograph of a middle-aged man. He had a sinister appearance and, when I looked closer, I saw why: his eyes had been coloured in with a marker pen, so that they were black.

I was puzzled. The photograph had been taken outdoors, perhaps by the sea – somewhere windy, anyway. The man was handsome, in a patrician sort of way, with a full head of greying hair, a bony, aquiline nose, and the kind of wrinkles that make a face look distinctive, lived in, rather than ground down and defeated. He was dressed in a leather jacket, the collar turned up rather raffishly against the wind. The ghost of a smile played around his lips. He wore the expression of a man who was pleased with himself and his place in the world, perhaps even a little disdainful of the onlooker. Even the blacked-out eyes failed to dispel his air of self-confidence.

I checked the envelope again to see if there was a letter inside, but it was empty. I turned it over and studied the postmark. It had been posted locally the day before. I wondered who on earth could have sent it, and why. I was curious, but not alarmed. Getting odd missives through the post is an occupational hazard in my job. Ex-clients, or members of their families, occasionally send me rambling, incoherent letters that are either effusive, abusive, or both. I usually glance through

19

them, put them to one side and, after a couple of weeks, send a polite note in response. In this case, as there was no address, it was clear I wouldn't even need to do that.

I slid the photograph back into the envelope, and put it in the 'pending' tray on my desk. I covered it with the letters I needed to keep from the morning's post, and threw the junk mail in the bin. Then I opened my coffee, blew on it, and took a sip.

The phone rang. I didn't pick it up, because I knew who it would be – Bob was away at a conference. The answerphone came on, and I listened.

'Jess, just calling to see how you are.' There was an anxious note in Bob's voice. Good, I thought. Serves him right. Let him suffer.

A month ago, Bob had returned from a business trip and confessed to me that he'd had a one-night stand. He'd said he'd resolved not to tell me, but after he'd got home he'd found he couldn't live with the guilt. He'd begged my forgiveness, explained that he wasn't unhappy with me, but that he'd been feeling frustrated in his career. It had been a pathetic attempt to boost his ego, he'd said. I hadn't been very understanding.

'And the girls,' Bob went on. 'I hope Nella's concert goes all right today. Tell her I'm sorry to miss it.' Pause. 'Give her my love, won't you. Wish her luck.' Another pause.

I'd asked him how old the woman was. About thirty, he'd said, shamefaced. Who was she, I'd wanted to know. Just a local translator, he'd told me. No one of any significance. That had disgusted me. A man of fifty-two, the head of the legal department at the Assembly, sleeping with a woman so much younger than himself, someone he regarded as unimportant. I hadn't enquired further. And I hadn't forgiven him, either.

'Your mobile doesn't seem to be working. Mine's on, if you want to call.' He sighed. 'Anyway, I'll be back later this evening. I'll get a cab from the airport. Be in about nine.' Silence. 'See you then. I'll bring you a surprise.'

I hoped it wouldn't be flowers. Bob knows I love flowers, so he'd been bringing them home, great bunches of them, waiting for me to put them in a vase and, when I didn't, doing it himself. Seeing them there, arranged cack-handedly on the mantelpiece, had made me want to cry. Or scream. I hadn't yet, except to myself. I was determined not to upset the girls. And I wanted to hold on to my marriage ... at least for the time being.

Bob hung up. I leaned forward and switched off the ringer on the phone, so I wouldn't be disturbed again.

I glanced at my watch. There was an hour to go until my first appointment of the day, an assessment of a new client. I decided to spend it doing some research on one of the regulars I had coming in later on, rather than letting my mind dwell on Bob, what he might be getting up to at the conference, and how I was ever going to forgive him for his betrayal.

I was reading a paper on Complicated Grief in the *Journal of Phenomenological Psychotherapy* when there was a knock at the door. I glanced at the clock. My new client had arrived a little ahead of time, but as it was his first visit – for an assessment, rather than a session – I put away my paper, picked up my notes, walked over to the door, and ushered him in.

I noticed immediately he walked into the room that he was a remarkably handsome man, tall and broad-shouldered, with a natural grace in the way he carried himself. I judged him to be in his late twenties, or thereabouts. He was wearing carefully ripped jeans, a black V-neck sweater with nothing on underneath, and a pair of running shoes covered in straps and bits of rubber. His shoulder-length hair was swept back from his face, and he had a day's stubble on his chin.

'Do sit down,' I said, indicating one of the armchairs in the corner of the room.

'Sorry if I'm a bit early.' He spoke in a low, polite tone.

'Not at all.'

He took the chair nearest the window. I sat down opposite him, glancing at my notes.

'Do you mind if I call you Gwydion, Mr Morgan?'

'That's fine.'

'And please call me Jessica.'

He nodded. Up close I could see that his eyes were green, fringed with thick, black lashes. I looked away. It seemed indecent to do anything else.

I waited for him to start talking. The way I was trained, that's what you're supposed to do. Wait for the client to initiate the conversation. You listen attentively, then you 'reflect back' – that is, repeat what they've just said, maybe paraphrasing it a bit.

Only I don't always do what I'm supposed to. Hardly ever, in fact. These days, after all my years of practice, I trust myself to do whatever comes naturally. So, after a short pause, I asked, 'How can I help?'

I was conscious of his eyes on me as I spoke. Normally, I dress quite formally for work, in fitted suits and smart blouses. My taste runs to high-quality vintage and reproduction outfits, which I go to a lot of trouble to track down and customize. But that morning, as it was a warm day, I'd dressed more casually, in a Forties-style printed cotton dress and high espadrilles. Now I began to feel self-conscious about my bare legs, and wished I'd worn something more modest.

'I don't know.' He ran a hand through his hair, in a gesture of frustration. 'It's a bit...' His voice trailed off.

Silence again. This time I didn't say anything. Experience has taught me that when someone comes to a grinding halt, something interesting is about to be said.

'It's odd... I don't know how to...' He blushed.

I wondered if it was going to be premature ejaculation. That's one of the commonest problems I see with men. Especially men under thirty, like this one. So I waited for an opportunity to help him to say it, if that's what it was.

He looked down. The thick, black lashes fluttered against his flushed cheeks. Eventually, he spoke.

'It's to do with buttons,' he said.

'Buttons?' I repeated the word quietly, evenly. Reflecting back, you see. Sometimes, of course, it's best to follow the correct procedure.

'Yes, buttons.'

I glanced down to see if there was a rivet on his jeans. If there was, it was hidden by his belt.

'Any particular type?'

He looked up at me, relieved that I hadn't laughed at him.

'The plastic ones are worst. The ones with four little holes. But I don't like any of them, actually.'

There was a pause.

'Well.' I gave him what I hoped was a reassuring smile. 'That's not as unusual as you might think. It's a well-known syndrome. It's got a name. Koumpounophobia.'

'Really?' He looked relieved. 'Koumpou... What was that?'

'Koumpounophobia. They made up the word for people who are so button phobic they can't say the word "button".'

'I see.' He smiled at me a little warily. 'Well, I'm not that bad. I can talk about buttons. I can't wear them, but I can cope with seeing them. From a distance. I won't touch them, though. And if they come loose. Or fall off...' He shuddered.

I'd come across cases of koumpounophobia before. They were difficult to resolve. Sometimes, if I couldn't get anywhere, I sent them over to Dougie, the cognitive behavioural therapist on the other side of the corridor. Meinir, the hypnotherapist on the floor above, was also pretty good on this kind of thing.

Gwydion sighed and passed a hand over his forehead. His glossy hair flopped forward over his face.

'It gets worse when I'm stressed.'

'That's very common, too.'

At this, he looked a little put out. People are funny like that, I've noticed. At first, they're pleased to find that they have a syndrome with an important-sounding name. Then they start to get worried that their complaint might not be exclusive enough.

'Actually, I am under rather a lot of strain at the moment,' he said. 'I'm working very long hours, finishing a series.' He stopped and gave me a searching look. 'A TV series.' He stopped again. 'I'm Danny in *Down in the Valley*. You've probably seen it.'

'Ah.' I nodded in a non-committal way.

Down in the Valley is a long-running Welsh TV soap. The girls watch it religiously. But I'd never sat through an episode all the way through, and I'd certainly never seen Danny appear onscreen. If I had, I would have remembered him.

He began to tell me about himself. As well as being Danny in *Down in the Valley*, he'd also starred in a film called *The War of the Dragon Kings* and had played several other screen roles, which, he said, I should look up on an Internet site called Curtain Call Casting. He was currently on the verge of a breakthrough in his career, having been offered a starring role in a major new period drama, an adaptation of the novel *Helen* by Maria Edgeworth, a contemporary of Jane Austen. He was very excited about it and was preparing to start rehearsals in three months' time. He'd come to me for help because he was worried that he wouldn't be able to cope with his costume – the buttons on the waistcoat, the jacket, and so on. His manner, as he spoke, was intense; he was articulate and sensitive, evidently deeply committed to his work. Despite – or because of – his reserve, he had a strong presence, and I could well imagine that he was a gifted actor. I could also see that he was very troubled by his phobia, afraid that he might let this longed-for opportunity slip through his hands.

When he'd finished I asked, 'I wonder, are there any other difficulties in your life at present?'

'How d'you mean?'

'Anything else worrying you?'

'Such as?'

'Well, relationships, for instance.'

'I don't have a girlfriend, if that's what you mean. I mean, there have been ... there are ... from time to time...' He looked away. I was surprised at his diffidence, given that he was such a good-looking man. 'But nothing serious. At the moment, anyway.'

'And your family?'

'I'm an only child. I have a very close relationship with my mother. My father...' He came to a halt.

'I don't get on with my father, as it happens,' he continued, after a short pause. 'He's a bit of an egomaniac.' He hesitated. 'But to be honest, I don't really want to go into all that. I just want to get this button phobia sorted, and get on with my life.'

I nodded. 'Well, I can see why, with this big part coming up. But I'm afraid if you're in a hurry, I'm not going to be much help to you. I'm a psychotherapist. What I do takes a long time and a lot of effort. And it doesn't always work.'

He looked surprised.

'You see, if you came to me, we would definitely need to look into your family relationships, especially those you find difficult.'

A flash of irritation crossed his face, but I continued.

'So if you want to deal with this quickly, you'd be better off seeing my colleague over the way. He has an altogether different approach. He'll help you identify your negative thought patterns, your specific fears, and so on, and take you through a set of exercises to try to change them. He may use a technique called exposure. First, you'll talk about buttons, then you'll see pictures of them, then you'll be asked to hold one, and so on, until you get over your phobia.' I paused. 'Is that the kind of thing you're after?'

He looked doubtful.

'It's actually very effective,' I said. 'And I can highly recommend this particular colleague.'

'The thing is...' He looked away, avoiding my gaze. 'It's not just the buttons.'

He seemed shy all of a sudden, embarrassed. The idea that he might have a sexual hang-up came back to me, but I put it to one side. Bracket your own thoughts, that's what you have to do when you're listening to someone. Put them in parentheses, and return to them later. It's a good rule, and one I try to stick to.

'It's hard for me to talk about it.' His voice dropped to a whisper.

I wondered what was wrong. In my view,

phobias about things like buttons and spiders are fairly easy to understand, though not to cure. They're the safe, convenient places we choose to store all our anxieties about the big things we can't control, starting with the fact that we're born, we die, and we don't know why. Getting scared of buttons is easier than getting scared of that. Until it gets harder, of course.

Eventually he raised his eyes and looked straight into mine. 'I'd need to know you better before I could...'

I tried to listen, but I began to feel like a startled rabbit trapped in the headlights of a car.

'I'm hoping to find someone...'

A car with very big headlights on a very dark, rainy night.

'...someone I can trust.'

I felt a sudden flush of heat rising up from my chest. I looked away, hoping it wouldn't spread to my face.

Counter-transference, I told myself. When you get emotionally entangled with your client, start to believe that you love or hate them with a passion. Just displaced emotion from other relationships in your life. It had cropped up rather quicker than usual in this case, even before the transference. (That's when the client starts to think they love or hate you with a passion.) But I wasn't too worried. I was pretty sure I could handle it. The situation, if kept well under control, could even prove enlightening, for both of us. As I said, I've learned to trust myself over the years.

Gwydion blinked, and I blinked, and the moment passed.

I glanced at the relief on the opposite wall. It was white, and calm, and serene. The circle seemed to sit naturally among the squares, quietly confident that it was in its rightful place.

'Well, Gwydion,' I said. I looked back at him and smiled my kindest, most sensible smile. 'I consider myself quite trustworthy. If you decide you want to come and see me, I'll do my best to help.'

2

I saw another four clients after Gwydion Morgan, all regulars, all spinning stories that still managed to fascinate and move me, whether the stories themselves or the spinning of them; and then I drove over to Nella's school. She was due to be singing at a concert that afternoon. She'd only recently taken it up – all the girls did it for music GCSE, she said, it was an easier option than learning an instrument – but so far I'd never heard her utter a note. On the rare occasions when she practised, she shut her bedroom door firmly, turned up the volume on her stereo, and forbade me to enter until she'd finished. And she hadn't wanted me to come to the concert, but I'd insisted on being there.

I was running late, so I drove over to the school a little faster than I should have done, swung the car into the forecourt and parked hurriedly. Then I ran over to the main hall, joining the last of the parents as they were filing in. I found a seat, nodding politely at the people I knew, and looked over at Nella. She was standing to one side of the stage with her classmates. When she caught sight of me, I waved discreetly, but she didn't wave back. Instead, she turned away and began to talk to her friends.

The teacher went over to the door, shut it, and the chatter in the room quietened down. Then he went up onto the stage and introduced himself, thanking us for attending. He seemed rather too grateful for our presence, which didn't bode well.

The first performers were two painfully shy boys with electric guitars, one of them chugging out a dull blues riff while the other improvised haphazardly over the top. While they were playing, my mind wandered back to the photograph I'd received that morning. Probably just a disgruntled client, I told myself, but all the same, it was odd. I'd have to try and find out who the man in the photo was; perhaps that would tell me who'd sent it...

Next up was a plump, ungainly girl with glasses, who sawed her way through a piece on the cello. She had the air of a young woman who hadn't got a lot going for her in life but was determined all the same to beat Bach's flibbertigibbet arpeggios into submission, and get herself an A-grade in the process. By the end of the piece, although it was excruciating to listen to, I felt like standing up and cheering.

Looking somewhat weary, the teacher came back onstage, sat down at the piano and announced that the singers would now perform. As Nella had predicted, they were all girls, like her.

Not a boy to be seen among them.

The first was a pretty fifteen-year-old with carefully streaked and blow-dried hair, whose mannered rendition of 'My Heart Will Go On' was note-perfect. Despite the song's nonsensical lyrics – not her fault, of course – and her absurdly dramatic gestures, her performance was greeted with wild applause. Afterwards, Nella shuffled out onto the stage, head bent, hair covering her face, hands stuffed into the pockets of her jeans.

I held my breath and my heart began to beat. I tried not to sit on the edge of my seat. As the teacher played the opening notes to the song, I willed her to look up at the audience, but she continued to gaze stubbornly down at the floor.

She began to sing. Her voice was a whisper, almost inaudible. I felt irritated, frustrated. What was the matter with my daughter? Why wasn't she confident, sure of herself, like the girl with the streaked hair? She was just as pretty, probably just as good a singer. If only she'd…

Then she raised her head. This time, her voice came out loud and clear. I swallowed. Tears came to my eyes. She had a beautiful voice, and this was the first time I'd ever heard it. For an instant, as she sang, she looked my way. She must have seen the emotion on my face, and it must have encouraged her, because, as she came to the final verse, she seemed to let go of her inhibitions and forget where she was.

When she finished the song she glanced up at me triumphantly, as the audience began to clap. I clapped along with them, as hard as I could. Somebody gave a cheer as she left the stage, and

I saw her laugh as her friends clustered around her, congratulating her.

The next pupil came on, a tall girl with a clarinet. I listened politely as she started her piece, but by now I'd had enough. As the notes cascaded out, the odd squawk and hoot escaping from the instrument, a feeling of intense heat came over me and I passed my hand over my forehead, closing my eyes for a moment. As I did, I saw Gwydion Morgan's thick, black eyelashes fluttering against his flushed cheeks.

The heat subsided, and I opened my eyes. Don't panic, I told myself. It's just hormones. And the shock of hearing Nella sing, so beautifully, so unexpectedly.

The clarinet let out a high-pitched squeak, and a ripple of laughter went through the audience. The girl began to giggle, stopping for a moment to fiddle with the neck of the instrument while the teacher waited patiently at the piano. The audience shifted on their seats, and a few of the parents got up quietly and left, having seen their children perform. I took the opportunity to slip out of the hall with them, giving Nella a quick wave as I went. I knew that if I went over and congratulated her, she'd feel embarrassed. She looked away, but I noticed her trying to suppress a smile.

Outside in the car park I walked quickly over to my car, unlocked the door, and was just about to get in when I heard someone behind me, calling my name. I turned to see a man in his thirties wearing a loose checked shirt and jeans. He was carrying a guitar case. For a moment, I didn't recognize him, and then, as he came up closer, I remembered him as a former client of mine.

'Emyr,' I said. 'Hi.' I paused for a moment. 'What are you doing here?'

I'm often buttonholed by ex-clients as I go about my daily business – Cardiff's a small place, after all – and usually I'm pleased to see them. But Emyr's slightly over-familiar manner had always made me feel a little uncomfortable.

'Same as you. Watching the show.'

He smiled and came up closer. He had a wide smile – rows of straight, white teeth – and light brown freckles on his face. He stood a head taller than me, and his hair was that golden auburn colour that you often see in Wales, despite the fact that the Welsh are always thought of as dark and short.

'Just like to see what the youngsters are up to,' he went on. 'Keeping my ear to the ground.'

'Youngsters.' Maybe that was the problem. Emyr had a penchant for teacherish words like 'youngsters'. He'd come to see me a couple of years before with low-level depression after losing his job, but as he'd simply wanted to fulminate about the injustice of the situation, rather than explore his reaction to it, there hadn't been much I could do for him, so he'd left after a few sessions.

'I saw your daughter sing,' he went on. 'She's a talented lass, isn't she?'

'Thank you. Yes, she is.' I was about to tell him that before today I'd had no idea that Nella could sing a note, but for some reason I thought better of it.

'So what are you doing these days?' I asked instead.

'I'm an A&R man. In a manner of speaking.' He gave a wry grin. 'I'm setting up a new community music project. Council grant. We're looking for youngsters who might like to use our studio. Twenty-four track, state of the art. Completely free of charge.' He fished in the pocket of his jeans, produced a slightly battered card, and handed it to me.

I glanced down at the card. It was garishly coloured and bore the legend 'Safe Trax' in a rather dated graffiti-style script that Nella, I felt sure, would dismiss as 'lame'. Underneath were his name and a contact number.

'Thanks.' I put the card in my bag. 'Well, good to see you again.'

'And you. Take care.'

I got into the car, nodded at him through the window, and moved off. As I drove through the gates I saw him turn to watch me, and then walk slowly back towards the school.

That evening, as a treat for Nella, I made the children's favourite supper: hamburgers and chips. We ate it sitting in front of the television. The hamburgers were actually venison – less saturated fat – but I'd never told them that; the buns were wholemeal; and I'd made the chips myself, in the hope that they'd be slightly healthier than the bought variety. I also put a small salad of lettuce, tomato and watercress on each of their plates, though I knew Rose wouldn't eat any of hers. But even if she didn't, at least I could console myself that I'd done my best. As Merle Haggard, Bob's favourite country singer, put it – Mama Tried.

After we'd finished supper and cleared away, Rose went into the kitchen to practise her clarinet, while Nella went upstairs to do her homework. After a few minutes, I knew, loud music would begin to emanate from her room, interspersed with quiet spells, when she'd be on her mobile. I'd recently decided not to intervene any more – after all, she was sixteen now – so, instead, I went into Bob's study and switched on the computer. Then I walked over to the door, shut it firmly, and returned.

I typed a name into the search engine: Curtain Call Casting. I hesitated for a split second, wondering whether I should really be doing as my new client had asked, and then clicked onto the site. I scrolled down a list, found his name, and then clicked onto his page.

At the top of the page was a publicity shot. The lighting was dark and moody, and Gwydion was standing face-on to the camera, wearing a tight white T-shirt and black joggers, worn low on the hips so as to reveal not only the waistband of his designer boxer shorts, but also a glimpse of muscular stomach beneath. His hair was tousled and his eyes were half closed, as if he'd just got out of bed.

Beside the shot was a column headed 'Quick details'. I glanced down at it and read off his vital statistics, or whatever they're called if you're a male actor. Playing age: 25. Height: 6 feet 1 inch. Weight: 12 stone 9 pounds. Hair colour: brown. Eye colour: hazel – no, they weren't, they were green. Build: medium. And that was it.

Underneath the publicity shot was a list of his acting roles. Apart from his role in *The War of the Dragon Kings*, and two cameos in films I'd never heard of, most of his appearances to date seemed to be in obscure Welsh television shows, including the redoubtable *Down in the Valley*. There were also credits for radio and TV commercials. I scrolled down further. As yet, there seemed to be no mention of the forthcoming part in the period drama.

Music began to thump from Nella's room upstairs. I decided to ignore it.

Underneath the vital-statistics column was a link to another site, so I clicked on it. It turned out to be a movie database, giving more details on *The War of the Dragon Kings*, along with another shot of Gwydion, this time dressed in little more than a loincloth. The film was a remake of one of the stories from the Mabinogion and, judging by the paucity of reviews, not a particularly successful one. I scrolled down to a message board at the bottom of the page, to look at the recent posts discussing his role in the film. Sadly, there was no mention of his acting skills. Instead, the first message, from a person called shelleewellee, posed the question, 'Isn't Gwydion a total dish', to which there was resounding affirmation from all and sundry, in no uncertain terms. The only comment that could possibly have been construed as an endorsement of his acting was from someone called gigigirl: 'that guy is well fit, what a grate film, the end was so sad I was reeching for a box of tishoes...'

The music from upstairs got louder. I wondered whether I should go upstairs and intervene after all. But once again I decided not to. It was time Nella learned to do her homework without my supervision, and suffer the consequences at school if she couldn't discipline herself. Besides, I had work of my own to do.

I began to feel a bit of a fool for having joined, however briefly, the cyber-community of Gwydion's half-witted schoolgirl (and boy) admirers, but instead of closing the page, I found myself scrolling up to a heading marked 'Trivia', which told me: 'Trained at the Royal Academy of Dramatic Art (RADA)'. At the end of this piece of information was a link marked 'MORE'.

I was about to click on the link when I stopped myself. Although Gwydion had given me permission to google him – in fact almost implied that it was my duty as his new therapist to do so – I felt I'd found out quite enough for the time being. He would need to tell me his own story in his own time, in his own words, and it wasn't fair to him to jump the gun like this. Or to me, come to that. It would be easier for me to help him, much easier, if I didn't arm myself with too many preconceptions about him.

Just then the door opened and Bob came in. He's a big, well-built man, and he's always a presence, a strong presence, when he enters a room. He still had his coat on, a proper tailored black topcoat, and there were drops of rain sparkling on the shoulders. His curly hair was slightly dishevelled, his specs pushed up into it, and there was an enthusiastic, boyish smile on his face. Whenever he came home he brought with him a scent of cold, fresh air, of unknown, far-off cities, of an exciting, eventful life lived outside the confines of our domestic world that made my heart jump. Not this time, though.

He was carrying a black paper bag with silver edging.

He walked over to the desk where I was sitting. 'Here,' he said.

I took the bag and peered at the contents. Inside, nestling in a cocoon of white tissue paper, was a potted gardenia.

'Thanks,' I said. I could smell the scent from the waxy flowers, but I didn't put my head down to sniff it, as I normally would have done. Instead, I put the bag down on the floor beside my feet.

'You're back then,' I said.

When he heard the flat tone in my voice, his face fell.

'Yes. No delays, for once.'

To cover his disappointment he gazed absent-mindedly over my shoulder at the computer screen. I followed his gaze, wondering how I was going to explain what I was doing. But when I looked back at the screen, I saw that Gwydion's website page had vanished. There was nothing to see except the screensaver, a holiday snap of the family in wetsuits, standing in descending order of height like a ridiculous row of penguins, somewhere on a windy beach in west Wales.

3

Jean, my first client of the day, was being boring. Very boring. It was a trick she pulled from time to time, especially when we'd been getting somewhere in the previous session. She would arrive and, after the most cursory greeting, begin to discuss some minor domestic problem in detail: a blocked drain, a bath plug that didn't fit, an odd noise coming out of the Hoover. Today, it was a faulty curtain rail.

'You see, you can't just mend the broken bit.' She sighed in exasperation. 'You'd have to find someone to make a completely new one. It'd cost a fortune...'

I nodded, but not, I hoped, in an encouraging way. I'd had enough of the curtain rail. We'd spent the best part of the session on it.

'And then there's the fitting, of course...'

I thought back to the paper I'd read on Complicated Grief. Complicated Grief is when, after more than a year, a person continues to behave as if their loss had only just occurred. I'd been reading it in the hope that I could somehow help Jean move on, but it didn't seem to be much use.

'I've no idea where I'll be able to find a man to fit it...'

My thoughts began to wander. A picture of Gwydion drifted into my mind. He was sitting on a horse, dressed in nothing but a skimpy loincloth, with a quiver of arrows strapped to his back. He was gazing into the distance, his tanned body slick with sweat. There was a smear of earth across his shoulder, as if he'd recently been tumbling in the dirt...

'I've looked in the Yellow Pages, but...'

He turned his head, his green eyes narrowing when he saw me...

'I can't find the right sort of person. Should it be a draper? A carpenter?...'

He pulled the horse round, and slowly rode towards me. I watched his muscles move under his skin as he came closer, until, finally, he bent down, reached out his hand, and...

'You're not listening, are you?'

Jean stopped talking.

It took me a moment to realize I'd been miles away.

'Of course I am.'

I was appalled at myself. What on earth was the matter with me, daydreaming – well, no, fantasizing – in the middle of a session? Obviously, Bob's fling had disturbed me at a deeper level than I'd hitherto been conscious of. I'd really have to stop this nonsense and get a grip, I told myself, especially as Gwydion – the real Gwydion, that is – had decided to start therapy with me, and was going to be coming in directly after Jean's session.

Jean sniffed. 'I suppose I must be very boring.'

There was a silence.

'No.' I chose my words with care. 'But perhaps it would help if you could talk more directly about your feelings.'

'That's what I've been trying to do.' She spoke

40

with real anger in her voice.

Jean had a point. If I'd been concentrating I'd have realized she was expressing her difficulty in remaking her life after her husband's death ('you can't just mend the broken bit'); her anger at her straitened economic circumstances ('it'll cost a fortune'); her fear that she would never find a new partner ('a man to fit'); and, underlying it all, her despair at being suddenly widowed at the age of sixty-five. It was my job to crack her codes, help move her on to the real issue at hand, and I hadn't been doing it.

She was in a huff now. She began to pick at the bobbled fabric of her zip-up top. It was navy-blue polyester, and she was wearing matching navy-blue trousers. The type they call 'slacks' in those catalogues full of smiling, healthy-looking elderly people with dull clothes on. Except that Jean wasn't smiling or healthy-looking. Her skin was blotchy and lined, and her hair was dirty, thin, and badly dyed.

'Well, as it happens, I'm really upset today. Not that you'd care...'

My ears pricked up. Now we were getting somewhere.

'Upset?'

'Yes. And tired. I couldn't sleep last night.'

'Couldn't sleep?'

'Do stop repeating everything I say,' she snapped. There was a pause. 'The thing was, I dreamed I saw Derek.'

This time I kept quiet. Derek was her late husband.

'He looked awful,' she went on. Her voice

41

began to tremble. 'So thin. Like he was when...' She broke off and began to sob.

There was a box of tissues on the coffee table between us. I leaned forward and pushed it in her direction. She took a tissue, wiped her eyes, and went on.

'He was begging me not to forget him.'

I glanced at the clock. Sure enough, our fifty minutes were up. In fact, we were slightly over time.

Damn, I thought. She's done it again. Jean had a habit of bringing up important material just as the session was coming to a close. Although the clock was in full view, she seemed entirely unaware of her pattern of behaviour.

I waited as she blew her nose, tucked the tissue into her sleeve, and settled back into her chair. She was about to continue when I interrupted her.

'I'm sorry, Jean.' I spoke softly. I tried to make my voice as kind and sympathetic as I could. 'We'll have to stop there for today, I'm afraid. Our time is up.'

I'd hoped to take a break before my new client, Gwydion Morgan, arrived. I like to have a few minutes to myself between sessions to jot down notes, check my messages, go over my schedule, nip to the loo, perhaps make myself a cup of tea if I get time. Eat a cachou. Smoke a cheroot. Drink a highball. Well, no, of course I don't smoke cheroots and drink highballs, in fact, I'm not altogether sure what a highball is, but, metaphorically speaking, that's what I like to do between sessions. Sit and stare into space and ponder for a while. Watch the shadows of the trees play on the ceiling. But on this occasion, I didn't get the chance. Because by the time Jean had composed herself and I'd escorted her out, Gwydion was sitting outside in the waiting room. She was late, and he was early.

It was the kind of situation I prefer to avoid. I don't like my clients meeting each other. They get jealous, and nosy, and start asking questions. The idea that I have other people to attend to never seems to occur to them until they actually bump into one another and have to face that reality. And when they do, they tend to take it out on me, one way or another. Of course it's all grist to the therapeutic mill, and shows me how clients deal with competition – sibling rivalry and all that – but, on balance, it gets in the way, and always makes me feel a little uncomfortable.

When Jean saw Gwydion she turned to me with a hurt, accusing look, before saying goodbye in a somewhat huffy manner; while Gwydion, for his part, gave me a sympathetic grin, as though to commiserate with me for having to deal with such a dreary-looking woman. To mollify Jean some-what, and put Gwydion in his place, I touched Jean's shoulder solicitously as I said goodbye to her, then glanced at Gwydion and politely asked if he would mind waiting until the time scheduled for his appointment before coming in.

Back in my consulting room, I picked up my bag, scrabbled through the contents, and brought out a lipsalve and a hairbrush. I couldn't find my powder compact, so I applied both without using a mirror. Then I walked over to my chair, sat

43

down, and looked up at the white-on-white relief on the wall, determined to meet him with the composure he would expect from me.

The circle was sitting, as ever, in its rightful place among the squares. But as I gazed at it, I began to notice that it was throbbing very slightly. The movement was almost imperceptible, but it was there. I'd never seen it before. The circle had always rested quietly in the middle, its serene stillness emanating into the squares around it. I told myself it was merely a trick of the light, but even so, it unnerved me. And then I began to feel an intense heat rising up from my chest into my neck, onto my face and along my arms.

Just then there was a knock at the door.

'Come in.'

The door opened and Gwydion walked in. This time he was wearing jeans and a leather jacket. Underneath it, I noticed, was a white T-shirt like the one I'd seen him wear for his publicity shot.

I gestured towards the empty chair opposite me. 'Do take a seat.'

He walked over to the chair and sat down. As he did, I couldn't help but see the curve of his chest underneath the jacket, outlined by the T-shirt. I looked away.

'Thank you.' He settled himself in the chair. There was a pause, and then he said, 'I'm not sure where to start.'

'Wherever you like.' I tried to keep my tone neutral.

He didn't reply. Instead, he looked at me search-ingly, trying to meet my gaze. I looked back as steadily as I could.

He sighed and ran a hand through his hair. 'Wherever I like...' He knitted his brow. For a moment he seemed to have forgotten me. 'Let's see...'

There was a silence.

'Well, I'll begin with something that's been bothering me. Something apart from the buttons. It's a dream I've been having – sometimes as often as twice a week.'

This was turning out to be a good day for dreams, I thought. And at least this one had been brought up at the beginning of the session, not the end.

'More of a nightmare, really,' he went on. 'I don't know what it relates to, but it scares me.' He stopped speaking, and started to chew his lip.

'Well.' I began to relax. Gwydion seemed to be the kind of client who could get straight to the point, instead of having to be coaxed to focus on the real issues at hand. And now that we were getting down to work, my silly fantasies about him seemed to have receded. 'Maybe you could start by telling me what happens in the dream.'

'Yes, of course.' He sat back in his chair, half closing his eyes and lowering his voice to a whisper. 'I'm a child. I don't know how old.' He paused. 'But I'm small. And the place I'm in is dark. Pitch-black.'

His eyes were completely closed now, and there was an expression of deep concentration on his face. I was surprised at how quickly he'd responded to my suggestion, but I put it down to his training as an actor.

'I'm locked in a box. Someone has shut me in

45

here. I can't see, and I can't breathe. I'm running out of air...'

Although he was deeply serious, and I didn't doubt his sincerity, there was also something a little theatrical in his manner. I couldn't help thinking that he'd begun to sound like someone from a book you'd find in the 'Painful Lives' section of Waterstones – *Daddy, Don't Do That Again*, perhaps. But then I glanced down and saw him scratching at the fabric on his sleeve, picking at it, twisting it in an ungainly fashion, just as Jean had done earlier, and I sensed that this was no performance.

'I want to shout for help,' he went on, 'but I know I mustn't. I have to be quiet. So I begin to count to myself in the dark. One, two, three, four...'

Gwydion came to a stop. He opened his eyes and looked at me. Then he closed them again.

'Five, six, seven ... I keep counting, until I reach ten.' He breathed in sharply. He opened his eyes again. 'And that's when I wake up.'

He passed a hand over his face, resting his palm for a moment over his eyes. Once again it was a slightly melodramatic gesture, but I thought I saw something genuine in it, something that I'd seen before with troubled clients. It's a particular kind of body language that speaks of exhaustion and defeat, of witnessing unresolved conflict on a daily basis. Conflict that you can't control, that makes your life a misery. It's the opposite of trying to create drama out of nothing. It's a kind of resigned stoicism. When you see it in young children it can be heartbreaking.

Gwydion was looking at me expectantly. Having told me his dream, he evidently thought I was about to give him chapter and verse on the meaning of it, like some kind of shaman. I suppose he wasn't far wrong. We psychotherapists are shamans of a sort. After all, Freud's first major work was a book on the interpretation of dreams. And if that's not shamanic, I don't know what is.

'Well, what do *you* make of it, Gwydion?'

Gwydion looked irritated. 'You're supposed to tell me, aren't you?'

'Am I?'

'Well, of course you are.'

I sympathized with his irritation. All this 'reflecting back' can get on your nerves. Parroting people's questions back to them. Repeating their confused, and confusing, statements. But unfortunately it's part and parcel of the way I work. Because I believe my clients know a lot more about themselves than I ever will. So it's not my job to tell them what's lurking in their unconscious. I simply try to make it possible for them to tell me what they know about themselves. And some things that they don't know they know, because they've never tried to explain them to anyone.

'I'd like to hear your own thoughts first.' I paused. 'You say it's a dream you've "been having".'

'Yes. A recurring dream. It gets worse when I'm tense.'

I thought for a moment. 'You say that, in the dream, you want to shout for help, but you feel you mustn't. Why's that, do you think?'

'Well, that's probably to do with my father. I

47

grew up frightened of him. He was a drunk with a filthy temper.' He frowned. 'Everyone knew, of course, but nobody cared. He got away with it, because of his reputation.'

'Reputation?'

'Oh, come on.' Gwydion rolled his eyes. 'Where have you been living? On the planet Mars?'

Perhaps, I thought, I should have followed that 'MORE' link on the movie database after all.

'Sorry, Gwydion, but I don't know who your father is.'

'Evan Morgan. The theatre director. You must have heard of him.'

I nodded. The name was familiar, but not being much of a theatregoer, I didn't know much about him.

'Evan's a great man. Supposedly. But as a father he's always been a complete bastard.' Gwydion spoke without anger. Or a kind of anger that was so old it had lost its fire. 'He's never taken the slightest interest in me. Or my mother. He's always been too busy working. And shagging his secretaries. Personal assistants, he calls them now. The latest one's younger than me.'

I nodded. There was nothing to say in response to this piece of information. A 'how awful' or an 'oh dear' might have been appropriate in a social context, but this was a therapeutic encounter, as it's called in the trade, and such lightweight commiserations were out of place.

Gwydion sighed. 'But I didn't come here to talk about him. Everything always comes back to him. This is about me.'

I nodded again.

'The thing is,' he went on, 'I really want to get to the end of this dream. I keep thinking, if only I didn't wake up before the end, I could find out what happened. And then maybe I could get myself sorted.'

'And what would that mean to you? Getting yourself sorted?'

'Well, being able to get a decent night's sleep, for a start. Being able to concentrate properly in the daytime so I can learn my lines. Not having to worry about whether I'll be able to handle this button business when it comes to dress rehearsal.' He shrugged. 'I'm sick of it. That's why I've come to you.'

I nodded. There was a silence, and then I said, 'There's probably a reason why you do wake up before the end of your dream.'

'And what's that?'

'Well, maybe part of you doesn't want to know what happened.'

He frowned. 'What, you mean because it might be too ... upsetting?'

'Yes. And until that part changes, you won't find out.' I hesitated. 'Because it won't let you.'

He didn't respond. Instead he looked down at the floor, a puzzled expression on his face. Then he leaned back in his chair and looked at me.

'You talk like a psychotherapist,' he said. 'But you don't look like one.'

This was a familiar tactic, changing the subject. But I didn't protest.

'Really?' I smiled, but I began to feel self-conscious again. 'And what does a psychotherapist look like?'

49

'Sort of mumsy, I suppose. Sensible.' He stopped for a moment. I began to wonder whether he was engaging in some kind of flirtation with me. 'Although that dress you're wearing is a bit...'

I was wearing a dove-grey woollen dress with a sweetheart neckline and pearl buttons down the front. I'd chosen it because I thought he might find the buttons a little less threatening than some. They didn't really look like buttons at all, more like ... well, pearls.

'...a bit...'

I didn't take up his cue. Instead, I let him grind to a halt, and then I said, 'Are you OK with these kind of buttons?'

'Yes, fine. Thanks.' He paused. He seemed mildly discomfited by my question. 'You know, I never asked you what your qualifications for this job were.'

'Oh. Well, as a matter of fact, I trained as an existential psychotherapist.'

'What on earth does that mean?'

'It's just a school of therapy. It emphasizes freedom. And choice. Rather than the idea that your life is determined for you by the circumstances of your birth.'

He nodded thoughtfully. 'Well, I agree with that.' He paused. 'Where did you train?'

'In London. At–'

He waved his hand. 'It doesn't matter. It wouldn't mean anything to me.' Another pause. 'And how long have you been doing this – what was it...? Existential...'

'Twenty years. More or less.'

'I see.'

He looked down at his lap, frowning. For a while, we sat there in silence together. And then, when the silence began to get too loud, he spoke.

'Sorry if I seemed rude. About your dress.'

'That's OK. You weren't.'

'And nosy. About your qualifications.'

'Not at all. You're right to ask. After all, you're entrusting yourself to me. I'm your therapist.'

He nodded. There was a short silence and then he said, 'You know that part of me you were talking about? The part that doesn't want to know what happened in my childhood?'

I nodded.

'I'm going to have to change that, aren't I? If I want to find out.'

'Probably.'

'And you think you can help me to do that?'

'I hope so. It depends on you, really. And whether, deep down, you actually want to change.'

'I do.'

He looked up at me and, for the first time, he smiled. It was a sweet, sincere smile, like a little boy's. I thought of the child in the box, blocking his ears and counting to ten. I smiled back at him, and then I looked away, up at the relief on the wall behind his head. I was inwardly congratulating myself on handling the situation so calmly, despite the fact that his remarks about my appearance had made me more uncomfortable than was usual with a new client. But, to my consternation, I noticed that the circle was still pulsating gently among the squares.

I was standing at the cooker, grilling mackerel

fillets for supper. Normally I enjoy cooking for my family in the evening; after a long day of intense encounters with emotional clients, I find it soothing to absorb myself in the simple rhythms of peeling, chopping, heating, stirring and tasting. And now that the girls are getting older – Nella just sixteen, Rose coming up to ten – I'm beginning to be a little more adventurous in my choice of dishes. Rose is still a fussy eater, of course, but I'm aware that unless I vary what I put in front of her, she'll never change.

When Bob was at home, the four of us usually ate supper together round the table, unless there was something special on TV. It's the way I was brought up. My mother always cooked a family meal in the evening, and I'd fallen into the same pattern. Bob did most of the shopping at the weekends, from a list that I gave him to take out. He followed it religiously, if a little unimaginatively, often phoning me from the supermarket to find out exactly what it was I wanted. He'd always understood, from the start, that my career was as demanding as his and, on a day-to-day basis, much more emotionally draining. Over the years he'd supported me every step of the way, especially when the children were young and I was struggling to set up my practice. He was good like that. Thoughtful. Considerate. Or used to be, before he started to go away on business so much, and this fling, moment of madness – whatever you like to call it – happened. In some ways, the fact that he'd always been so devoted in the past made his confession come as more of a shock. I couldn't piece it together, make sense of it, try as I might.

'Could you clear away now, Bob?' I tried to keep the tension out of my voice. 'We're going to be eating soon.'

'What was that?' He glanced up.

I bent to turn one of the fish, and as I did, a drop of hot oil spat out at me, narrowly missing my eye.

'Can you give me a hand here.' I wasn't shouting, but I'd raised my voice. 'Supper's almost ready.'

'OK, sorry.' He picked up the laptop and moved it to the sideboard, laying it down next to a bowl of fruit. I noticed that he didn't close it. 'What do you want me to do?'

'I don't know. Lay the table or something.' The fish began to smoke. 'Just help.'

Bob walked over to the kitchen window and opened it a fraction to let out the smoke. Then he got some knives, forks and glasses out of the dishwasher and began to lay the table. When he'd finished he came over and stood beside me.

'Plates?'

'Here.' I picked up the plates, which were warming above the hob, and pushed them at him.

He took them and stood beside me for a moment.

'Look, I'm sorry about bringing all this work home. I've got a ton of stuff to get through. It's never-ending.'

I don't like people hovering next to me when I'm cooking, so I waved him away.

'All this bloody red tape,' he went on, standing back. 'Committees. Focus groups. Panels. I really don't think I can stand it any more.'

'Well, leave then.' I bent to turn another fish. The oil sputtered up, but this time I leaned away to avoid it. 'Go back out on your own.'

'I don't see how I can. I'm at the top of my tree, there's nowhere else to go.' He paused. 'And the salary...'

'Oh, stuff the salary.' I was impatient. 'We could manage. We always did before.'

Bob stood holding the plates for a moment, a hurt look on his face, and then went off to lay the table.

We often had this conversation, but normally I was more sympathetic. It always ran the same way. He'd complain about his job, and I'd remind him that, only a few years ago, he'd been an independent political lawyer who loved his work; that since he'd taken the job at the Assembly, ostensibly a big promotion, he'd been miserable, bogged down in the bureaucracy. We'd talk about the fact that if he decided to quit the job, he could take on some big political cases again, maybe do some consultancy work. Recently I'd felt we were getting somewhere, that he was beginning to make up his mind. But since his fling with the translator, I'd lost interest in his dilemma.

I turned the last fish over, opened the oven and poked at the baked potatoes. When I looked up, I saw Bob at the sideboard, peering at his laptop screen.

'What are you doing?' I asked. The irritation in my tone was obvious.

'Just closing this down.'

'Well, can you go and get the girls, please?'

Bob went out into the hall and called up the

stairs, while I laid the fish on the plates and brought them over to the table, along with the baked potatoes and some steamed greens. I knew Rose wouldn't eat the greens, but at least these days she didn't scream until I took them off her plate, as she'd done when she was a toddler. Then I got a big jug of water, filled each glass, and put it in the centre of the table. Before I'd finished, the girls came cantering down the stairs and into the kitchen.

There was a short lull as I took off my apron and we sat down to eat, each of us finding what we needed to accompany our meal: butter, salt, pepper, mustard, tomato sauce. I felt a momentary, but nonetheless satisfying, sense of achievement as I watched my family prepare to eat the carefully planned, delicious, yet nutritious meal I'd made for them.

My satisfaction was short-lived, however. I'd noticed that Nella was looking unusually cheerful, her cheeks slightly flushed, and then she burst out with her news.

'I've been spotted by an A&R man,' she said. She savoured the words, which were evidently new to her.

'What's an A&R man?' Rose picked up the tomato sauce and put a huge dollop of it on the side of her plate. Then she began to spread it over her fish.

Nella ignored her.

'It's a talent scout, Rose,' Bob said. 'A person who looks out for good singers and musicians, to make a record.'

'He says I've got a fantastic voice,' Nella went

on. 'He wants to make a demo and send it to a TV producer in London.'

'That's wonderful.' Bob grinned at her delightedly. 'When did he hear you sing?'

He leaned over and cut off a piece of butter for his potato. A rather large piece, I thought. I wondered whether I should buy a low-fat spread instead.

'It was at the school concert.' Nella was all smiles.

'I was so sorry to miss that, sweetheart.'

Nella shrugged. 'Mum was there, weren't you?'

I nodded, slowly coming to the realization of what had happened at the concert after I'd left.

'Yes. You were great, Nella. Your singing was absolutely beautiful.' I hesitated for a moment. 'What's his name, this ... this A&R man?'

'Emyr. Emyr Griffiths.'

My heart sank.

'He's got his own recording studio, twenty-four tracks, and he's going to put together some backing tracks, and we're going to do my Billie Holiday song and maybe some others, and then...'

Nella chattered on excitedly, but I was only half listening. I'd been hoping this situation wouldn't arise. I hadn't given her Emyr's card, and there had been a reason for that.

You see, in his sessions with me, Emyr had explained why he'd lost his job as a teacher. One of his pupils, a teenage girl, had developed a crush on him, confessed her undying love, and burst into tears when he'd rejected her. He'd tried to console her, putting a solicitous arm round her shoulder as she wept, whereupon she'd promptly reported him to the head teacher. The head had been sympathetic, but because he'd actually touched the girl, she'd been forced to dismiss him. Emyr had never found work as a teacher again, and that was why he'd become depressed. The whole situation was very unfair, and I'd sympathized with him. He'd seemed a decent enough man, if a little naive. But all the same, I had to admit, when it came to my own daughter... Well, mud sticks, doesn't it...

'We're going to go up to London to meet this producer. He's a manager as well...'

Nella was becoming more animated as she outlined Emyr's plans for her rise to fame.

'I don't know about that, Nella,' I cut in, before I could stop myself. 'You're far too young to be going up to London with a complete stranger. And anyway, you need to be concentrating on your schoolwork at the moment, with your exams coming up...'

Nella stopped talking. A sullen look came over her face, and she began to play with her food, pushing it around the plate with her fork.

Bob tried to make amends. 'All Mum is saying, love, is that we need to take this step by step...'

Nella put down her fork and glared at me. 'You just don't want me to be happy, do you?' There were tears of anger in her eyes. 'You're so overprotective. None of my friends get this kind of shit from their parents...'

'She said shit,' Rose murmured, gazing down at her fish, now entirely coated in tomato sauce.

'Come on, Nella, don't be so touchy. Nobody's stopping you doing anything.' Bob's tone was placatory. 'We're just trying to make sure...'

Nella got up from her chair, pushing it back so that it scraped loudly across the floor, and marched out of the room, slamming the door behind her.

There was a long silence.

'Shall I go after her?' Bob said.

'If you want to.' I put down my knife and fork, suddenly exhausted. It had been a long day. 'I'd leave it a while, let her cool down.'

'Why did you jump down her throat like that? When she was so excited about it all?' Bob's tone was perplexed, rather than accusing.

'I'm sorry, I didn't mean to. It's just that...' I paused. 'It's nothing to worry about, really. I'll tell you later.'

Rose looked up from her fish, with interest.

'Nella's probably got a point,' I went on. 'I think maybe I am being a little over-protective.'

'Well, that's natural enough.' Bob began to mash his butter into his potato. 'You're a mother. It's your biological destiny.'

'What's a biological destiny?' Rose piped up.

'It's something you can't avoid,' I replied. 'Like being a woman. Or a man.'

Rose looked confused, but I was too distracted to explain further. Bob came to my rescue.

'It means, Rose, that if you're a mother, you have an instinct to look after your children and protect them from danger. You can't help it. Even when your children find you really annoying.'

'That's right,' I said. Hearing him explain it, I felt less guilty that I'd been so insensitive, pouring cold water on Nella's plans like that.

'We'll just tell Nella that she's too young to go to London with this guy on her own,' he went on. 'I'll offer to drive them up in the car, hang around in the background, keep an eye. I'm sure she'll be fine with that.'

I nodded, knowing that she wouldn't.

We ate in silence for a while, or at least Bob and I did. Rose was busy helping herself to more tomato sauce, and I was doing my best to ignore the fact. For the time being, I'd had enough of dampening my children's enthusiasms, be they for pop stardom or lashings of tomato sauce.

'That's enough.' Bob leaned over the table and took the sauce bottle from her hands.

I smiled at him, grateful that he'd stepped in. Even when I was angry with him, I couldn't help acknowledging that he was wonderful with the girls. He adored them, and they adored him, despite – or perhaps because of – the fact that he was away so much these days. So I wondered whether I should try harder to make amends, if only for their sakes.

Bob got up from the table. 'I'll go and talk to Nella. And by the time I get back, Rose, I want you to have eaten up all your fish. If you do, we'll go on the Wii and do a bit of Dance Party.'

He struck a John Travolta pose and Rose laughed. I laughed too, involuntarily. He noticed, caught my eye, and gave me a conspiratorial wink. As he did, a startlingly clear image came into my mind.

He was talking to a young woman. She was wearing a headset, speaking into it. She was blonde and slim, with perfectly made-up blue eyes and frosted pink lips, and she was smiling, showing her whitened teeth. She was wearing one of those tiny dresses young women favour these days, just a sliver of brightly coloured fabric hanging off her tanned limbs, the asymmetric cut revealing, and then concealing, the shape of her body as she moved. Yet she looked genuinely innocent, as if it were completely natural for her to be showing off so much flesh while she worked. He was smiling back at her, talking too, nodding encouragingly, keeping his eyes on her face. Then I saw him get up and walk over to her. He reached forward, took her hand, drew her towards him, and...

Just a local translator. No one of any significance. Bob's words echoed through my head, along with another few, that I'd added. *False. Treacherous. Deceitful.*

'If that's all right with you, Jess.'

I realized Bob was talking to me, waiting for a reply.

'OK,' I said, looking away. 'But don't keep her up too late. It's nearly her bedtime.'

4

I've got a set of rules for my job. Number one: never get too involved with your clients. Two: never arrange to see them outside the session. Three: never take calls from their family. Four: never visit them at home. Five: well, the list goes on. But I do make exceptions when I think a client

60

is at risk. So when Arianrhod Morgan, Gwydion's mother, phoned me to say that he was suffering from deep depression and she feared he was suicidal, I took her seriously. She was distraught, wanting to find out whether his behaviour had given me cause for concern when I met him.

I told her that he hadn't seemed unduly depressed when I'd seen him, and went on to ask her a few routine questions, such as whether he'd made any suicide attempts in the past, or had spoken of a specific plan, such as taking an overdose, to which she replied that he hadn't. However, she said, he'd been lying in bed, refusing to leave his room, and apparently unable, or unwilling, to speak to anyone. He no longer got up in the morning, washed himself or got dressed. And in the last few days he'd virtually stopped eating. She'd sounded genuinely upset, and had begged me to come down and see him. I got the distinct impression that she was exaggerating about the suicidal tendencies but, just to double-check, I decided to make a visit. Normally I would have discussed the situation with my supervisor – all practising therapists, however experienced, are supposed to have an hour or so of supervision every month – but she had recently taken a sabbatical and I hadn't got round to finding a new one, so for the time being I was on my own.

It was a wet, blustery day as I swung the car onto the M4 and headed west, out of Cardiff towards Carmarthen, the roads enveloped in the kind of swirling mist that makes words like 'Mabinogion' spring into your mind unbidden. As I passed the factories and wind-farms out on the hills I realized that, despite the sober purpose of my journey, I was glad to be getting out of the city for the day. It's something to do with the landscape, I reasoned. West Wales holds a kind of glamour for me: the brooding black mountains; the ruined castles; the huge beaches with their sweeping tides; the Celtic crosses looming out of drunken churchyards; the white stone cottages with their black slate roofs... Let's edit out the boarded-up shops, the smashed phone boxes, the toothless junkies, the pubescent parents, just for the moment. They're not part of this particular story.

I passed the turning off to Porthcawl, the traffic thinned out, and a solo piano recital came on the radio. Chopin, I thought, by the sound of it. I wondered what the piece was. It could have been a prelude, a nocturne, or a scherzo for all I knew. Or even a polonaise, an ecossaise, a mazurka. I'd missed the announcement, I hadn't been listening. But whatever it was, I found it immensely sooth-ing. The lack of drums, or words, or mid-Atlantic nasal wails was especially appealing to me. I sighed, relaxed back into my seat and hitched up my skirt. It was a dogtooth-check, kick-pleat num-ber, a little tight at the hips, that I'd teamed with a cream silk blouse – no buttons – a cashmere sweater and lace-up brogues. I put my foot on the accelerator.

As I drove along the sea road I saw the satanic mills of Port Talbot, its tall chimneys coughing out a pall of yellow smog that hugged the coastline for miles, and the words 'chimney-sweeping' came into my mind. That's what Anna O, the first psychoanalytic patient, called her therapy with Dr

Breuer, Freud's predecessor. (She also coined the term 'talking cure'. In this game, it's the patients who do all the work, including naming the treatment.) A thorough clean-out, I reflected, that's all Gwydion needs. A chance to blow away the cobwebs, get his deep fears and anxieties off his chest. He'll be able to talk to me. Hold my hand, in a purely metaphorical sense though, as it happens, Dr Breuer actually did hold Anna O's hand, listening to her for hours as she lay on her bed in the dark, telling him fairy stories. I wasn't planning on doing that, of course. Modern professional ethics prevent that sort of thing and, besides, it didn't end well between Breuer and Anna O, as is well documented. But all the same, I was certain I could help Gwydion. Come to him in his hour of darkness, his time of need. And even if I couldn't, I was determined to try.

I got to Creigfa House, the Morgan place, in the early afternoon. It was a few miles away from a tiny fishing village, perched on a clifftop in solitary splendour, overlooking St Bride's Bay. Before announcing my arrival I stopped the car on the side of the road and peered at the house through the big iron gates. It was tremendously grand. A darned sight grander than I'd expected. One of those Jacobean piles with tall chimneys, pointy gables and castellated whatnots all the way round the roof. It looked like something out of a fairy story. There were latticed windows everywhere, and barley-twist pillars around the porch, and carved stone garlands drooping down over the front door. But impressive as it all was, when you looked more closely, you could see that parts of it, especially on the wings, were crumbling away. The kind of house that, however much money you spent on it, would always be falling to pieces. Nevertheless, it was still beautiful. Unique. Rococo. Baroque even.

I hesitated for a moment. The house looked intimidating, as those marauding lords had intended it to do all those centuries ago. And there was an air of melancholy about it, too. I had a sudden urge to run away, but instead I forced myself to press the buzzer, speaking into the grille, giving my name, and resisting the temptation to say something silly like 'Open, sesame'.

Immediately, as if by magic, the gates swung apart, closing again behind me as I passed. As I drove up the path to the house my heart began to thud. The tyres crunched on the gravel. There were peacocks strutting about on the front lawn. As I passed, one of them flipped up its tail, spread its feathers, and shrieked at me. It was all tremendously gothic. (Rococo, baroque, gothic? Make your mind up, Jessica.)

At the end of the drive there was one of those round lawns with a flowerbed of regimental marigolds in the middle of it. I stopped the car, turned off the engine, picked up my bag, got out and looked around, hoping the peacock wouldn't attack me. Then a woman emerged from beneath the garlands.

'Dr Mayhew.'

She was slim, tall, dark-haired. Her face was lined, a little weather-beaten even, but finely chiselled, with high cheekbones and a wide brow.

'Mrs Morgan. Good to meet you.' I put out my hand.

'Arianrhod, please. And you.' She shook it firmly. I noticed that the skin on her fingers was rough, like a gardener's.

'Where shall I park the car?'

'Oh, leave it there.' She turned and ushered me towards the doorway of the house. 'Do come in.'

Inside, we walked down a dark corridor with great stone slabs on the floor, until we reached a modern, well-lit kitchen. Arianrhod sat me down at the kitchen table, pushing a pile of books, newspapers and letters to one side to make space for me. Then she went over to the stove and put the kettle on.

'Lovely place you've got here,' I said to her back.

'Thanks,' she replied, not turning round. 'It's a lot of work, but I ... we love it.'

I registered the hesitation. I wondered where the marauding lord was, and whether he would show up at some stage.

I watched Arianrhod as she moved around the kitchen, making the coffee. It was hard to guess her age. She was dressed simply but elegantly, in jeans, a navy sweater and a pair of battered brown loafers. Her hair was loosely tied back, and she brushed a strand of it away from her eyes from time to time. She moved around quickly, like a young woman, but when she turned to me, with her face under the lights, I realized she must be in her early fifties at least.

'Milk? Sugar?'

I said no to both. She brought a cafetiere to the

table, along with two cups and a plate of biscuits, and sat down opposite me.

'I'm so grateful to you for coming. I know it's asking a lot. But I'm so worried. Gwydion's always had his low moods, but he's never been as bad as this before. His GP hasn't been much use – he doesn't seem very good on this kind of thing.'

'That's OK.' I paused. 'Where is he, by the way?'

'Upstairs in his bedroom. As usual. I'll take you up in a minute.' She rummaged in her pocket and brought out a plastic pouch of tobacco. 'Mind if I smoke? I'll go outside if you want.'

'Don't be silly. It's your house.'

She pulled an ashtray towards her. 'They're your lungs.'

I waved away her objection, but I appreciated her asking.

She began to roll herself a cigarette. I felt envious as I watched her. I gave up smoking years ago, but I still miss it. Not so much the taste, or the sting of the nicotine as it hits your lungs, or that light-headed feeling as it courses round your brain, just the conspiratorial element of lighting up with another person over a coffee or a drink, and shooting the breeze.

Arianrhod appeared to have read my thoughts. She waved at the pouch. 'Help yourself.'

'No, thanks. But I'll have a biscuit.' She passed me the plate. They were good-quality shortbread fingers, buttery and crumbly. I took one, dipped the end in my coffee and munched away. Arianrhod continued rolling.

'So how is Gwydion today?' I said, after a while.

'Oh.' She took a lighter out of her pocket. 'Much

66

the same. But he says he'll see you.' She lit her cigarette, drawing in a deep breath and exhaling slowly. 'Thank God.'

I couldn't help breathing in with her. The tobacco smelled warm, delicious, with just a hint of that acridity that would later turn the air in the room sour.

'You know, I really can't take much more,' she added. Blue smoke swirled around her dark head and she waved it away with a delicate hand. Then she took another puff and blew out again. More smoke, this time blue-grey, to match her eyes. It was all rather beautiful, I thought. Though dangerous to the health, obviously.

'Well, I'm not surprised,' I said. 'It's hard work being with someone who's having a ... a little bit of a wobble.'

She gave a short laugh, almost despite herself. 'So that's what you doctors call it, is it?'

'I'm not a doctor. Not a medical one, anyway.'

'Oh.' She sighed, took another drag of her cigarette and rested it on the rim of the ashtray. 'Well, do you mind if I call you Dr Mayhew, anyway? It makes me feel secure.'

I was touched. 'Call me whatever you want,' I said. 'Within reason.'

She laughed again. I sensed that my presence was beginning to cheer her up. I began to feel better, to think that my visit might possibly be useful, not only to Gwydion, but to his mother as well. So far Arianrhod was turning out to be a much easier proposition than I'd imagined. But then I looked down and saw the rough skin and the nicotine stains on her fingers and I was reminded that none of this was going to be easy.

There was a long silence. The cigarette was still burning in the ashtray, the smoke emanating from it thin and pungent. When it finally went out, Arianrhod didn't bother to relight it. Instead she rose to her feet, as though she'd suddenly come to a decision.

'Come on,' she said. 'Bring your coffee, if you like. I'll take you up now.'

Arianrhod led me upstairs, through narrow corridors with beamed ceilings and uneven floors, until we came to the door of Gwydion's room. She knocked, but there was no reply, so she opened it gently.

'Gwydi? Dr Mayhew's here to see you.'

I peered into the room over her shoulder. It was dark, the curtains drawn. I could just make out a bed beside the window.

'She'd like to talk to you.'

There was an almost inaudible groan from the bed. Arianrhod opened the door wider, stepped aside, and gave me a little push into the room.

'Good luck,' she whispered. Then she closed the door behind me and left.

I stood by the door for a moment, my eyes adjusting to the dark. I wasn't sure what to do. So I stayed there and said, in what I hoped was a reassuring voice, 'Gwydion, it's me, Jessica. Would you mind if I came over and sat beside you for a while?'

There was another groan that I took to be assent. I walked quietly over to the bedside, drew up a low armchair and sat down.

68

Gwydion was lying in bed with his eyes closed. He was unshaven and his hair was greasy. His complexion looked sallow, unhealthy. Underneath the bedclothes I could see that he was wearing a sweater, a scarf, a dressing gown and pyjamas. The room was rather draughty – it was that kind of house – but it certainly wasn't cold. I wondered if he often overdressed like this, or whether this was something new. The button phobia flashed through my mind, but I couldn't make anything of it.

There was a long silence. Interminable. I looked around the room. It had obviously been Gwydion's since boyhood. Ranged around the shelves on the walls were piles of comics, a Game Boy, a chess set. Propped in a corner was an ancient cricket bat, taped up along the bottom where the wood had cracked. Sitting on a chest of drawers was a sheep's skull and a homemade catapult. It all looked idyllic, reminiscent of the kind of childhood you read about in books, but seldom actually encounter, where tousle-haired boys make dens in the woods, and the worst that can happen is a scraped knee after climbing a tree, or a chill after playing out in the rain: healthy, happy, carefree. Except that I knew from looking at the figure lying in the bed that it wasn't. Or if it was, that something had gone very wrong along the way.

'I've had the dream again.' I jumped as Gwydion spoke. He still had his eyes closed.

'Yes?' I said. I tried to sound encouraging, without being pushy.

Silence fell once again.

'This time there were voices.' Gwydion spoke

in a low whisper.

'Voices?'

'Yes.' He frowned. 'I'm in the box again,' he went on. His voice was a monotone. 'It's dark. I can't see anything, but I can hear...' He stopped. He appeared to be making a tremendous effort to remember something. 'Two voices ... a man's and a woman's...'

He stopped talking and turned his face to the wall.

We sat there in silence for a while. Then I said, 'Gwydion. Would you mind opening your eyes for a moment and looking at me?'

I don't know what made me say that. Irritation, probably, that he hadn't had the manners to open his eyes, say hello, register my presence. But the minute I'd spoken, I regretted it. There'd been a distinct note of impatience in my voice, which I hadn't managed to disguise.

He turned over, his back to me.

My irritation increased. I started to wonder whether he was having me on, whether this was all some absurd game he was playing. Of course, I should have known better: people struggling with mental illness do play games, run rings around their therapists and everyone else; it's part of the illness. So if Gwydion was play-acting, there was probably a good reason for it. And if he wasn't, I was being unkind. Whatever the case, in my impatience I'd risked losing my chance to find out what that reason might be.

'I'm sorry, Gwydion.' I paused. 'I shouldn't have said that. It doesn't matter whether you look at me or not. Just carry on talking. I'm listening.'

But Gwydion remained facing the wall, saying nothing.

He went on saying nothing for the next half-hour, and I went on kicking myself inwardly for interrupting him in mid-flow. But eventually my impatience began to leave me, and instead a deep sadness came over me. Here was this young man, in his prime, lying in a darkened room, letting his life slip slowly by, unable to grasp it, to savour it. And no one seemed to be able to help him, to reach him, least of all me.

I looked over at the window, and saw that, behind the curtains, the sun had come out. A tiny ray of sunlight was beginning to creep along the window ledge. I thought of a fragment of poetry that I knew, one that my mother had taught me as a child.

I remember, I remember,
The house where I was born,
The little window where the sun
Came peeping in at morn...

With a start I realized that, in my reverie, I'd spoken aloud. Then I heard Gwydion's voice, finishing the verse.

He never came a wink too soon,
Nor brought too long a day,
But now I often wish the night
Had borne my breath away...

As he whispered the words, tears filled my eyes. Tears for Gwydion in his anguish, and for some-

71

thing else as well: for the sudden realization that my mother had never taught me the second verse – hoping to shield me perhaps from the pain of growing up, from the ultimate powerlessness of her love, and keep me a while longer in the safety of childhood. She'd done her best for me in those early years, I realized now. Like most mothers. Like Arianrhod, most probably. And if it hadn't been good enough, well, that was the world's fault, and growing up's fault, not hers.

'About the dream, Gwydion.' I was whispering, to keep the urgency out of my voice. 'Was it exactly the same – or was there something else? Some little detail, perhaps, however small, that might help us to find out what's wrong ... what you're running from?'

Gwydion remained facing the wall, motionless.

'Anything else you want to tell me?'

He shook his head, but he didn't turn round.

I felt suddenly exhausted. I needed to get out of the dark, airless room and back into the daylight.

'Gwydion. I think I'm going to go now. Unless you want me to stay.'

He shook his head again.

'You've got my phone number. You can call me any time you want. Or...' I hesitated a moment, then said, rather recklessly, 'or I can come back to see you here.'

There was no response, so I got up and walked over to the door. I stood there for a moment, waiting to see if he would speak to me before I left. But he didn't, so I opened it and walked out into the corridor, closing it quietly behind me.

5

When I went downstairs I found Arianrhod in the kitchen. She asked how I'd got on, and I told her that Gwydion hadn't said much, except to tell me about a dream he'd been having. She seemed disappointed, and asked me if I could possibly stay the night and talk to him again in the morning. I refused, saying that I had to get home, which was true enough: Bob would be working late, and I'd need to organize the girls' evening, and catch up on some papers myself. At that, she looked even more downcast, and then suggested I might like a walk around the grounds before I left, to stretch my legs before the drive home. I agreed, even though I knew that what she really wanted was a chance to discuss Gwydion further with me, and I was somewhat reluctant to do so.

We went into the hall to get our coats – the weather had cleared, but there was still a nip in the air – and were just about to set off when the lord of the manor himself appeared. He drove up in a Range Rover, slammed on the brakes, jumped out, and opened the boot to let out two large liver-spotted dogs.

'Who the hell's parked their bloody car in the–?' he burst out. Then, seeing me, he stopped.

He was a well-built, good-looking man in his late fifties or so, with exactly the same luminous green eyes as his son.

'Evan. This is Dr Mayhew.' Arianrhod seemed unsurprised by his outburst. 'Dr Mayhew, my husband, Evan Morgan.'

I nodded at him.

He cleared his throat and thrust a hand out towards me. 'How d'you do.'

We shook hands briefly. He looked remarkably youthful, I noticed, and remarkably like Gwydion, except for the lines on his forehead and temples, his jutting cheekbones and the lilac shadows under his eyes. But there was nothing of Gwydion's insecurity in his demeanour.

He let go of my hand and turned to Arianrhod. 'Is Gwydion out of bed yet?'

'Not yet, no.' An anxious note crept into her voice. 'But he'll be up sooner or later, I'm sure...'

'So, no joy, eh?' He turned to me, a look of exasperation on his face. 'I really don't know what we're going to do with him. Lying around in bed all day, like a teenager. Still tied to his mother's apron strings. I despair of him sometimes...'

I didn't reply, but I felt my anger rising. No wonder Gwydion has problems, with a father like this, I thought.

'I hope you can help him. It's time he pulled himself together. Made his own life, away from here.' He looked me in the eye as he spoke, and I felt a flush start to rise from the back of my neck. He seemed to be sizing me up, assessing my competence, whether as a woman or a doctor, or both, I wasn't sure.

'Dr Mayhew and I were just going for a stroll, before she goes home,' Arianrhod said. There was a subtle touch of martyred patience in her tone.

She paused. 'We won't be long. We'll take the dogs, if you like.'

'Whatever you want.' He gave a sigh of frustration. 'I've got Rhiannon coming over in a minute.'

At the mention of Rhiannon, Arianrhod looked pained, but did her best to hide it.

'We've got a ton of work to get through...' He paused, as if he'd suddenly remembered I was there. 'Goodbye, Dr...'

He looked at me again, registering my discomfort, a faint smile playing about his lips.

'Mayhew,' I reminded him. 'Jessica Mayhew.'

He nodded curtly, then walked off towards the house, his boots crunching on the gravel. As I watched him go, I realized with a shock why he looked so familiar. It wasn't just his similarity to Gwydion, or the fact that I'd probably seen his face in the papers or on TV. He was, without a doubt, the man in the photograph I'd been sent, with the blacked-out eyes.

Arianrhod and I set off across the lawn, the dogs circling us in their excitement at the prospect of another walk. Then they ran off ahead, on the trail of some scent or other, darting back to us from time to time as we headed out into the walled gardens overlooking the sea.

For a while, neither of us spoke. My mind was racing. I knew now who the man in the mystery photograph was, but I still didn't know who had sent it, or why.

'I'm sorry about that,' Arianrhod said at last, when we were out of earshot. 'Evan isn't the most patient of men. He gets upset whenever Gwydion's ... ill. He worries about him. And it tends to come out in ... well, an odd way. He's very fond of him, really. He doesn't mean any harm.'

I nodded, but I didn't reply. I was still puzzling over the photograph. Then it came to me. It must have been Gwydion who'd sent it. It had arrived the morning he first came to see me, after all. He was obviously unstable, and he hated his father – he'd told me as much at the last session we'd had. And clients quite often send me notes they've written in advance, rather than bringing up difficult issues in the session. This was evidently just a variation on that theme.

I felt a sense of satisfaction. Although I'd brushed it aside at the time, the question of the photograph, and the message beneath it, had been at the back of my mind ever since it had arrived. Now I could cross off that small but irritating anomaly in my life.

We reached a high stone wall.

'This way.' Arianrhod opened a small wooden door set into it, and ushered me through.

Gardens by the sea are strange places. There's a beauty to them, but they're not comfortable, domestic, tamed. The salt wind stunts the trees, twists them out of shape, and the shrubs, bushes and plants wear a tough, embattled air as though struggling for their right to survive. Arianrhod's garden was no exception, but the stone walls facing out to sea helped to shelter it. It had been carefully planted too, with an emphasis on architectural form, on the contrasting shapes and colours of branches and leaves, rather than flowers. And the design of the garden was a pretty one, a series of walled squares, each connected to the next by a little wooden door, with narrow paths that led around the lawns and beds.

I'm not much of a gardener myself – I'm reserving it for my old age, when I'll have more time – but I could see, as we walked around, that a lot of work had gone into maintaining the place. The lawns within each walled square were mown, the edges of the beds clipped, the leaves raked into neat piles in the corners. It was as lovingly cared for as such a windblown spot could be.

'Do you do this all yourself?' I asked, as we walked into the final square, which was evidently the kitchen garden.

'Well, there's a man who comes in to do the lawns.' Arianrhod brushed the hair out of her eyes. 'But that's all.'

'It must be a lot of work.'

'It is. But I like it.' She reached up and dead-headed a rose as we passed. 'It's peaceful out here. Relaxing.' She paused. 'I'm so keyed up most of the time. What with Gwydion and...' She hesitated.

I sensed there was about to be an intimate revelation, possibly about Evan, but I headed it off at the pass.

'Well, it's lovely. You've obviously got an eye for this sort of thing.'

I wasn't being unsympathetic, but I didn't want to talk to Arianrhod about her husband. She wasn't my client, Gwydion was. And if there were problems in the family, which there evidently were, I'd rather hear about them from the horse's mouth than the horse's mother.

Arianrhod seemed to get the message, and changed the subject. 'Do you want to go out and look at the view from the clifftop?' she asked. 'It's pretty spectacular.'

'Fine,' I said. I felt the urge to get away, before Arianrhod decided to confide in me further, but I didn't like to refuse. Besides, I wanted to look out at the sea before I left. I wanted to store it up in my mind for future use. If I take a long look at something beautiful during the day, I'm often able to recall it in detail when I'm in bed at night, and it helps to get me off to sleep. It's a trick I've learned, and I sometimes recommend it to my clients as a cheap alternative to Temazepam.

We walked through another small wooden door out onto a narrow clifftop path, which led through a dense thicket of gorse bushes and brambles to a small clearing. We stopped there and looked out over the vast expanse of slate-grey sea, stretching far off into the hazy horizon beyond.

It was, indeed, spectacular. The tide was out, and below us was a dizzying drop down to the exposed seabed, a sheet of cratered rock like a slimy brown moon, pitted, turreted, treacherous. Around it hung a curtain of yellow cliffs, the soft limestone layered like mortarless bricks on a half-demolished building.

Without thinking, I caught my breath and took a step back from the edge of the cliff. There was no form of fencing or hedging between us and the abyss, and I wished there had been.

'I know,' said Arianrhod. 'It's a bit over-whelming, isn't it?'

'I'm fine,' I said. 'As long as I keep away from

the edge. I don't have much of a head for heights, I'm afraid.'

We gazed out in silence at the sea. Then I looked down and noticed there were some steps and a handrail cut into the side of the cliff, leading down to a jetty that stuck out over the rocks below.

'Can you get down there?' I asked. 'Not that I'm thinking of trying.'

Arianrhod laughed. 'It's safer than it looks, actually. We often go down and swim off the jetty out there in the summer. Even at this time of year, if the weather's good. The sea's warmed up by now. I mean, when I say warm...' She laughed again. She seemed to have a habit of ending, or rather not ending, her sentences with a laugh.

She led me over to the top of the steps, and I peered down at them cautiously. Now that I was close up to them, I could see they were cut quite deep into the rock. With one hand on the rail, they'd be fairly safe, if a little slippery. Even so, it was a very long way down to the sea.

'I really must be getting on,' I said. 'I'd like to be home before it gets dark.'

'Of course. It's getting late. I hadn't realized...' Another unfinished sentence. Another laugh.

I was about to turn and go when I noticed there was a little plaque at the top of the steps, with a name and a date inscribed on it: 'Elsa Lindberg 1971–1990'. Below it were some words in a foreign language. A Nordic one, by the look of the As with little circles on the top, and the Os with umlauts over them.

'What's this?'

'Oh.' She paused a moment. 'Very sad. A young

79

girl, a tourist from Sweden, I believe. It was a long time ago. There've been a few casualties here over the years, I'm sorry to say. Mostly people who swim out too far. The currents can be very treacherous.'

There was something offhand in the way she spoke that contrasted with the usual intensity of her manner. I wondered whether the accident had upset her more than she was letting on.

'I can imagine.' For a moment an image of the girl, and of her cold, lonely death out there in the slate-grey waters, flashed through my mind. But it didn't do to dwell on it, so after a moment I added, 'Come on. Let's go.'

As we walked back up the path I took a last glance down at the steps and out to sea. In the short time we'd been there the tide seemed to have moved in, stealthily, without me noticing, so that the water was now approaching the bottom of the cliffs. I shivered involuntarily. I was glad to be leaving.

6

When I got home, after a tedious drive back up the motorway, the house was empty. I checked my phone and found two messages. Bob was working late – no surprise there – and Nella had gone out with her friends. Rose, I knew, was off on a school outing to see a play. They'd both arranged for Bob to pick them up on his way home. There was nothing for me to do, no one who needed me. I could relax if I wanted to, please myself, have some 'me' time, as the women's magazines call it: pour myself a drink, take a long, hot bath, cook myself a dish the girls don't like – risotto, perhaps, or soup – read something undemanding, and get an early night.

Tonight, however, I didn't want any 'me' time. I wanted to be out and about, with people around me; lights; noise; chatter. Anything to prevent me from thinking too hard, to dim the memory of my trip to the Morgan place: that odd house, those odd people, and my odd part in their lives. And, luckily enough, it was Friday.

A group of my friends, all women, meet up regularly on Friday nights for a drink at our local arts centre. Sometimes we eat there, or take in a film, but mostly we just sit around talking, winding down at the end of a busy week. There are about six of us in all, but often one or two of us are missing. It's a relaxed, simple arrangement: you go if you feel like it, and not if you don't. I made a quick phone call to one of them, Mari Jones, to check she would be there, and when she told me she would – but later, after she'd eaten – I decided to do the same.

When I got to the arts centre it was already getting on for ten. The place was packed, but my friends had found a table in a quiet corner of the foyer. I said hello, asked if anyone wanted a drink, took a couple of orders and went up to the bar. After a moment's deliberation I decided to have a half of Reverend James, the local brew, named after a Victorian saver of souls with a sideline in selling beer.

I brought my drink back to the table and sat down. The conversation was in full flow, dominated as usual by Mari. Mari is an actress with a steady career in Welsh-language theatre, television and radio. She's loud, and funny, and glamorous; and if sometimes she talks a little too much and laughs a little too long, I make allowances for her, because she's warm and expansive, and generally larger than life. Sitting next to her was Sharon, an American academic who works at the university. The polar opposite of Mari, Sharon is quiet, thoughtful and bookish. Yet the pair are close friends, probably the closest of the group. The others who had turned up that night were Polly, a full-time home-maker – well, it's better than 'housewife', isn't it? – and Catrin, who runs a vintage-clothes shop in the Arcades and is the source of many of my outfits.

I listened as Mari held forth, laughing with the others as she mimicked the absurd pomposities of the theatre director she'd been working with that week. As time went on, the conversation around the table became more animated, but I found it hard to join in. My head was full of what had happened that day. I couldn't discuss what I'd seen of Gwydion and his family life, of course, because he was my client, but I couldn't put it out of my mind either. So, instead, I began to probe Mari on the subject of the Morgans' place in the acting world.

'Your director. He's not this guy Evan Morgan, is he?'

'No.' Mari gave a wry grin. 'Why d'you ask?'

'Oh, no reason. He's the only Welsh theatre

director I've ever heard of, that's all.'

'I wish it was.' Mari sighed. 'Evan's brilliant, absolutely brilliant. Best director I've ever worked with, actually.' She paused for a moment. 'Strange guy, of course. Used to have a terrible drink problem. Vile temper at times. And he's a dreadful womanizer.'

She hesitated. I waited. I knew there was more to come. Mari isn't the soul of discretion, which I suppose was the reason I'd been pumping her for information.

'In fact, I had a bit of a–' She stopped in midsentence, a coy smile playing about her lips.

I didn't say anything. I had a feeling she wouldn't need prompting.

'It was nothing, really,' she went on, after a brief pause. 'Just a quick fling, years ago. There was no future in it.' She sighed again. 'A lot of fun, though, at the time.'

I waited again. And there was more, as I knew there would be.

'Haven't seen him for ages.' She hesitated. 'There was some kind of scandal, I seem to remember, a while back. Something about ... I don't know, a young girl. Surprise, surprise. Anyway, it was all hushed up. He's doing incredibly well for himself these days – up for a knighthood, apparently.' Another brief pause. 'But he's not a terribly happy man, by all accounts. Dreadful marriage. His wife's one of those posh Anglo-Welshies from up the borders.'

Mari stopped, took a sip of her gin and tonic, and continued. 'Arianrhod Meredith. She was very young when they got together. Very beautiful. Evan had great ambitions for her at first, but she ended up just being his wife, giving parties for his friends...'

I felt a stab of sympathy for Arianrhod, but Mari was in full flow now and I knew better than to interrupt.

'And then, when she got older, and lost her looks, that was it. She dropped out of sight completely. Stopped socializing, everything. She's pretty much of a recluse these days, I believe. But she and Evan are still together. And he's still putting it about, so I hear.' She frowned. 'Shit relationship, but somehow it's lasted.'

'Any children?' I shouldn't have asked, but my curiosity as to what she'd say got the better of me.

'Just one son, Gwydion. Absolutely gorgeous, like his dad used to be. Sex on a stick. Jesus, I wouldn't mind...' Mari checked herself. 'He's a good actor, too. Could do a lot better for himself, if he used his father's contacts, but he won't. Apparently he absolutely hates Evan, because of the way he treats Arianrhod. You can't blame him, really.'

I didn't ask any more questions. Gwydion was my client, and listening to Mari's gossip about his family set-up made me feel curiously disloyal.

Sensing my reluctance to pursue the conversation, Mari shrugged, then picked up her cigarettes and her lighter. 'Listen, I'm going outside for a fag. Back in a mo. I'll get you a drink on the way back, if you like. What are you having?'

'I'm fine, thanks. I'm driving.'

She rolled her eyes. 'Well, take a cab home. Leave the car here. It's Friday night, isn't it.'

84

Leaving her car somewhere and coming back to get it next day was the sort of thing Mari did regularly. Now in her late forties, she was still drinking, smoking, staying out late, getting up late, pleasing herself. She was divorced and her children had left home, but she didn't seem to be lonely. She was immensely sociable, and continued to have various romantic liaisons on the go. In some ways I envied her, but I knew I wasn't in the least like her. I like socializing, up to a point, but I also need peace and quiet, and time to think. And if I didn't have a family to go home to at night, I'd definitely be lonely. Very lonely.

'I think I'll get back actually,' I replied. 'I'll come out with you.'

I said my goodbyes, apologizing to Polly that we hadn't had time for a proper chat, but she didn't seem to mind. She and Catrin were deep in conversation with Sharon and hardly looked up as we left.

Outside, it was raining. We stood under the eaves of the building, and Mari lit up, inhaling deeply. She held the smoke in her lungs for a moment and then exhaled slowly, with a sigh of pleasure. I watched, envious of her ability to savour the sensation.

'Can I have one?'

Mari looked surprised. 'But you don't smoke.'

'I know. But I'll have one anyway.'

She offered me the pack and I took a cigarette. She held out the lighter and I bent forward, shielding the flame with my hand.

'Anything wrong?' she said as I straightened up.

'Yes,' I said. I sucked on the cigarette, then blew

85

out the smoke, coughing a little as I did. 'Bob's been unfaithful to me. He's slept with another woman.'

'Bloody hell. What happened?'

I hesitated. As I've said, Mari's not the soul of discretion. But she's not malicious, not in the least, and I needed to talk to someone. What's more, I was still so angry with Bob that, to be honest, I didn't care who knew what he'd done.

I took another drag on the cigarette, even though my head was starting to spin.

'Well, he went off to this conference a few weeks ago. In Munich. When he came back he was in a weird mood, and then, after a few days, he confessed that he'd had a one-night stand.'

'The bastard.' Mari was outraged. 'Who was she?'

'One of the translators at the conference. German, I think. Younger than me, a lot younger. About thirty. "Someone of no significance", he called her.'

'Has he ever done this before?'

'No.' I paused. 'At least, he says he hasn't. Though I'm beginning to wonder...'

She reached out and took my arm. 'Listen, I'm sure he's telling the truth. This is a one-off. Bob's a decent guy. He's devoted to you and the girls, anyone can see that.'

'I know he is,' I said. 'And he's feeling terribly guilty. I wish I could talk it through with him, let it go. But I can't. I keep imagining what she looked like ... what exactly happened ... what they did...' I stopped.

'I wouldn't go there, if I were you, *cariad*.' Mari

squeezed my arm.

'But why would he do this?' I went on. 'After all these years. I thought we were OK together. I thought...'

'Was anything wrong between you?'

'No.' I took another puff of the cigarette. It was making me feel nauseous, but I soldiered on.

'Sex all right?'

I thought about it. 'Well, OK. Nothing spectacular. But quite ... serviceable, I suppose.'

There was a short silence, and then Mari laughed. 'Serviceable, eh? Well, maybe what you both need is a bit of a shakeup.' She hesitated. 'Why don't you give him a taste of his own medicine? Have a little dalliance of your own.'

'Don't be ridiculous.' I was taken aback. 'I'd never do that.'

'Why not?'

'Because ... well, because I'm just not interested in other men.' I paused. 'I used to be, of course. Rather too much, actually. But these days I never think about that kind of thing.'

'Really?'

'Yes, really.' For an instant a picture of Gwydion in his tight T-shirt flashed into my mind, but I dismissed it. 'I'd never dream of risking my marriage. I've got the girls to think of. It would be completely irresponsible.'

'No one's asking you to run off for good, are they?' Mari paused. 'And Bob's hardly in a position to complain. If I were you, I'd take advantage of the situation. You've got carte blanche now. Enjoy your freedom. It's probably the last taste of it you'll get for a long while.'

I was shocked. 'But that's childish, Mari. Childish and dangerous. Marriage isn't a power game. And it isn't just about sex, either.' I realized I was beginning to sound sanctimonious, but I carried on all the same. 'It's about love, and trust. And...' I did my best to finish the sentence, but the words didn't come.

Mari gave a wry smile. 'Well, maybe you're right. Maybe things have changed since I last had a husband.'

She shrugged, taking a last drag of her cigarette. Then she threw the butt down beside mine, where it lay soaking in a puddle. Together we looked out at the car park, watching the rain running off the roof in front of us. Then she said, 'Come back in for a drink, Jess. I think you need one. Or several.'

'No,' I said. I gave her a kiss on the cheek. 'I'm tired. I'm going home. Thanks for listening.'

'Any time.' She put her arm around my shoulder and gave me a hug. 'Let me know how things go.'

'I will.'

She turned to go back indoors, and I ran out into the rain, giving her a little wave as I went. Then I got into my car and drove home, down the dark streets to the house, waiting quietly for me in the rain, under the lamplight.

The following Monday, back in my office, I was waiting for Jean to turn up to her session. She was already half an hour late. Normally she'd have been there early, sitting outside in the waiting room, giving me a reproachful look if I happened

88

to pass by, as though to express her dissatisfaction that I couldn't even give her an extra five minutes of my time. So I knew it wasn't like her to miss a second of her session, let alone more than half of it.

I felt irritable, restless. Much as Jean frustrated and bored the hell out of me, I was discomfited at being stood up by her. The trouble is, when my clients don't turn up for sessions, I never feel relieved, no matter how difficult they've been. I feel I've failed. That I'm no good as a therapist. And sometimes, of course, I worry that they may have taken a turn for the worse.

That wasn't likely to be the case with Jean. She wasn't the depressive type. Too angry, too indignant about the unfairness of her situation – becoming a widow, just as she and her husband had retired, were looking forward to taking it easy. Too furious with me, and my lack of ability to help her. No, Jean's absence wouldn't be caused by chronic depression; rather, it would be... I thought of what she'd told me, about her husband appearing to her in the dream, thin and pale, as he had been before he died. He'd been – what was it she'd said? – *begging her not to forget him.* Which meant ... yes, of course. Obviously. That she *was* beginning to forget him. And feeling guilty about it.

I sighed, and was just about to turn away from the window when I caught sight of my elder daughter walking down the street towards the coffee shop. By her side was a man with auburn hair whose face I couldn't quite see. He was taller than her, a grown man, not a schoolboy. I wondered what she was doing with him, and whether she was

89

skipping lessons. Then, as he turned to open the door of the shop for her and went in behind, I realized with a shock that it was Emyr Griffiths.

I felt a rush of anger, and my heart began to thump in my chest. I had an urge to run downstairs and accost them in the coffee shop, ask Nella what on earth she was doing bunking off school, and order Emyr to leave her alone.

There was a knock at the door. It was my next client of the day.

A sudden panic came over me as I remembered the story of why Emyr had been sacked from his job, but I managed to overcome it. He hasn't done anything wrong, I reminded myself. Nothing was proved against him. And Nella's sensible enough. She can handle the situation. She's probably discussing SafeTrax with him, or something equally innocent. Nevertheless I stayed at the window for a few more moments, staring intently at the coffee shop, as if my maternal gaze could protect my daughter from afar, until I heard another knock.

I went over and opened the door.

I hadn't been expecting Gwydion Morgan to turn up for his session. Just three days earlier he'd been lying in bed, face to the wall, refusing to speak to me. But to my surprise, he arrived on the dot, clean-shaven, hair freshly washed. Somehow, he'd rallied, got up, got dressed, and driven all the way up from Pembrokeshire to see me. I couldn't help feeling pleased, despite my anxiety about Nella.

I waited until he had settled himself. There was an uncomfortable silence, so I broke it.

90

'So.' I paused, hoping he would initiate the conversation.

'So.' He smiled. He seemed pleased to see me.

I smiled back, in what I hoped was a kind, understanding way. And then, infuriatingly, I felt a sudden warmth rising up from my neck, flushing my cheeks.

'You look well,' I said.

'I'm feeling a bit better, as it happens.' He appeared not to notice the fact that my face was on fire. 'Thanks for coming down to the house, by the way.' He ran a hand through his hair in that by now familiar gesture.

I nodded again.

'It did help.'

'I'm glad.' I tried to sound non-committal.

'Aren't you going to ask me why?'

'If you want to tell me.' I paused. 'But not if you don't. You're free to talk about anything you like in the session, you know.'

He narrowed his eyes, his head on one side, as though sizing me up. 'Am I?' he said. 'Right. Thanks.' There was more than a trace of bitterness in his voice.

He lapsed into silence. I thought of going over to the window, on the pretext of opening it to get some air, so I could check what was happening at the coffee shop, but instead I forced myself to think about the matter in hand. I began to wonder what Gwydion's evident anger was all about. I knew from the photograph he'd sent me – an issue I was going to have to raise with him sooner or later – that he was furious with his father. And then there was the transference, of course. Something to do with the relationship with his mother, Arianrhod, that he was projecting onto me. A notion that he was at my beck and call, at her beck and call, even when we were telling him that he was free to do as he pleased. Something like that...

He turned his gaze away from my face and looked down at the floor. 'I didn't like it that you'd been in my room, seen me in that condition.' He hesitated. 'It was my mother who asked you to come, not me.'

'Yes.' I said. 'Well, I can understand why you might feel angry about that.'

I wondered whether to apologize for the intrusion, but decided against it.

'I don't feel angry, not really.' He sighed. 'Just kind of ... embarrassed.'

'There's nothing to be embarrassed about,' I said. I spoke quietly. 'We all have our off days.' I paused. 'And that's what I'm here to help you with.'

'I know.' He cleared his throat, as though to indicate that the subject was now closed. 'Anyway, I'd like to try and talk some more about the dream.'

I nodded encouragingly.

He closed his eyes. 'Let's see... Where did we get to last time? I'm in the box. It's dark. I'm frightened.' He knitted his brow, as though concentrating hard. 'I can hear the shouting, getting louder and louder. A man's voice, and a woman's. Then...'

He came to a halt.

'Go on.'

'Then ... there's a scream. The woman's voice, screaming. And the man's voice, deep, rough, angry ... shouting back.' He pressed his fingers into his forehead. 'And then ... a sudden jolt. The box moves, as though it's hit something hard. I squeeze my eyes tight shut, hold my breath. I want to call out, but no one must know I'm here...'

He put both hands over his face. I could see that they were shaking slightly. Then, to my surprise, he began to sob, great choking sobs that at first shook his shoulders, and then the whole of his frame. I leaned forward over the low table between us and pushed a box of tissues towards him. I would have liked to put my hand on his arm, but I didn't feel that was appropriate, not in this case.

'It's all right, Gwydion.' My voice sounded curiously disembodied. I've noticed that happens sometimes in my sessions, at moments of crisis. Everything seems to slow down, and sound, even the sound of my own voice, comes to me as though from far away.

'I can't do this,' he said. His voice was muffled behind his hands. 'It's too much to ask. I just can't.'

It's too much to ask. I wondered what that meant. There was something odd about all this, I felt sure. Something that didn't quite add up.

'I'm sorry,' he said. Or rather gasped, as he pulled a tissue out of the box, still hiding his face from me. He wiped his eyes and blew his nose. As he did, his body was still trembling with after-shocks, or aftersobs, or whatever they're called, those great quivering breaths that children give once they've stopped howling but haven't quite

93

finished the job.

Finally, he took his hand away from his face and looked at me.

'I'm sorry, Jessica, but I really can't go on with this.' He was trying to steady his voice, but there was still a quiver in it.

I said nothing. I doubted that he meant it. When clients say they can't go on, it usually means we're getting somewhere, and that, on the contrary, they're about to spill the beans at last. All I have to do is sit tight and listen, maybe push the tissues over from time to time, as when it gushes out, it's generally a pretty messy business. But not this time. To my surprise, Gwydion didn't continue. Instead he got up to leave.

'Gwydion, come on,' I said. 'You don't have to rush off like this. Just stay for a moment. In silence, if you like. You don't have to say anything.'

'No, I'm sorry. I think I'd better be off.' There was still a tremble in his voice, but I could see that his mind was made up.

He walked over to the door.

I watched him go. For the second time that day I felt as though I'd been slapped in the face. I hadn't expected this, hadn't seen it coming. I tried to think of something to say, something to keep him there, but nothing came to me.

He opened the door. I thought for a moment he was about to go out without so much as a good-bye, but he turned and said, 'I'm sorry about this. It's not your fault. You're a decent person. Trying to do your job. That's why...'

There was a silence as his sentence trailed off in mid-air.

'Why? Why what, Gwydion?'

He glanced away from me and, just for a second, I saw that there was regret, real regret, written all over his face. He had the air of a little boy who had done something wrong and had been caught out. I had no idea why. Gwydion had lost me. And now I was losing him.

I tried another tack.

'Gwydion,' I said. 'Before you go, can I ask you something?'

He nodded.

'Did you send me a photograph of your father in the post?' I hesitated, then decided not to elaborate.

He looked nonplussed. I wasn't sure whether that was because he was feigning ignorance or because he had no idea what I was talking about. Either way, I wished I hadn't brought up the subject.

We stayed there for a while, him hovering at the door, me sitting on the edge of my chair, both of us knowing that this moment was a turning point – and both of us seemingly unable to seize it, make sense of it, move forward with it.

Then he walked out of the door, shutting it quietly behind him.

When I got home, after my evening sessions, Bob was on his way out. Rose was upstairs in bed, asleep. I could hear music coming from Nella's room, so I went up to talk to her.

Outside her door I stopped and listened. She was playing the Billie Holiday song she'd sung at the concert.

95

I knocked. As usual, she didn't reply, so after a short pause I opened the door and walked in.

'Hello, love.'

Nella was at the computer. She didn't turn her head.

I went over and sat on the bed. 'How's it going?'

She was deep into Facebook, a smile playing over her lips as she read a message from a friend.

'Listen, I need to talk to you a moment.'

She turned to look at me. I could see from her expression that she was miles away.

'It's just that...' I hesitated. 'I saw you going into the deli opposite my office today. With Emyr Griffiths.'

'So?'

'Well, I just wondered ... you know ... what you were doing there. At that time of day. Out of school...'

'I'm allowed out when I have a free period.'

'Really? Aren't you supposed to be working, though?'

She turned back to the computer, offended that I was quizzing her. 'I was working. The meeting was about my future career.'

'Oh?'

She looked up, a shy smile on her face. She was excited, although she was trying not to show it.

'Emyr's going to put me up for *Jazz Quest*.'

'What's that?'

'It's this new TV show.' Her eyes seemed to widen as she spoke. 'Like *X Factor*, but not lame.'

'That's fantastic news, darling.' I did my best to sound enthusiastic. 'Well done.'

Nella stopped hiding her smile and beamed happily at me.

'He thinks I'm star material. This producer he knows in London is a consultant for the programme, he chooses who goes on. He says he's really excited about me.'

'Has he heard you sing?'

'Not yet, no, but Emyr's told him...'

'Nella,' I cut in. 'I hope you're not going to take this the wrong way.' I spoke as gently as I could. 'But I'd be careful if I were you. You're sixteen now, you're a very pretty girl, and ... well...'

Nella began to scowl. 'Oh, right. So what you're saying is, they're not interested in my singing, they just–' She broke off. 'Thanks, Mum. That's very supportive, I must say.'

I sighed. 'Look, I'm sure they do admire your singing. You sing beautifully. But I'm just warning you...'

'You're being ridiculous.' Nella was getting angry now. 'You treat me like a child. I can look after myself, you know.'

'Of course you can. It's just that there've been some rumours about Emyr.' I hesitated. 'There was some kind of fuss at the school he used to teach at, some business with one of the girls, and he ended up getting the sack. I don't think he did anything wrong, actually, but there was a suspicion he might have. That's all I'm saying, Nella. I just want you to be aware of the situation.'

'Fine. Thanks for telling me.' She turned away, leaned forward to the speaker on her desk and turned up the music.

I got up, walked over to her and put my arm

97

round her shoulder.

'Lovely song,' I said. I kissed her lightly on the cheek. 'Is that the one you're going to do for the show?'

Nella didn't reply.

Instead she slipped her shoulder out from under my arm, signalling that our conversation was now over.

7

The following week Gwydion was back. I was pleased, but not altogether surprised. Clients quite often cut short a session, leaving in distress, only to reappear the following week as if nothing has happened. It's all part of the transference, the acting out of ancient emotional dynamics and, on the whole, one just has to sit tight and prepare for a bumpy ride. But it can be unnerving for the therapist, wondering what's going to happen next – particularly when a client seems to be on the brink of finding out what lies at the root of their problem. Or when the counter-transference, as in this case, seems especially powerful.

The knock on my door came at the appointed hour. I ushered Gwydion in, showing him to his chair and sitting down opposite, in mine. He was wearing his jeans, as usual, and a thick navy-blue sweater. He looked a little tired, I thought. There were shadows under his eyes, and a faintly distracted air about him, but otherwise he seemed calm enough.

For a moment we sat together, saying nothing. I sensed that he was savouring the quiet calm of the room, as I so often did during the day. The tree outside the window cast its shifting shadows on the wall and, as the silence deepened, we could hear the faint rustle of its leaves.

'Winter's coming,' he said. 'You can feel it in the air.'

I nodded, not wanting to break the silence yet. There's always a moment, at the beginning of a session, when I feel a sense of anticipation, excitement almost; as if the familiar map of that person's life, and mine too, has been lost, left behind somewhere, for the moment, so that the two of us can begin, in the peace of the consulting room, to redraw it, seeing and understanding it for the first time.

'I'm sorry I walked out on you last time,' he went on, looking down at the floor. 'I just felt I'd had enough. But now ... well, I realize I'm not going to resolve this on my own. I need your help.'

He glanced up at me. As he did so, his pupils seemed to widen and darken. I held his gaze, looking straight back at him. For once, I didn't feel flustered. I simply acknowledged to myself that I couldn't help responding to him as a normal woman does to an attractive man, that these subterranean currents of emotion pass through us all from time to time, however unwelcome or inappropriate they may be. And that, besides, there was something more important going on here: Gwydion was a sensitive, vulnerable human being in need of someone to help him, someone he

99

could trust. I needed to show him I was that person.

'Let's go back to the dream, shall we?' I said. 'Have you dreamed any more of it?'

'No. I'm stuck. Every time I get to the jolt, I wake up.'

'You said last time that, before you felt the jolt, there was shouting going on. A man's voice and a woman's voice.'

'Yes.'

'Do you know who the voices belong to?'

'I'm not sure.' He looked away. 'I mean, the man's voice could be my father's, of course. It's angry, like his used to be when I was a child.'

'And the woman's?'

'I don't know.' He shrugged. 'I suppose it could be my parents arguing. They did, a lot, when I was a child. But I don't really recognize the woman's voice.'

'What about the sudden jolt? What could that be, do you think?'

'Again, I can't really say. I mean, my father had a bloody awful temper, but I don't remember him ever hitting my mother. Or me.'

I thought for a few moments. 'You say you were in a box. In the dark. I wonder what that's about.'

'Well, my parents didn't lock me in a box, if that's what you're getting at. They weren't cruel to me. The worst they did was ignore me.'

'They? You mean, your mother ignored you, too?'

He looked confused for a moment, as if he'd spoken out of turn. 'No. No. She was always very good to me. We were – are – very close.'

'In what way?'

He seemed surprised at my question. 'The usual way. She looks after me, worries about me. Like mothers do.'

He paused. I sensed that he didn't want to discuss the matter further.

'No, it was Evan that was the problem,' he went on. 'His whole life revolved around his work. He was away so much, we hardly ever saw him. And when he came home he was always surrounded by people. Actors, mostly. He never made any time for me.'

There was a silence, and then he added, 'He really didn't know me. He just wanted to show me off, as his son. I suppose he was proud of me, in his own way. He used to try to get me to entertain his friends, teach me little routines, set up puppet shows, that kind of thing. But he was always so impatient. He'd get angry when I couldn't learn a line, or a dance step. He frightened me, undermined my confidence. I used to end up dreading the whole business.'

I thought for a moment. 'And yet, as an adult, you went into acting.'

He gave a wry smile. 'Strange, isn't it? I suppose you could say he was my role model, in that respect. And perhaps I did inherit whatever talent I have from him.' He paused. 'He still tries to teach me stuff, says I can use his contacts, but as regards my career, I don't involve him at all. I don't want his help. If I make it, I'm damned if I'll give him the satisfaction of thinking he's had anything to do with it.'

He spoke with such bitterness that I couldn't

help feeling a little sorry for Evan. He'd obviously been a distracted father, wrapped up in his own world, but he seemed, in his naive way, to have loved his son.

'So, going back to the dream, and this couple arguing,' I said. 'You say your parents' relationship wasn't violent. What was it like, then?'

'He treated her with utter contempt.' A harsh note came into his voice. 'From as far back as I can remember, he had one affair after another.'

'How did you know that?'

'I just knew. Children sense these things, don't they? Some woman who's always coming round to the house, laughs a bit too loud, touches your father's shoulder a little too often. Your mother looking hurt and humiliated. And then at night, hearing the arguments going on downstairs, while you lie there in bed, frightened and upset.' He paused. 'She really suffered. Evan had no shame. He never hid his philandering. Each time he was unfaithful he'd come home and confess, swear that he'd never do it again. She forgave him every time. It was pathetic.' He lowered his voice. 'I hated him for what he did to her. Still do.'

I began to feel less sorry for Evan. In fact, hearing how he'd treated his wife, repeatedly humiliated her in front of her son, made my gut clench in anger.

'The thing is, it's still going on. He's got this girl Rhiannon now. He's quite open.' He waved a hand dismissively. 'But to tell the truth, I'm past caring about it. There's nothing I can do. My mother's not going to leave him. They're just going to go on as they are, as far as I can see, to the bitter end.'

We fell silent. Eventually I spoke.

'I think you do care about it, though, Gwydion.' My tone was tentative. 'I think this conflict became part of you when you were growing up. That's what happens to children when their parents fight. That's what you're still carrying now, inside.' I paused. 'And maybe the jolt...'

'In the dream?'

I nodded. 'It could be something that actually happened, of course. Or perhaps something that you wish would happen? So that the conflict can be resolved at last.'

'Maybe.' He didn't look convinced.

There was a short silence, and then he began to talk about the upcoming rehearsals for the drama series. He'd have to miss the next session, he said, as he was wanted for meetings with the director, but he was keen to press on as quickly as possible after that: he needed to get the button phobia under control before dress rehearsals started, and he was still troubled by the dream, which woke him up at night, leaving him too tired to focus on his work properly during the day. I felt for him. He was in a rush to solve these pressing practical problems that threatened to ruin his career. It seemed irrelevant, at such a juncture, to be delving into old family conflicts that couldn't be changed – he had a life to get on with.

And yet I knew, from past experience, that there was no real alternative for Gwydion. Sooner or later, when things are wrong in our lives, there comes a jolt. The call of conscience, as Kierkegaard named it. We can ignore it and carry on, constrained perhaps by our decision, limiting our horizons, or we can see it as an opportunity to put things right. Whether Gwydion was going to be able to respond to the call, I didn't know. But if he could only get to the end of his dream, I thought, there was a good chance he might be heading in the right direction.

We talked some more, mostly about the button phobia and the costume he was going to wear for his role as Granville Beauclerc, the male lead in the drama series. He said it was likely to feature metal buttons on the waistcoat and jacket, and horn ones on the shirt, sewn on through a shank at the back, rather than through holes in the buttons themselves. He explained that they wouldn't be the worst type for him, and that he'd probably be able to manage once he had buttoned himself into his costume. We went on to discuss practical issues, such as how he might contrive to be alone when the buttoning took place, or whether someone else might do the buttoning for him, and then it was time for him to go. We said goodbye, and I wished him luck with his upcoming meetings; he seemed reluctant to leave, and I, too, was sorry to see him go, aware that his absence the following week would interrupt the steady progress we had been making in our sessions.

After he'd gone I went over to my desk to catch up on my correspondence before my next client came in. But instead of scrolling through my emails, I sat for a moment looking at the screen-saver, a drawing of our house and garden that Rose had brought home from school as a young child.

My session with Gwydion, as so often happens

with a client, had raised a few issues of my own. I thought of the sudden jolt in his dream, the call to conscience as I'd interpreted it, telling him that something fundamental was amiss in his life, something that he needed to address immediately. Could that apply to me? Was Bob's infidelity the jolt I'd needed to show me that our marriage was in trouble? Perhaps it was his way, albeit uncon-sciously, of telling me that. I'd responded sensibly, or so I'd thought up to now. I hadn't shouted and screamed, hadn't threatened to leave. I'd behaved like a responsible adult, a parent, not a jealous lover, aware of how much was at stake, how much would be lost – for all of us – were we to fight and part. But in truth I was angry with him. Seething with rage, to be more exact. My gut reaction to Gwydion's description of Evan's philandering had told me that. If I was to be honest with myself, I needed to acknowledge my anger, find a way to express it, not simply turn away from it for fear of the destruction it could cause. The problem was, how was I going to do that, without wreaking havoc in my life?

'Bob, I'm thinking of going away for a few days.'

'Mmm?' Bob looked up from the paper. We were sitting at the kitchen table after breakfast, reading the Saturday papers.

'I need a break.' I picked up my coffee cup and warmed my hands on it.

'Good idea. Where shall we go?'

'No. Not us. Me. On my own.'

He put down the paper, pushing his specs up into his hair as he did.

'Jess, when are you going to stop punishing me?' There was a look of genuine anguish on his face. 'I've said I'm sorry. I've done my best to make amends. What more can I do?'

'I'm not punishing you. I just want to be on my own for a bit, that's all.'

'Look.' He sighed. 'I made a stupid mistake, and I regret it terribly. But I'm sure we can work this out. Why won't you talk to me, let me explain?'

'We have talked about it.' I took a sip of coffee. 'You had a one-night stand. I've accepted it. You've said it won't happen again. I believe you. There's nothing more to say.'

'Oh, for God's sake!' Bob was exasperated. 'You're a psychotherapist, aren't you? You're supposed to believe in people expressing themselves, communicating. Why can't you do it yourself?'

'Psychotherapists are just the same as anyone else, Bob.' My voice was beginning to rise. 'They get pissed off when their husbands cheat on them. They feel jealous. Hurt. Resentful. We're not bloody saints, you know.'

'OK, fair enough. But you're just not giving me a chance here. We need some time on our own together. I'm sure that would—'

'I don't want time on my own with you, Bob,' I cut in. 'To be quite honest, I can hardly bear the sight of you at the moment. But, as it happens, I want to stay married to you. I don't want to lose all this.' I gestured around the room. 'Or upset the girls.' I paused. 'I'm sure this feeling will pass. You'll just have to let me get it out of my system in my own way.'

He was about to reply, but just then Nella walked in. There was an uncomfortable silence. She walked over to the fridge, opened the door, got out a carton of juice and poured herself a drink.

'Are you two having a row?' she said.

'Yes,' I said.

'No,' Bob said. We spoke in unison.

'I see. Well, don't let me interrupt you.' She shut the fridge door, picked up her drink, took a biscuit from the tin on top of the fridge and walked out.

There was a silence. We were both feeling ashamed about quarrelling in front of Nella.

'Nella's getting rather sarky these days,' Bob said, changing the subject.

'Just adolescent stuff, I think.' I did my best to sound conciliatory. 'She's very touchy at the moment. I tried to talk to her the other day about this so-called A&R man...'

'What about him?' Bob looked concerned.

I'd already told him that Emyr had been sacked from his job, and why. I'd said I thought it was unfair, that there was a kind of hysteria in schools these days about the issue of physical contact between teachers and pupils. However, I hadn't yet said that Emyr had also been my client; I hadn't wanted to worry him – or to disclose confidential information unnecessarily.

'I wasn't going to mention it before, but he came to me for a few sessions a while ago.'

'Oh? What for?'

'Nothing much. Just mild depression after losing his job.' I paused. 'I only saw him two or three times, but he seemed fairly normal, as far as I could tell.'

Bob frowned. 'Is he trustworthy, do you think?'

I thought for a moment. I pictured Emyr standing in the car park burbling on about youngsters and Safe Trax.

'Well, he's a bit of a twit. But pretty harmless on the whole, I'd say.'

'Good. Better keep an eye, though.'

There was another silence, this time a long one. Then Bob spoke.

'When do you want to go off?'

'I thought towards the end of next week maybe, and over the weekend. If you could look after the girls.'

'Of course.' He thought for a minute. 'Although, hang on, I've got a meeting on the Saturday morning...'

'Tough,' I said. 'Cancel it. Or take Rose along with you.'

He nodded silently.

'It'll be a good opportunity for you to spend time with Nella,' I went on. 'I think she needs a bit of input from her father right now. Maybe you can talk to her about this man Emyr. I don't want to be the one who's always breathing down her neck.'

He nodded again. Then he glanced at his watch.

'I'd better go up and change. I promised I'd take Rose out for a game of tennis this morning.'

He got up from the table, looking miserable.

'Make sure she puts her sun cream on, won't you. And her hat.'

'Of course.' He paused. 'I thought we might go

108

out for lunch somewhere afterwards. The three of us.'

'Sorry, I've got to get through this. Take her on your own, she'll like that.' I went back to reading the paper.

He came over and put his hand on my shoulder.

'Go off on your trip, Jess,' he said. 'Don't worry about the girls, I'll take good care of them. It'll be fun.' He paused. 'Just come back and try to forgive me, OK?'

In my mind's eye I saw him lean towards the translator, take off her headset, and whisper something in her ear.

'OK.'

He waited for a moment, hoping perhaps that I would reach up and take his hand, but I stayed motionless.

'See you later, then.'

'Later.'

I didn't look up as he left.

I spent the next couple of hours sitting at the kitchen table on my own, drinking tea and reading an essay by the French psychoanalyst Jacques Lacan snappily entitled 'Of Structure and the Inmixing of Otherness as a Prerequisite to Any Subject Whatsoever'. I was trying to put Bob and the translator out of my mind and, after a while, I managed to do so.

I have to admit, reading Lacan is a bit of a secret vice, as far as I'm concerned. I'm well aware, of course, that in many ways the man's a pretentious bore; he takes the idea of the Freudian slip a little too literally, going in for a lot of heavy-handed Gallic wordplay, which makes his jokes just about as funny as a Jacques Tati film. But even so, there's a lot I like about the guy: his insistence, like Freud, on paying attention to the precise words we use, the language we speak, as a way of penetrating the barrier between what we know about ourselves and what we don't; and that strange French concept of *jouissance*, of pleasure that is also suffering, the pursuit of which dominates our lives, disrupts them, makes us want to live more rather than less, whatever difficulty, misery, or disaster, that may bring.

Probably we would all be quiet as oysters if it were not for this curious organization which forces us to disrupt the barrier of pleasure or perhaps only makes us dream of forcing and disrupting this barrier.

I was just about to tear myself away from *jouissance* and galvanize myself into action when the phone rang. I picked it up.

'Hiya, *cariad.* Mari here. How's it going?'

'Not too bad. You?'

'Oh, bearing up... Can you talk?'

'Yes. Bob's out playing tennis with Rose.'

'Any developments?'

'Well, I've decided to go away for a short break. Without the family.'

'Good thinking.' She paused. 'Where are you going?'

'I haven't decided yet. But it won't be west Wales.'

She laughed. 'D'you want me to come with you?'

110

I thought about it. 'No. I think I need some time on my own, actually. But thanks for offering.'

We went on to chat about this and that. Mari told me she was up for a part in a new film about the early life of Shirley Bassey, set in Cardiff in the Fifties. She was hoping to play Bassey's mother, the redoubtable Eliza Jane, and had been practising her accent for the audition. Then she asked me about how Nella's singing was going, and I told her about Emyr Griffiths. I said I was worried about him, explaining how he'd been sacked from his job at the school, but I didn't tell her that he'd come to me as a client afterwards. As I've said, Mari isn't the most discreet of souls. She advised me not to worry, to let Nella get on with her life, as I knew she would. Then she asked me how things were going at work.

'Actually, there's something going on with one of my clients.' I hesitated, not wanting to break my rule about patient confidentiality. 'I can't really tell you about it, but it involves that director you told me about, Evan Morgan.'

'Oh yes?' Mari sounded intrigued.

'Didn't you mention there was some kind of scandal about him and a young girl. Way back?'

'That's right. She was working for the family at the time.' Mari gave an ironic laugh. 'The Swedish au pair. Priceless, isn't it.'

'She was Swedish?'

'As far as I remember. There was some kind of accident. She went off swimming on her own. Drowned, out there in the bay behind the house...'

My mind was racing. So the Swedish tourist that Arianrhod had told me about wasn't a

111

tourist at all. She was the family's au pair.

'I really can't remember the details. But the family were upset about it,' Mari went on. 'And of course, there was the suspicion that...'

'That what?' I pictured the photograph of Evan Morgan, with the blacked-in eyes, and felt a cold fear rise up from my belly.

'Well, you know what he was like.'

'What d'you mean? You think he had something to do with the accident?'

'Of course not. No, that there'd been some hanky-panky between him and the girl.' Mari sighed. 'It wouldn't have looked good if that had come out. Not in the circumstances.'

'But wasn't there an investigation?'

'I suppose there must have been. But the family managed to hush it up, or that's what was rumoured. They're a pretty influential lot, the Morgans, aren't they?'

I pictured the little plaque at the top of the cliffside at Creigfa Bay, the unfamiliar script with its circles over the As and dots over the Os. I wondered who had put it there. Her parents, most probably, as a memorial. I wondered what it said and, if I could find out, whether it would tell me anything more about the girl who had drowned out there in the grey waters.

Mari began to press me for information as to who my mysterious client might be. She must have thought she was being subtle, but it was clear to me that she was simply looking for gossip. So I brought the conversation to a close, telling her that I was running late, that I had a ton of household chores to do, and that we'd have to talk another time. She sounded disappointed, but I rang off all the same.

Damn, I thought, as I put the phone down. I went over to the table and began to clear up the breakfast things. Outside, the sun was still shining. I'd been looking forward to getting out there, pottering about in the garden in a haphazard way, perhaps hanging out the washing if the weather held. Now I had this to think about, and I knew I wouldn't be able to relax.

I stacked the plates and cups by the dishwasher and started to load it, pondering on the problem as I did. Why had Arianrhod lied to me about the girl? Was it to shield her husband from a sex scandal, or for some other, more obscure, reason? Could Gwydion's recurring dream, about the man and the woman fighting, be connected to the accident? And, most disturbing of all, could Evan Morgan have been involved in the girl's death?

I looked out of the window at the garden. There was a lot that needed doing. Cutting back, mainly. I'd been planning to tackle it that morning, striding out into the sunshine brandishing the secateurs, restoring order, shape and beauty to the sprawl, but now I felt overwhelmed by the task. It began to seem like an impossible chore, a doomed attempt to gain control over encroaching chaos.

Sometimes, in these gardening situations, you just have to tell yourself to carry on. Bust through the feeling of helplessness, hopelessness. Go down the 'Yes, we can' route. Ignore the 'No, we can't' option, even if that's the more realistic response. So I did. I put on my gardening boots, donned my scruffiest jumper, arming myself with a hacksaw, secateurs and a penknife, and went out.

For two hours I sawed, and chopped, and clipped, and heaped, and piled, and dragged, and tidied, and as I did, some phrases from the Lacan paper kept coming into my head:

Life is something which goes, as we say in French, 'à la dérive'. Life goes down the river, from time to time touching a bank; staying for a while here and there, without understanding anything ... and it is the principle of analysis that nobody understands anything of what happens.

When I'd finished I cleared away some dry, dead wood and built a small bonfire at the end of the garden, by the compost heap. I set light to it and watched it burn. It caught fire quickly and began to crackle. As I watched the flames leap up, and the smoke curl into the sky, a sudden realization came to me. The photograph of Evan had been sent to me as a plea to find out what had really happened, and whoever it was from, I felt impelled to accede to its request.

It began to rain. I poked away more vigorously, but the flames died and the bonfire began to smoke. I heard a crack of thunder in the distance. I looked up and saw that the sky had gone dark.

Nobody understands anything of what happens.

As the downpour gathered momentum, I picked up my tools and ran for cover, back into the house.

8

The air hostess came past – cabin attendant, I think they're called nowadays – and I ordered another gin and tonic. I like to drink when I fly. Cramming yourself into a metal tube hurtling through the sky begins to seem like tremendous fun, which it never does when you're sober. I also like to take drugs. Betablockers, Temazepam, that kind of thing. I'd take cocaine too, if it wasn't illegal. For me, it's all part of the holiday. I know I'm a respectable psychotherapist and mother of two, but as far as I'm concerned, when I step onto a plane I leave all that behind. It's something to do with being up in the clouds, I think, unable to lift a finger to help anyone, however dire the circumstances. It's an intoxicating feeling, even without chemical enhancement.

I took a hefty swig of the G&T, put my head back, and closed my eyes, listening to the dull roar of the engine, the low chatter of the passengers and the soothing clink of the ice cubes in my drink. I gave a sigh of satisfaction. I was on my way to a beautiful city I'd never seen before. I was going to stay in a comfortable hotel overlooking the sea. There was no one with me, no husband, no children. I had no responsibilities. I was out and about in the world again, alone.

After I'd spoken to Mari on the phone, and found out that the girl who'd drowned in the bay

115

was in fact the Morgans' au pair, I'd felt a compulsion to investigate further. In fact it had become something of an obsession. I knew that, to some degree, I had my own agenda here, that I was doubtless projecting my anger at Bob onto Evan, the philanderer par excellence. However, I was genuinely moved by Gwydion's story. I wanted to help him, and time was moving on: he was due to start rehearsals in only a few weeks, and unless he could get the insomnia and the button phobia under control before that, he might well struggle to cope. Moreover, I was convinced that the dream held the key to his problem. I'd come to believe that the jolt, as well as representing his desire to heal the rift between his parents, and thus within himself, might actually be a memory of a real, traumatic event that had occurred in his childhood – an accident, perhaps, that had been covered up, and lied about, by Evan.

I'd searched the Internet for information on the accident, but found nothing, so I'd gone to the local-history section of the library to see if there had been any reports in the newspapers at the time. Eventually, after scrolling through endless rolls of microfiche, I'd found a brief mention in the *Western Mail*, giving a short description of the incident: that a couple walking their dog had found a young woman's body on the beach, that the police had established she was Elsa Lindberg, a nineteen-year-old student from Stockholm on holiday in the area, and that she'd drowned as a result of being swept away by the current while swimming on her own 'outside the designated safety area'. At the end of the report was a comment from the girl's mother, Solveig Lindberg, who'd said simply, 'I am devastated by the loss of my daughter.'

I'd managed to trace Mrs Lindberg on the Internet. There were a lot of Solveig Lindbergs, and I'd spent quite a while looking for the right one, but finally I'd found her. She was based in Stockholm, heading a campaign to stop the planting of genetically engineered trees. I'd contacted her by email, established that she was the mother of Elsa, told her I was a psychotherapist, that I'd come across some information concerning the accident in the course of my work, and asked if she'd be willing to answer a few questions about it. She'd replied, saying that she was keen to talk to me, but didn't wish to communicate about it by email. That was when I'd come up with the idea of going to the psychotherapy conference in Stockholm for my break.

That was over a week ago, and now here I was on the plane. The pilot came on the intercom, announcing that we would soon be landing and saying that the weather in Stockholm was fifteen degrees, fine and set fair.

I smiled to myself and looked out of the window. Far below, I could see the sea, glittering in the sunshine. Everything's going to be fine, I told myself. I'll go to the conference, and see Mrs Lindberg on the Sunday. In between, I'll just unwind: explore the old town, the Gamla Stan, visit museums and art galleries, rummage through second-hand clothes shops and market stalls, sit in cafes drinking coffee with cinnamon buns ... and generally savour my brief moment of freedom.

117

There's something about the light in Stockholm. That's what I remember about it now. I suppose most of the time the place is swathed in cloud and rain, but when I was there, the sun shone out of a clear blue sky each day. It was different from ordinary sunlight, though. It was crystal-clear, cold and sharp, with a kind of merciless intensity that was at once exhilarating and intimidating: a northern light made for frozen wastes, tundra and taiga, wolves and bears and caribou, not for ordinary human beings going about their daily lives in a busy city. And the way it hit the buildings, sideways-on, was different, too: it came from a strange position in the sky, or so it seemed to me. The sun was high up, so high up that you couldn't see it at all, except as a dazzling white expanse that you had to look away from quickly before it burned your eyes. It was a dangerous sun, a dangerous sky; not that it wished you harm, of course, it couldn't care less whether you lived or died. You were nothing to that sky, a mere speck, beetling about with all the other specks on the face of the earth below.

Somehow, living under that sky for those few days, and coming to understand its impassive nature, began to make me feel fierce and reckless. It didn't help that, where I was staying, near the old part of the city, the streets and passageways between the imposing buildings echoed with the footsteps of passers-by; or that ravens circled around the tops of them, cawing, especially when night began to fall; or that, everywhere you looked, you could see the sea, glinting in the glare,

118

mocking your landlubber habits, beckoning you to set sail through frozen waters and ice floes and glaciers to unknown, undreamed-of lands. During those few days in Stockholm something stirred in me – a spirit of adventure, I suppose. I began to realize how constrained, how small, how domestic, my life was, and to long for ... I'm not sure what. Not something better – I'm quite contented with my lot, on the whole – but definitely something bigger. In Lacan's words, I'd been 'quiet as an oyster', hiding under a rock on the seashore, and now, the clear light and crisp air of Stockholm had woken me up, and I began to want things oysters don't want. Pleasure. Excitement. Conflict. Pain. *Jouissance*. In short, *more* – although more of what, I wasn't quite sure.

The hotel, as I'd hoped, was simple and comfortable, all painted-wood interiors, fluffy towels and crisp white sheets, with a lovely view over the water that I could see from my bed when I woke up in the morning. The first two days I attended the conference, a series of scientific papers on the nature of mindfulness, the approach *du jour* in current psychotherapy. They were concerned to show that meditation and other practices borrowed from Buddhism have proven neurological benefits, alleviating all sorts of mental and physical illnesses, from depression and anxiety to psoriasis and tinnitus, by reducing chronic pain and stress. Most of the lectures were fascinating and instructive, and I was glad I'd attended. In the evenings there were parties and dinners, where I bumped into former colleagues and met a host of new ones. They were a lively bunch, all in all, and I thoroughly enjoyed being with them, but I didn't arrange to meet up with any of them over the weekend. I wanted the rest of my break to myself.

Over the next two days I changed my mind as I pleased: decided to sleep in, but got up early; set out for a must-see museum, only to be distracted by a little street market on the way; skipped lunch, napped in the afternoon, and spent the evening sampling strange fish dishes in a fancy restaurant, high up in a tower that you had to take a lift to get to. For the first time in years I was able to dither to my heart's content: I spent hours deciding on what souvenirs to bring home, and finally settled on some adorable fingerless mittens for the girls, trimmed with embroidered Lapland ribbon; a crimson felt beret with a black grosgrain bow, in mint condition, for myself; and a bottle of aquavit for Bob. It was deeply satisfying not to make plans; not to have to negotiate anything; not to consider anybody's likes or dislikes, moods or whims, except for my own. And after a while, as I'd hoped, I began to forget about Bob and the translator, and instead immersed myself in the city and its past, walking its cobbled streets, gazing out to the still, blue waters that encircled them, and letting images of Vikings, Valkyries, swan maidens, medieval warlords, megalomaniac kings and stern, frock-coated pastors run through my head.

On the Sunday, as arranged, I went to the Vasamuseet to meet Solveig Lindberg for lunch. She'd told me that she'd wear a bright pink jacket, so that I could recognize her. She'd said she was in her sixties, with grey hair. I'd described myself as dark-haired, in my forties, and said I'd be wearing

120

Fifties-style tortoiseshell sunglasses, whatever the weather.

I got to the restaurant a little ahead of time, but Solveig Lindberg was already there, waiting for me. I noticed her immediately I walked in. She was wearing the pink jacket, as promised, sitting at a table for two and studying the menu. When I went over and introduced myself, she got up, extending her hand to shake mine. She was tall and slim, dressed in a loose charcoal-coloured sweater and trousers that perfectly complemented, and toned down, the pink.

'I'm so glad you've come,' she said. She seemed excited. 'Here, do take a seat.'

I did as she asked.

'Can I get you a drink?'

I took off my sunglasses. 'I'll have a beer, thanks.'

She waved the waiter over. Judging by her angular face and her greying, ex-blonde hair, she was well into her sixties, but she looked the picture of health and elegance, with piercing blue eyes, smooth skin, and lines only in places where lines look good.

She ordered my drink and we made small talk, chatting about the weather, what I thought of Stockholm, and so on. When the waiter came back we ordered our food. Then, as he walked off, she laced her fingers together, leaned forward slightly, and cut to the chase.

'So. You wanted to talk to me about my daughter's death.'

Usually, I've noticed, people avoid the word death when speaking of a loved one. They say 'passed away', 'left us', or some such euphemism.

121

I wondered briefly if it was a cultural difference, whether the Swedes were perhaps more pragmatic about this kind of thing, or whether Mrs Lindberg herself was unusually forthright.

'Yes.' I paused, wondering how best to begin. 'I can't tell you how I came across this information, but let's just say, I've got a client who may or may not be affected by it. I want to help him, so I've decided to look into it further. For reasons of confidentiality, I'm unable to say more than that. I'm sure you'll understand.'

She nodded.

'Now, it's been suggested to me that the accident wasn't fully investigated. I don't know anything about it myself, though. That's why I'm here. To ask you.'

'I'll tell you whatever you want to know. I don't mind talking about it.' She picked up her glass of water and took a sip. 'In fact, I'm glad of the opportunity. I don't get much of a chance to discuss it these days.'

There was a silence. I looked down at her hands, noticed she wasn't wearing a wedding ring.

As if reading my thoughts, she went on, 'After Elsa died, I split up with her father. She was our only child.'

I nodded, but said nothing.

'He remarried, started a new family.' She paused. 'I never did. I'm not sure why.'

She stopped talking. I decided not to ask her why the split had occurred. I thought I probably knew. Put simply, there are times when, for a couple who have lost a child, love doesn't do the job. When parents are suddenly plunged into misery together like that, they sometimes find the best way to deal with it is to get away from each other, make a new start, carry on alone or with somebody new. That's the plain, unvarnished truth. It isn't very palatable, of course. But there it is.

'You see,' she went on. 'Andreas – that's Elsa's father – was angry with me. He thought I couldn't accept that Elsa's death was an accident. That I couldn't cope with the idea emotionally.'

I noticed, rather irrelevantly, that her command of the language was remarkable. Like many Scandinavians, she spoke better English than the English.

At this point the waiter brought over our food. It looked good, but for the moment neither of us touched it. I sensed that she was about to make a revelation.

'Mrs Lindberg,' I began. 'You don't have to tell me anything you don't want to...'

'Solveig, please.' She reached over and laid a hand on my arm. Lightly, politely, but there was an urgency in her gesture. 'The thing is, I do. I do have to tell you. Nobody else will listen to me. Elsa's death was not an accident. I'm convinced of it.'

I nodded again, non-committally this time. The psychotherapist's art mainly consists of nodding non-committally, and I'd perfected it over a couple of decades. I'm pretty good at it now. Though I must admit, it isn't that hard.

She picked up her knife and fork, and began to eat. I did the same, feeling somewhat confused. I wondered whether Solveig's husband had been right to suspect that perhaps she was in denial. I'd hoped, when I'd first seen her, that I'd finally come across a success story: someone who had overcome tragic misfortune, escaped from the slough of despond that ensues in its wake. Now I began to wonder whether she'd found another way to cope, by simply pretending that some evil unknown hand had caused Elsa to drown. Denial. Paranoia. Both common neurotic symptoms with a single, and very useful, purpose: to shield us from pain, to flee from the glaring, terrible reality of life – that bad things happen, all the time, to some people and not others, quite randomly, and for no good reason at all.

'So what do you think happened?' I took another sip of beer. A small sip, because it was strong, and rapidly going to my head.

Solveig put down her knife and fork. 'Elsa went over to Wales that summer as a tourist, that much is true. She went with a friend from university, Ingrid. While they were there they met a local family, the Morgans. They offered the girls free board and lodging in return for looking after their young son, Gwydion, and helping around the house. It's a lovely place, right on the coast, and the weather was glorious that summer. Elsa liked it so much that she decided to stay on for a few weeks more, after Ingrid came back to Stockholm.'

I noticed that Solveig had clasped her hands again, lacing her fingers together.

'Actually, I was rather excited when she told me about the Morgans,' she went on. 'They were unconventional, arty types. An actress and a director, very well off. They're quite famous in Wales, I believe.'

124

I nodded.

'And Elsa seemed happy, so...' Solveig's voice trailed off for a moment, as though she was lost in thought, then resumed. 'Anyway, what could I do? She was nineteen years old, an adult. She wasn't under my control any more. And she was pretty good about keeping in touch. She phoned us quite often, wrote to us once or twice. She seemed to be having a wonderful time. Playing tennis. Sailing. Swimming.' Solveig came to a halt.

There was a silence, and then I said, 'Did she often swim in the bay? The one behind the house? I've heard the currents are quite treacherous out there.'

'Yes. But I don't believe she drowned. Because, you see...' Solveig picked up her beer and took a sip. 'Elsa was a very strong swimmer. And we Scandinavians ... we teach our children about the dangers of the sea. They have the rules drummed into them from when they're babies. She'd never have taken any risks.'

'Even so.' I chose my words carefully. 'Teenagers ... young people ... they're sometimes a bit head-strong, aren't they? They do take risks. We all know that.'

Solveig shook her head. 'I'm certain that she wouldn't have.' She paused. 'When ... it happened ... I went over to Wales to see for myself. I went to the bay. It looked safe enough, on a calm day. And the weather had been good the day she drowned. I checked.'

She stopped, picked up her knife and fork, and started to eat again. I followed suit. Then, after a while, I asked, 'So what do you think did happen?'

Solveig grimaced. 'I still don't really know. The police were totally unhelpful. There'd been a brief inquest, showing that the cause of death had been accidental. She was a teenager, which is a high-risk group for drowning, and they'd found traces of alcohol in her body. So that, as far as they were concerned, was that.'

'Could she have been drunk, perhaps?'

'No. The alcohol traces were very slight. As I said, she knew the dangers.'

'Did they find anything else?'

'Some injuries to her head.' Solveig's voice trembled slightly. 'Some bleeding.'

'Really?'

'Consistent with drowning from natural causes, apparently.' She seemed to be recalling the words of the report. 'The head injuries were due to buffeting in the water, and the bleeding was passive, caused by internal congestion as a result of the head-down position of a floating corpse.'

The head-down position of a floating corpse. The words hung in the air.

'It sometimes causes diagnostic confusion,' she continued, a bitter edge to her tone. 'In fact, as I found out, it's very difficult to establish from the autopsy exactly what happened in a case of drowning. You have to look at the circumstances. I thought they were suspicious, so I went back to the police.'

'And?'

'The inquest had ruled out suicide or homicide, so they refused to investigate further. They were polite enough, but I could tell they thought I was overreacting, that I was simply distraught at the

126

death of my daughter. And they were obviously friendly with the Morgans, wouldn't say a word against them.' She paused. 'The family themselves were no better. They completely clammed up. The mother seemed to be in a terrible state. Tearful, incoherent. The father...' Solveig came to a halt.

I waited.

'Have you ever met him?'

'Only once, briefly. I can't say I took to him.'

'Well, then ... I thought he was a lying bastard.' Solveig spoke in an even tone, but there was a quiet anger in her voice. 'He claimed that Elsa must have gone swimming the previous evening, as night was coming down, on her own. The macerated condition of her skin, established by the postmortem, was consistent with his story. He said she must have got into difficulties because of the current. Or maybe that she'd had cramps. That they hadn't noticed her absence until the morning. I didn't believe him. It didn't ring true.'

'Are you sure about that?'

Solveig looked straight into my eyes. I looked back, into the piercing blue, and thought of the sea and sky and Elsa drowning somewhere between them, cold and alone, without her mother to comfort her. 'I am. I didn't trust him an inch.' She paused. 'To tell you the truth, he tried to flirt with me. As if he thought he could distract me from investigating my daughter's death. In front of his wife, as well. I found it disgusting.'

I shook my head in disbelief.

'So what happened in the end?'

'I couldn't get anywhere. I stayed on for a while,

saw to all the arrangements, had Elsa's body flown home. Put up a plaque at the spot where she died. Andreas didn't come over to help, couldn't cope with it. Then I went back to Stockholm. Got through the funeral, somehow. Tried to forget. Lost my husband. Began a new career. Carried on. As people do.' Solveig finished her meal and pushed her plate away. 'Dessert?'

'No, thanks.' I'd been enjoying my meal, but my appetite had suddenly vanished. 'Shall we just have some coffees?'

Solveig nodded, waved the waiter over and ordered the coffees. Then she opened her bag and took something out.

'Would you like to see a picture of her?'

For a moment I didn't know what she was talking about. Then I realized that she was holding a photograph of Elsa.

'Yes. Of course.'

Solveig handed over the photo. It was in colour, rather battered at the edges. The girl was fair-haired, with long, slim arms and legs, like her mother. The same elegant, Nordic bone structure. She was wearing a sky-blue sweater, and she was laughing hard.

'She's lovely, isn't she? She looks like you.' I started, realizing I'd spoken in the present tense, as though she was still alive.

I handed the photo back. As I did, my eyes filled with tears. I thought of my own children, and imagined how terrible it must have been – must still be – for Solveig to bear the loss of her daughter at such a young age, with her whole life still ahead of her. And I felt a shiver of fear when

128

I thought of Nella and what might be happening at home with Emyr and *Jazz Quest*, and the manager, producer, or whoever he was. I'd given Bob strict instructions not to let her make any decisions about the audition while I was away, but of late I'd begun to realize that she was reaching a stage where she might well decide to take matters into her own hands.

Solveig leaned towards me and put her hand on my arm once again. This time, her grip was firmer.

'Help me find out what happened, Jessica. Please. I need to know. I've done everything I can. You live over there. You could help me.'

'Well, I'll try. But I'm not a detective.'

'I know, but I'm sure you realize there's something wrong here. That's why you've come to see me.'

I didn't deny it.

'I knew someone would come one day,' she went on, letting go of my arm. 'These things never stay hidden forever.'

For a second, three images passed before my eyes. I thought of Gwydion lying in his bed, his face to the wall. Of Arianrhod in a cloud of blue smoke, twisting her fingers in her sleeve. Of Evan Morgan, standing on the driveway of the mansion, frustrated and angry.

'Look,' I said. 'I think you may be right. It's possible you haven't been told the whole truth about what happened.'

I wondered for a moment what on earth I was getting myself into. I made sure not to mention what I already knew of the family – patient confidentiality and all that. But I also thought it wise not to get her hopes up at this stage. I wasn't convinced there had been foul play, if that was what Solveig was getting at. So I chose my words carefully.

'If you like, I'll try to find out a bit more. But I warn you, I can't promise anything.'

'Thank you.' Solveig spoke lightly, but I could hear the intensity in her tone.

The waiter brought over the coffees. While we drank them we went back to making pleasantries. Then, after a while, she looked at her watch and said she had to go.

When she got up to leave, she shook my hand. Then, impulsively, she leaned forward and kissed me on the cheek.

'Goodbye,' she said. 'And good luck.'

'Thanks.' I put my hand on her arm for a moment. 'I'll keep in touch.'

'Mind you do.'

She gave me a last smile. A cheerful, encouraging smile. Then she picked up her bag, slung it over her shoulder, and left.

9

Bob came to the airport to collect me. He was in a buoyant mood, evidently expecting an immediate rapprochement between us. He hugged me tightly when I saw him, took my suitcase, and put his arm around me as we walked to the car. As we drove home, he told me that all had gone well with the girls over the weekend: he'd taken Rose out and about with him on Saturday, and on the Sunday he'd invited his mother over for lunch. Nella had helped him cook the meal. They'd had a chance to talk, and she'd told him that there was nothing to worry about. Emyr was just trying to help her get her singing career off the ground, she'd said. She was practising for the audition, and she'd let us know when it came up. In the evening, Bob said, he and the girls had watched a film on TV. Rose had snuggled up to him on the sofa, and Nella had leaned against him and put her head on his shoulder, the way she'd used to do when she was little.

'That's nice,' I said. My anger towards him was thawing a little since my brief adventure in Stockholm. 'Maybe I should go away more often.'

Bob laughed, but he shot me a nervous glance. 'Feeling any better?'

'I don't know.' I thought about it. I did feel calmer. The break had done me good, helped me to move on from my feeling of helpless resentment towards him. 'I think so.'

'Good.' He leaned over and patted my knee. 'Now, tell me all about Stockholm.'

I told him about the city: the blue skies; the glittering islands in the sea; the pretty little hotel by the water's edge; the cobbled streets of the Gamla Stan; the restaurant in the tower with the panoramic views; the grandiose wooden warship in the Vasamuseet, which I'd visited after my lunch there. Built in the seventeenth century by King Gustavus Adolphus, it had so many gun

131

decks perched on its narrow keel that it toppled over and sank on its first outing. The ambitiousness, and foolishness, of the endeavour had made a strong impression on me. The way that nobody – architects, shipbuilders, naval strategists, political advisers – had dared to tell the king that the ship wouldn't stay up in the water, even in port. The way that armies of sailors were employed to run up and down the decks when he visited, to make it look as if it could keep steady.

'You'd like Sweden.' I paused. 'Maybe we could go together some time.'

I didn't mention that everything there was fiendishly expensive. That had been a shock to the system, not to mention the bank balance. And I didn't mention who I'd had lunch with at the Vasamuseet, either.

When we got home, Rose bounded up to greet me, glad to have me back. Nella was too, I could tell, although she pretended at first not to have registered my absence. They both loved the mittens, and Bob was gracious enough about the aquavit, opening it and pouring us an aperitif. The house was tidy, and Bob had cooked a casserole for supper. Nella had made a salad, and Rose had iced some fairy cakes for afters, as she called it. We ate together, and I felt more relaxed than I had done in a long time. Looking around the cosily lit kitchen, it seemed impossible that anything, anything at all, could destroy this little unit: Bob, me, and the girls. But that night, when we went to bed and Bob tried to make love to me, the translator came back again.

She was wearing her headset and her tiny dress.

Bob was in his suit, his specs perched on the end of his nose, looking serious. He was sitting at a desk, with his name on a little sign in front of it. The translator was smiling at him. He was smiling at her. Every time he spoke, she repeated his words. He liked hearing her voice, shaping the outline of his sentences in her language. She liked fashioning them for him, presenting to all the people listening, polished and buffed. Then the scene changed and I saw a bed, a hotel bed like the one I'd slept in during my stay, only this one was wider, and grander, and in it were Bob and the translator, and the headset had come off, and the tiny dress...

'I'm sorry,' I whispered. 'I'm not quite ready yet.'

In the days that followed I somehow didn't find time to tell Bob about my meeting with Solveig Lindberg in Stockholm. There was a lot to do on my return, catching up with work, getting the household running again, ferrying the girls here and there. But the real reason I kept silent was that I hadn't decided what my next step should be. Of course, keeping the meeting secret was a small matter, or at least that's what I told myself at the time. But even so, it weighed on me, because up to that point I hadn't, on the whole, kept secrets from him – even insignificant ones.

Nella seemed in a cheerful mood. At night we heard the Billie Holiday song coming from her room, and her voice, singing along with it. She was evidently practising hard for *Jazz Quest*. Then, one evening towards the end of the week, after I'd got home from work, she appeared in the kitchen dressed in a tight, short skirt and a skimpy T-shirt, her face plastered with make-up.

'Mum, I need a lift. Over to Fairwater.'

'Now?' I glanced at my watch. It was already six o'clock.

'Yes.'

'But what about supper?' I said. 'And home-work?'

'I'll get something to eat over there. And I've done my homework.'

'OK, then.' I could see no reason why she shouldn't go out for a couple of hours. 'Where shall I drop you off?'

'At my friend's.'

'Which friend?'

'Tamsin.'

'Who's she? I've never heard of her before.'

Nella sighed. 'Mum, I've got a lot of friends, you know.' She spoke slowly, as if talking to a halfwit.

I nodded. 'How will you get back?'

'I'll call you.'

I thought for a moment of giving her my time-worn lecture about not being a taxi service, but decided not to bother.

'All right,' I said. 'Come on, then. Let's go.'

We went into the hall. She picked up her bag and stood by the door while I put my coat on. Nella watched me, but she didn't get her own jacket.

'You're not going out like that, are you?' I said. 'You'll freeze to death.'

Sometimes, when I talk to my elder daughter, I seem unable to express myself without coming out with every cliché in the book. I could have said, 'Can I pass you your jacket?' or something like that. But instead I always seem to parrot the same old hackneyed lines. I wish I could stop myself, but I don't seem to be able to. Perhaps it's some ancient mothering – or smothering – instinct, wired into the DNA.

'Are you sure you don't want to borrow a cardigan?' I continued, as we went outside, got into the car and drove off. 'I think there's one in the back.'

Nella ignored my remark. Instead, she flipped down the visor above her head and began to inspect her face in the mirror, even though it was dark and she could hardly see.

'You could put it in your bag. Just in case.'

'In case of what, Mother?' Nella always calls me 'Mother' when she's annoyed with me. 'I'm getting out of the car and going into someone's house. Then I'm going out of someone's house and getting into the car. What do you expect to happen on the way? A biblical flood? A hurricane? And if it did, how would the cardigan help?'

I nodded, duly admonished. Nella was right, in a way. And I was right, too. I could see her point, but she wasn't going to be able to see mine, not for a long time yet. So it was useless to pursue the issue.

We drove along in silence. I thought about mentioning the fact that her eye make-up was a little heavy, but decided against it. When we got to Fairwater she flipped the visor back into position, registered where we were, and directed me into a quiet, well-lit modern estate with neat lawns in front of each detached house.

135

'Park here,' she said. 'And turn round.'

'Which house is it?'

'Oh, one of those.' She waved an airy hand.

'What time do you want picking up?'

'I said. I'll call you.'

'Mind you do. Before eleven, please.' I leaned over and pecked her on the cheek.

She got out of the car and shut the door. I could see she was waiting until I drove off before going up to the house, so I turned the car round and headed slowly back down the road. As I did, I glanced in the rear-view mirror and saw her walk up the pathway to one of the houses. When she got to the door, it opened. A figure was framed in it, illuminated by the light in the hallway. The figure of a man with curly, reddish hair. I squinted into the mirror, trying to see who it was, and then I recognized him: Emyr Griffiths.

I started as the car tyre bumped the side of the road. By the time I'd steered the car back onto the road and turned the corner, the house, and the figure in the doorway, were lost to view.

As soon as I could, I parked the car on the roadside, fumbled in my bag for my mobile and called Nella. Her phone rang, but she didn't answer it. I tried again, but she still didn't pick up, so I texted her, telling her to phone me immediately. Then I sat waiting for a reply, getting angrier and angrier. Nella had lied to me. She'd told me she was going to see a girlfriend, but she wasn't, she was visiting Emyr at his house... If she didn't call, I decided, I'd go back, knock on the door, and demand to know what was going on.

The mobile rang.

'What is it?' Nella sounded irritated.

'Look,' I said, 'you told me you were going to see your friend Tamsin. But you're in that house with Emyr Griffiths...' I stopped, realizing that my voice was rising.

'So? Tamsin's here too. We're talking to Emyr about our recording session.' There was a pause as Nella walked away from whoever it was that was listening to the conversation and lowered her voice to a whisper. 'And you can stop spying on me.'

'I'm not spying on you. I'm just trying to make sure–'

'Listen, Mum, I'm fine,' she cut in. 'Calm down.' She spoke as if reassuring a lunatic. 'Don't call me again.'

'OK. But whose house is it?'

'It's Emyr's house.'

'You didn't tell me that.'

'Well, I'm meeting Tamsin here – at the studio. It's in the house.'

'Fair enough. But you should have explained.' I paused. 'Don't stay out too late. When will you be back?'

'I'll keep you informed.' With that, Nella switched off her phone.

I drove home feeling angry, wondering whether I'd overreacted. Nella hadn't exactly lied to me, but she hadn't told the truth either. When I got home I busied myself helping Rose with her homework and, after she'd gone to bed, sat watching TV, my mobile in my hand. It didn't ring, but at precisely five to eleven Nella let herself into the house. As she came in through the front door, I

137

heard a car drive off down the lane.

'Oh, so you got a lift,' I said, coming into the hall.

Nella nodded, put down her bag, and headed towards the kitchen. I followed her.

'I'm sorry I panicked,' I said, as she cut herself a slice of bread and began to spread it with peanut butter. 'But I just wish you'd explain what you're doing, that's all. I worry about you. Emyr...' I stopped, then started again. 'Well, we don't know him very well, do we?'

Nella waved the knife impatiently. 'I don't want to go into this right now, Mum. I've got a lot on my mind.'

I didn't respond. It was clear that discussing the issue further would only lead to an argument. So I decided to go up to bed.

'Turn out the lights when you go up, won't you,' I said. 'Dad's away in London tonight.' Then I added, as I walked down the hallway, 'And remember, Nella. I don't like being lied to. Don't do it again, please.'

The next day I was too busy to dwell at any length on my altercation with Nella. I had a new client that morning, filling Jean's old slot, and after that Gwydion was coming in, after missing last week's session. I wondered what kind of mood he'd be in.

At eleven o'clock precisely there was a knock on my door and he walked in. He was wearing a hooded top, jeans and his strappy running shoes. He looked relaxed and confident.

'Welcome back,' I said as he sat down in the chair opposite.

'Thank you,' he said.

'So? How did it go?'

'Fine. Very good, actually. The director and I just seemed to click. He's very sharp, very intuitive. We worked on the script, made some changes.' He smiled. 'I've never really worked with the top people before. This is a new level for me.'

'Well, that's great.' I paused. 'No sleeping problems, then?'

'No.' There was a note of excitement in his voice. 'The thing is, Jessica, since I last saw you, everything's changed. You see, I've got to the end of the dream.'

'Oh?'

'I know what happens now.' He paused. 'Can you remember where we were with it?'

'I think so.'

Clients often do this. They expect you to remember the exact details of their inner landscape at a moment's notice, forgetting that you may have dozens of other inner landscapes currently on your books. But, for reasons to do with my own inner landscape, I did remember the main features of Gwydion's dream, quite accurately.

'You were in the box. The dark space. You were afraid. You could hear voices above you, shouting. And then a sudden jolt.'

'That's right. I'm down there in the dark.' As usual, he got straight down to business, closing his eyes and lowering his voice to a whisper. I noticed that he'd begun to talk in the present tense. 'I'm terrified. Afraid I'm going to die. And then ... outside the box, right outside, a splash. A loud splash, as though something heavy, like a body, has fallen into water. The box moves again, and I realize that it's floating on the water. With me inside it.' His voice began to tremble slightly. 'I begin to scream, louder and louder. Nobody comes, nobody can hear me, so I scream as hard as I can. And then, suddenly, I wake up.'

There was a silence. I didn't break it, but my mind was racing. It was all beginning to make sense. Gwydion hadn't been locked up in a box, as he'd described it, but had been down in the hold of a boat while some kind of altercation took place upstairs, on deck – an altercation between a man and a woman that ended with a splash: with something, or someone, jumping – or being pushed – overboard. What if the man's voice was Evan's? And the woman's Elsa's?

Gwydion opened his eyes and looked at me. There seemed to be a kind of relief written on his face, as though he had come to the end of a task, pleased that he'd accomplished it satisfactorily.

'So, what do you think?' he asked.

I batted the question back to him, as is my wont. 'What do *you* think?'

He frowned. 'It's about my father, obviously. About something that happened way back, before I can remember ... something bad...'

I nodded. Again, as is my wont.

'I know I used to go sailing with Evan on his yacht when I was very young. I can dimly re-member being taken out in it from time to time. I hated it as a kid, apparently. Still do. I suffer terribly from seasickness.'

I steered him back to the dream. 'But you can't remember this particular incident. Not consciously, anyway.'

'No, not at all. Perhaps I was very young at the time. I don't know.'

Silence fell once again. And, once again, I began to put two and two together. Could Evan have taken Elsa out on the yacht and pushed her over the side? Left her to drown in that cold sea, while he sailed on with his young son in the hold below. But if so, why? What would have been his motive?

There was a short silence. Then I said, 'Let's go back to the woman's voice. It definitely wasn't your mother's?'

'Definitely not.'

'No one you recognized?'

'No.'

I tried a different tack. 'What was the voice like?'

'High. Young. She was kind of giggling at first. I suppose they must have been drinking. And then, when he turned nasty, it got higher. Panicky. She gave a loud scream before she ... before I heard the splash.'

I nodded. That seemed to make sense as well. Mari had told me that Evan had a reputation as a drunk and a womanizer. As one of his many conquests, she'd had first-hand experience of it. And I myself had witnessed his bad temper on my brief visit to the Morgan place. What if Evan had taken Elsa out on the boat, made a pass at her, and then flown into a rage when she'd rejected his advances? Fought with her, pushed her off the boat by accident? Or, worse, done it on purpose, in a drunken fit of violence?

'Can you remember what happened after you

141

heard the splash?'

'No. Not a thing.' Gwydion looked pensive. 'I'm sure the dream is about a real event. And I'm going to find out what it was.' He paused. 'I feel better already for having got to the end of it. It hasn't come back since. I'm sleeping like a baby.'

'Good. I'm glad of that.'

'In fact,' he went on, 'I feel so much better, I don't think I need to come and see you any more.'

I was taken aback. Much as I was pleased at Gwydion's progress – most of which, admittedly, seemed to have occurred without my help – I hadn't expected this curt dismissal. I'd thought, now that he'd returned, that I was on the whole journey, the whole ride with him again, not just jumping on and off for one stop. Besides, my curiosity was getting the better of me. I wanted to find out the end of this story, where it went from here.

'So you feel you can cope on your own now?' I did my best to sound encouraging.

'Yes. You've helped me make a start. Now I think I just need to get on with my life.'

I'd been through this many times before. As a psychotherapist, the counter-transference whether positive or negative, ensures that you feel keyed in to your client's life. You can't imagine how they're going to manage without you. Or, if you're honest, the other way round. As I said earlier, being a therapist is a bit like being a parent. If you do your job well, sooner or later you get the boot. Only with clients, these people that you've come to know so well – perhaps better than their lovers, families and friends will ever know them – you wave goodbye to them for good. No weekly phone calls, no holiday postcards home, no family reunions. When they walk out of your door, that's it. Forever. It's a bit hard to take sometimes.

Gwydion looked at me and smiled. A warm, open smile, one that I hadn't seen before on his face. 'Thanks for all your help, Jessica.'

I smiled back. 'Well, you seem to have done most of the work by yourself.'

'Not really. It was important having you here to talk to.' He paused. 'But now I realize I've got to do this next bit on my own. I've got to find out what the dream was all about. I think I must have witnessed an accident. Maybe even...'

His sentence hung in mid-air. I waited, but he didn't finish it.

'There's nothing wrong with me now,' he went on. 'I was definitely traumatized by whatever happened back then. But now I've begun to remember what happened, it's as though a great weight's been lifted off my mind.'

'And the button phobia? What about that?'

'Oh yes.' He frowned.

'Has that resolved as well? As a result of ... getting to the end of the dream?'

'Not entirely. No.' He paused. 'But I've decided to take your advice about that. I've arranged a course of treatment.'

'Oh?' I couldn't help feeling a little hurt that he hadn't booked in with one of my colleagues in the building, as I'd suggested.

'Yes. Somewhere nearer home.'

'That makes sense.' I paused. I wanted to find

out more, but I felt I'd asked him enough questions. 'Well, then...' It was time to bring the session to a close.

Gwydion got up from his chair, and I stood up, too, to bid him goodbye.

'Good luck. All the best.'

I held out my hand. But to my surprise, instead of shaking it, he took it in his, and held it for a moment.

'Goodbye, Jessica,' he whispered. He moved towards me and kissed me lightly on the cheek. As he did, I caught the scent of his body, his hair. It smelled warm, intimate, familiar, like the top of a baby's head – a baby of your own, that you've loved intimately, passionately, ever since it was born. I realized I'd been subliminally aware of it from the minute he'd walked into my consulting room for his first session. Pheromones, they're called. Sexual, maternal, primal, biological sort of things. You can't mask them with scent, deodorant, shampoo. They don't smell bad, or good, for that matter. They just smell like themselves, unique to that being, whoever or whatever it is. And whether they come from a baby, a potential mate, or a mortal enemy, you can't help responding to them, like an animal.

'Goodbye, Gwydion.' I wondered for a moment which one he was, deep down in my psyche. A child. A lover. A potential threat. Or perhaps, most potently, a mixture of all three.

A sudden dizziness overcame me. I closed my eyes, trying not to rock back on my feet. As I did, I felt his lips brush across my cheek until they reached my mouth. I could feel his breath, warm and sweet, on my face. My heart began to thud in my chest. I knew that if I moved towards him, even infinitesimally, we would begin to kiss, as lovers do. But I didn't move a muscle.

We stayed like that, neither of us moving, as though suspended in time. Then I felt his hand slip out of mine, and when I opened my eyes he was walking towards the door, his back towards me. I watched, half in relief, half in regret, as he opened the door, walked out into the corridor, turned the corner, and was gone.

10

The following weekend Bob and I took the girls out west, to Pembrokeshire. We always go to the same spot, renting a small bungalow that overlooks the beach, with a breathtaking view over the sea. We'd stayed there many times before, and the children had always loved the place. I'd often wondered whether they actually preferred it to our own house, festooned as it was with fake barometers, china flower baskets and homemade pinecone decorations, most of which seemed to feature hedgehogs dressed in human clothing. But now, of course, I reflected rather sadly as we walked in, they were getting a little too old to enjoy that kind of thing. Nella hadn't wanted to come at all. The house, and the beach below, were no longer much of a draw for her – she was growing up, and leaving such simple pleasures behind.

That said, Bob and Rose seemed happy enough to be there. They both love surfing, and the moment we arrived got into their wetsuits, picked up their boards and disappeared off down to the beach, keen to catch the last waves of the season, while the sea was still relatively warm. It was far too cold for me, though, so I stayed behind in the house. Nella, never much of a sportswoman, stayed with me. Most of the time she mooched about in her room, practising her singing, or sat in a chair by the window, wrapped in a duvet, texting her friends on her mobile phone, her headphones clamped over her ears. Meanwhile I made myself busy, making beds that didn't need making, labouring over the simplest of meals. And when there was nothing more to do, I sat beside her at the window with a book, or gazed out at sea, watching the two small black specks of my husband and younger daughter bobbing in the waves below.

Mostly I thought about Gwydion and what he'd told me during his last session. It seemed likely to me that, as a young child, he'd been on the boat when Elsa met with her fatal accident, and as such was a witness. It also seemed possible that Evan had caused the girl's death. If that was indeed the case, I wondered what I ought to do about this explosive new information.

As a psychotherapist, my legal position was fairly clear. A client who tells you, in confidence, that he or she is about to commit a murder must be reported immediately, and if a client threatens to commit suicide, you may also need to take action. Otherwise, you're perfectly at liberty to keep shtum, whatever lurid tales your clients may tell you. Gwydion had talked to me in very general terms about an incident that had occurred years ago. No one was about to get the chop in the near future. So, in formal legal terms, there was really nothing that I needed to do.

As a citizen, though – a good citizen – wasn't it my moral duty to inform Gwydion of certain facts concerning his past that he didn't appear to know about? That, perhaps, his parents were keeping from him? The main one being that when he was a small child, a teenage girl, Elsa Lindberg, who had been his au pair, had drowned in the bay right outside the house, possibly on a boat trip she'd taken with Evan. Moreover, that I'd spoken to Solveig Lindberg, the girl's mother, and she was convinced that the Morgan family were lying about the circumstances of her daughter's death.

On the other hand, telling Gwydion this information would mean revealing that I'd been nosing around in his past without his knowledge. If I admitted that I'd been talking to people behind his back – people like Mari Jones and Solveig Lindberg – he might, quite understandably, feel angry and betrayed. And I didn't want that.

Of course, as well as the revelations about his past, there was the way we'd parted to consider. As I sat gazing out to sea, I imagined what it would have felt like, had his lips touched mine, had I made that tiny movement towards him, responded to his advances. More than once, as I watched the waves crash on the shore, he held me in a passionate embrace, pressing his body against mine and ... and then... Well, I tried not to feel too guilty about what I imagined next. Fantasizing is a healthy, normal part of our sexual lives, isn't it? An essential part, as far as most of us are concerned. Nothing wrong with that. But in this case it was accompanied by a foolish, adolescent daydream about him falling madly in love with me, and me falling madly in love with him.

Just an emotional reaction to what had happened with Bob and the translator, I told myself. A way of getting my own back. And a response, perhaps, to the taste of freedom that I'd experienced in Stockholm. It would pass soon enough. What was confusing the situation, of course, was that Gwydion had been my patient. And that, through my encounter with him, I'd now become embroiled in the Morgans' murky past, in trying to discover what exactly had happened to that young girl out in the bay all those years ago.

It didn't help that the cottage where we were staying was only a few miles from the Morgan place. I was only too well aware that it would be easy enough for me to pick up the phone, say that I was in the area and casually suggest that I drop in for a visit. But I didn't. Instead, I sat at the window, looking out to sea, in a state of indecision.

On Sunday morning I decided to act. The Elsa Lindberg mystery was still on my mind, and I knew that, if I paid a quick visit to the Morgans, I might be able to find out more. It seemed foolish not to take the opportunity now that I was so near; so I took it.

I got up and dressed casually, but carefully, in brown cords and a dark green, cable-knit sweater,

148

fixing my hair, Land Girl-style, with a kirby grip to one side. Nella was in bed, and I knew she would stay there until midday at least. Bob and Rose were eating breakfast, waiting for their wetsuits to dry and planning their next sortie into the waves. I made an excuse, saying I was going to the village to get some provisions, and that I'd come back to cook lunch later on. Then I got into the car, swung out onto the road and headed over to the Morgan place.

On the way I stopped and called ahead. Arianrhod answered the phone. I told her I just happened to be in the neighbourhood and wondered if Gwydion was there and whether I might drop in for a quick chat. I could be there in about fifteen minutes. She sounded surprised, but said that, yes, Gwydion was at home and they would both be happy to see me. She seemed reasonably friendly, but all the same I couldn't help feeling nervous as I drove along the country lanes towards the house. I knew I was going to have to talk to Arianrhod about what had happened, maybe even confront her with the fact that she'd lied to me – well, not lied, exactly, but withheld the truth – and I wasn't quite sure how I was going to go about it.

It was only when I drove up to the imposing iron gates and pressed the buzzer that I began to wonder whether visiting the Morgans that day was such a good idea after all. If there was going to be any kind of confrontation between myself and Arianrhod, being on the family's home ground would definitely put me at a disadvantage. I might have done better, I reflected, as the gates opened and I drove through, to ask Gwydion, or Arianrhod, or both of them, to come and see me in my consulting rooms, although that would perhaps have seemed a slightly odd request. But it was too late to change my mind now. I was here, and I was going to have to face the music. Or the Morgans were. Unless, of course, I sidestepped the whole issue, and pretended I was just here to pass the time of day and discuss the joys of holidaying on the Pembrokeshire coast. Which would have been odder still.

I parked the car on the gravel pathway, making sure to avoid Evan's preferred spot. Once again, one of the peacocks strutting about on the lawn came towards me, head jerking, emitting a shrill cry. I got out, banging the car door, and watched it scuttle off. Then I turned to see Arianrhod emerging from one of the flowerbeds beside the lawn.

'Welcome back.' She came over to me, a wide smile on her face. She seemed genuinely pleased to see me.

I smiled back. 'I hope I'm not disturbing you.'

'Not in the least. Just a bit of weeding.' She held up her hands. They were covered in dirt. 'I could do with a break. Come on in.'

We walked over to the front door and she pushed it open with her elbow. I followed her down the dark hallway to the kitchen. Once we were there, she sat me down at the kitchen table, went over to the sink and started to wash her hands.

'Tea? Coffee?'

'I'll have whatever you're having.'

'Coffee, then.'

I watched as she dried her hands and arms on a towel. She looked flushed, her hair slightly dishevelled, and she was wearing a scruffy gardening jumper that was fraying at the wrists.

'Gwydion will be down in a minute. Do you want something to eat?'

'No, no. I haven't got long. Got to get back to the family and cook lunch. We're staying just down the road from here.'

We chatted amicably about the nearby villages and beaches, which were the best places to stay, which the ones to avoid, while she busied herself with getting the coffee. Then she brought it over, two cups and a cafetiere, with a bottle of milk and a packet of digestive biscuits.

'All I've got today, I'm afraid,' she said. She sat down opposite and began to pour me a cup.

I took a biscuit and, when she passed over my cup, dipped the edge of it in the steaming liquid. I noticed, when she took hers, that she did the same. This time, it seemed, she was treating me in a more informal way, with the bottle of milk and the packet of biscuits on the table – more as a friend than as Gwydion's therapist.

For a few moments we munched our coffee-soaked biscuits in silence. I was sorry to have to break the moment of relaxed intimacy, but eventually I did.

'Arianrhod, there's something I need to ask you.'

'Hmm?' Arianrhod took a small tube of hand cream out of her pocket and squirted a little of it onto her palm.

'The Swedish tourist who drowned. The girl you

151

mentioned last time I was here. When we were standing on the clifftop looking out at the bay.'

She nodded slowly, looking a little baffled as to where this was leading, and began to rub the cream onto her hands.

'I found out...' I paused again. Still no reaction. 'That she was working for you that summer as an au pair.'

'Really?' she said. She looked up, a puzzled expression on her face. 'Was she? I don't remember that.'

'But you must remember.' I kept my tone level. 'The girl was working for you and then she drowned. That's not the sort of thing anyone forgets.'

'No, of course not.' She paused. 'I suppose it's possible that she might have been here at one time. Before the drowning, I mean.' She worked the cream into a rough, calloused patch on her forefinger. 'But we had so many au pairs in those days. There was always some girl or other here, helping out.'

She stopped rubbing and put the top back on the tube of cream. I noticed her hands were trembling slightly.

It seemed clear to me that she was lying, and I wondered if she was doing so to protect Evan in some way, possibly to do with the scandal. But I decided, for the moment, to let it go.

'How's Gwydion?' I said, changing the subject.

She looked up at me. 'He seems a bit better,' she said. 'But not terribly communicative at the moment, I'm afraid. To me, anyway.'

'Has he...' I hesitated, not sure how to put my

152

next question. 'Has he been asking you about ... about his childhood?'

Again, the puzzled look. 'How d'you mean?'

'Gwydion seems to think that something traumatic might have happened to him when he was young. Something that might have caused his ... issues.'

'No. He hasn't spoken to me about this.' She put her hand to her brow, as if in thought, but there was a nervous, febrile quality to her gesture. 'And I can't think of anything that might have–' She broke off. 'I don't know what's keeping him. Hang on, I'll go and get him. Won't be a sec.'

Arianrhod got up quickly and walked out. I waited, thinking she'd be back shortly, but she wasn't. After five minutes she still hadn't returned. I had a feeling this might all be going to take some time, that things were getting more complicated than I'd anticipated, so I took out my phone and quickly texted Bob to say I'd got held up and wouldn't be back until later that afternoon. Then I went over to the kitchen window and looked out over the lawn.

One of the peacocks had lifted its tail, fanning it out in front of a nervous-looking dowdy brown peahen, which was running about ineffectually in front of it, apparently trying to escape. As the cock turned, I saw the extraordinary upholstery on its back, two sturdy brown wings and a thick fan of grey feathers holding up the delicate canopy above. I watched, fascinated, as the courtship proceeded, the peacock strutting this way and that, little by little closing in on the hen as she searched for a way out.

153

As the minutes ticked by, I realized there must be some kind of discussion going on between Gwydion and Arianrhod, perhaps an argument. I wondered what they might be saying to each other.

The peacock began to bear down on the hen, cornering her by the edge of a flowerbed. He began to shake his tail feathers, rippling them so that the emerald greens and blues flashed in the sunlight, waving them this way and that until they dazzled her. Then he stepped forward to cover her. I looked away.

Gwydion came into the kitchen. Alone. He was dressed in his Sunday-in-the-country clothes, a pair of faded cords and a baggy woollen cardigan over a T-shirt that looked as though it had shrunk in the wash. There was a day or two's stubble on his cheeks. He seemed a little nervous. There was a slight flush to his cheeks, and he moved quickly, as though impatiently, in anticipation.

'Jessica. Good to see you. What are you doing here?'

'I'm staying nearby, so I thought I'd drop in. See how you're getting on.'

He came over and was about to kiss me on the cheek, but then thought better of it. Shaking hands would have been too formal, so we stood there by the window for a moment, feeling foolish – or, at least I did.

'Why are you really here?' he said. His voice was low, almost a whisper. Like Arianrhod, my visit seemed to have thrust him into a state of nervous anticipation.

'You ended our session so abruptly. I wondered why.'

I didn't mention what had happened at the end of the session, but that question, too, hung in the air.

'I thought I'd explained. But listen...' He paused. 'I was going to call you.'

'Oh?'

'Yes. I've been wanting to ask my mother about the dream. About the woman. And Evan.' His words seemed to come out in a rush, as though he was afraid that the moment would pass and he'd miss his opportunity. 'But...' He paused. 'I can't seem to raise it with her. I think it would help if you were present when I talked to her.'

I took a deep breath. 'Well...'

Sometimes therapists call parents or other family members in to discuss a problem with a client. It's a well-established practice, though not one I've ever used. I wasn't sure what I thought about it. On the whole, as I've said, I prefer to steer clear of the family baggage and deal with clients as individuals. I'm an existentialist, after all – by training, and by preference. Of course the family issues matter tremendously, but when a soul's in trouble, for whatever reason, it's usually better to keep them out of the proceedings, in my view.

'Please, Jess. Help me. I can't do this on my own.'

I let out my breath, as gently as I could. It wasn't a sigh, more a gesture of resignation. 'OK.'

He smiled in relief. 'Good. Great. She's waiting in the sitting room. I told her we'd be coming in together to talk to her. Come on.'

155

I felt slightly outmanoeuvred. A little resentful, even, that Gwydion had seen fit to jump the gun like that, assume that I would act as chaperone while he confronted his mother.

'All right. But you must understand, Gwydion, that sooner or later you're going to have to face her on your own. Without me.'

'Of course.' He began to walk out of the kitchen, and I followed.

'And your father?' I continued, as we walked along the corridor. I kept my voice low. 'Is he going to be in on this?'

'Evan's away.' Gwydion kept his voice at normal volume, unconcerned about being overheard.

'Well, I would have thought...'

We came to a door. Gwydion stopped in front of it, listened for a moment, and then knocked.

There was a voice from the other side of it. 'Come in.'

He opened the door a crack. 'Ready?' he asked, in a kind of stage whisper.

I thought that was odd. But the Morgans were an odd lot, no doubt about it, so I didn't give it a great deal of attention. 'Ready,' came the reply.

Gwydion opened the door and we walked in. Arianrhod was sitting on a large sofa and got up to greet us. She looked tired, worried, but, like Gwydion, there was also an air of excited anticipation about her that seemed out of keeping with the situation.

It was a big, airy room, rather grand, with French windows that gave out onto the lawn, and an open fireplace at one end. Over the mantelpiece was a large oil painting of a young, slim, dark-

156

haired girl wearing a diaphanous garment that could have been a nightie. Whatever it was, it didn't cover very much, anyway. It was a modern piece, all angles and shadows and odd perspectives, so at first I didn't realize who it was. Then I saw that it was Arianrhod as a young woman, as she must have been when she met and married Evan.

Arianrhod sat us down, me in an armchair, Gwydion in another, and herself on the sofa. The room was cold. There was no fire burning in the grate. But the chill seemed appropriate for what was obviously going to be an uncomfortable conversation.

'So, Gwydion.' Arianrhod spoke calmly. I thought she seemed more self-possessed than usual. 'You've told me you need to talk to me. And that you need Dr Mayhew – Jessica – here to help you do that.' There was a hint of derision in her voice, but only a hint.

Gwydion sat forward on the edge of his chair. 'There's something I've remembered, Ari.' I noticed that he called her by her first name. 'You know in the dream, where I hear the shouting, and the splash?'

Arianrhod nodded. It was clear that he'd discussed the latest developments in the dream with her already.

'Well, I know who it is now. The man who's shouting is Evan. And the girl... The girl is an au pair we had, called Elsa.'

I hadn't told Gwydion that the au pair's name was Elsa. He must have found out for himself. Perhaps from the plaque by the cliffside. Or

157

maybe Arianrhod had told him minutes before, during their confab while I was in the kitchen.

'I must have been about five or six. Evan took me out on the yacht with Elsa. He was at the wheel, teaching Elsa to steer the boat, and I saw them kissing. I felt sick, so I went downstairs to the cabin to rest. But I didn't sleep. The boat was rocking, and I could hear Evan and Elsa talking and laughing on deck. Evan was drunk. I hated it when he got like that. I was scared of him.'

Arianrhod looked down at her hands, a look of shame on her face.

'Anyway, I could hear him getting drunker. And Elsa seemed to be joining in. And then it began to turn nasty, as it always does with Evan.' Gwydion's voice trembled, and he began to speak a little faster. 'I heard shouting. Evan had got into one of his rages. And Elsa started screaming. Then I heard a bang, and a splash, like a body hitting the water. Evan started to crash about on deck, swearing. The boat lurched this way and that, and I wondered if he was going to be able to sail it home. I was terribly frightened. I thought we were going to die, that we were all going to drown.' Gwydion paused. 'And that's all I can remember. Nothing after that.'

There was a silence. Then Arianrhod spoke. 'I'm so sorry, Gwydi. I should never have–'

'No, you shouldn't.' Gwydion raised his voice. 'You should never have let him take me out in that boat. I used to dread it every time. The man was a drunken bastard. You should have put your foot down. Protected your son. But you never did, did you? You never stuck up for me. Not once.'

'I did try...' Arianrhod's voice was a whisper.

'No, you bloody didn't. You were completely craven. Still are...'

Arianrhod's face crumpled. She hunched her shoulders, and her body seemed to shrivel into her frayed jumper. I felt for her. She was evidently partly to blame for what had gone on in the past, but, as so often happens, her son seemed to find it easier to direct his anger at her, rather than at his father.

'And the worst thing is, you've lied to me.'

'Lied?' Arianrhod looked up. 'What do you mean?'

'You knew perfectly well what happened. Evan took Elsa out on that boat to seduce her. I saw them kissing, I can remember it distinctly. The dream unlocked my memory of that. And then, in the dream, I heard them arguing. Evan must have pushed Elsa over the side, left her to drown, and sailed off without her. I was down below, I heard the jolt as she hit the water. That's real, too. That's what's been waking me up every night for as long as I can remember.' Gwydion's voice had begun to rise. 'He was responsible for her death, the bastard. But you helped him cover it up. You both lied about it – to the police, to everyone. Lied to me. You never thought about how it would affect me, witnessing a murder.' Gwydion was shouting now, pointing his forefinger at his mother. 'That's why I've been so screwed up all these years. I've been driven half mad, and all this time you've been hiding the truth from me.'

'No, Gwydi.' Arianrhod was near to tears. 'I didn't know...'

I decided to intervene. 'I think what Gwydion's saying, is...'

I paused as they both turned to me. They seemed, momentarily, to have forgotten my existence.

'Well,' I went on, 'there are just a few facts that need clearing up here. Elsa Lindberg was your au pair, wasn't she, Arianrhod?'

'Yes.' Arianrhod nodded. She seemed to have accepted that there was little point in denying it now. 'I'm sorry I lied to you earlier about that. I didn't want you to know about the scandal. I thought...'

'And she did go out sailing with Evan and Gwydion, didn't she?'

Arianrhod nodded again.

'And then there was ... an accident?'

Gwydion held his head in his hands.

'What was it?' I tried to speak as gently as I could. 'You must tell us. For Gwydion's sake. He really does need to know.'

Arianrhod began to cry. She was obviously doing it to deflect Gwydion's criticisms and my demands but, all the same, there was a genuine element of distress in her reaction which made it seem callous to keep pressing the point.

I scrabbled in my bag and passed over a tissue. Arianrhod blew her nose and dabbed at her eyes. We waited until she'd composed herself, and then she began.

'It wasn't a murder, Gwydi. Evan told me what happened when he came home. He said that he and Elsa went out on the boat, and that he'd made a pass at her – he was honest enough about that.

160

It was a sunny afternoon, and as they were quite close to the shore she'd said she was going to jump off the boat and swim home. He'd told her not to, but she'd insisted. He'd tried to sail in behind her to make sure she was all right, but he'd lost her.'

She stopped. Gwydion was still looking at her angrily.

'Honestly, Gwydion, this is the truth.'

'What happened then?' I tried to get Arianrhod back on track with the story.

'Well, Evan came home, bringing Gwydi with him. I put Gwydi to bed, and we waited for Elsa to reappear. Waited up all night. Next day, her body was found washed up on the beach.'

'And yet you never told the police that she'd been on the boat with Evan.' I tried not to sound judgemental, but it was incredible. 'Why was that?'

Arianrhod hung her head. 'Evan persuaded me to keep quiet about it.' She looked up, beseech-ingly, at her son. 'You see, it would have been a terrible scandal. If people had known he'd gone out on the boat with that girl – she was so young, just nineteen – and tried–'

'And tried to shag her?' Gwydion cut in.

'Please.' A tear rolled down Arianrhod's cheek. 'Try to understand, Gwydi. It wasn't Evan's fault. He wasn't directly responsible for her death, but it would have looked bad, wouldn't it, if people had found out?' She paused. 'I was just trying to be a loyal wife. It would have ruined his career... I would have lost everything...'

At that, Gwydion got up and walked out of the room.

Arianrhod didn't try to stop him. Instead she

161

bowed her head, covering her face with her hands. I sat there, watching her, as Gwydion went out, slamming the door behind him. I wasn't sure what to do. So, for a few moments, I did nothing.

Then she spoke, from behind the hands. 'Go after him, please. He'll be going out to the bay. See if you can calm him down.'

I thought of the cliffs above the bay, and a sudden fear ran through me.

'All right,' I said. 'I'll try. See you later.'

I walked quietly over to the door and opened it. When I looked back, she was still sitting, hunched and silent, in front of her portrait.

11

I caught up with Gwydion as he crossed the lawn, heading towards the gate in the wall that led out to the bay. When he saw me he said nothing, but slowed his pace a little so that I could fall in with it. We let ourselves through the gate and onto the path, then walked to the edge of the cliff and looked out to sea. It was a murky day, the mist hovering over the water, a great, grey-brown mass of sea and sky and mud and sand and rock, with no features to distinguish one from another. A place where someone trying to swim home, in the cold water, with the darkening sky above, could easily get lost, and cold, and tired; a place where disorientation, and numbness, and despair would come quickly, so quickly that they might never have reached the shore.

Gwydion was still too upset to speak to me. Instead he stared out to sea, narrowing his eyes against the wind. For a while I did the same, standing in silence beside him, hoping that he'd start to talk. When he didn't, I walked over to the top of the steps cut into the rock, and peered at the inscription on the little plaque. I studied the name, Elsa Lindberg, and the dates, 1971–1990, as if they could tell me something I didn't already know; and then I scanned the words below, with the unfamiliar Js and Gs and little circles and umlauts over the letters, wondering what they meant.

Gwydion came up behind me. 'It's a poem,' he said. He spoke in a low, tentative voice, as though still not sure whether he had managed to calm himself. 'I found a translation. It's by a woman called Edith Södergran. Late nineteenth century.' He began to quote the lines in English. '*On foot, I had to cross the solar system, until I found the first thread of my red dress.*' His voice was trembling a little. He hesitated for a moment, composed himself, and then continued. '*I sense myself already. Somewhere in space hangs my heart. Sparks flow from it, shaking the air, reaching out to other speechless hearts.*'

There was a silence. *The first thread of her red dress.* The words made me think, not of defeat, of Elsa Lindberg drowning out in that cold sea, succumbing to the waves, but of victory – of the bright, uncompromising light of Stockholm, shining down on swan maidens, and Valkyries, and warrior women riding out through the frozen

163

wastes, up and out into the stars, through time and space, to avenge the dead.

'Strong stuff,' I said. 'Very Nordic. When did you look it up?'

'Oh.' He seemed nonplussed for a moment. 'Just recently.' He paused. 'Shall we go down the steps? I'd like to show you the beach.'

I hesitated. As I've mentioned, I don't have a great head for heights. And there was something particularly menacing about the bay below that put me off exploring it further. The way the cliffs rose up from it, layered and crumbling like half-demolished buildings. The way the sheets of rock on the beach jutted up, pitted and grey, like a lunar landscape. When you looked down at the beach from above, it seemed primordial, like an ancient seabed: you could imagine landslides, and volcanoes, and earthquakes, and huge tectonic plates shifting there, like a crack in history, in time itself.

'I don't know,' I said. 'I really ought to be getting back...'

He grinned at me. 'You're not scared, are you?'

'No...' I began.

He raised his eyebrows in amusement.

'Well, perhaps, a bit.' I peered down at the steps. 'They look awfully steep. And slippery.'

He went down to the steps, turned to me and held out his hand. 'Come on.'

I waved away his hand. 'I think it's safer if I hold on to this,' I said, gripping the handrail.

'I'll walk in front. That way, I'll break your fall. Not that you're going to fall, of course,' he added, seeing my look of dismay.

164

We picked our way carefully down the steps. Once we were walking on them, the cliff face that they were cut into didn't look so dizzyingly steep. And they were quite safe, I told myself, as long as you clung on to the handrail to stop yourself slipping. Ahead of me, Gwydion walked along without even touching the rail. He'd obviously been down here many times before. But for me, it seemed fraught with danger, and it wasn't until we'd reached the bottom that I let go of the rail, venturing out tentatively behind him onto the jetty below.

I followed him down to the end of the jetty. It led over the beach, which was covered in slimy clumps of seaweed and crusty turrets of barnacles, into the sea. Not a great place for swimming, I thought. Or anything else, for that matter. The kind of place that reminds you how glad you are to be living in comfort and safety in the twenty-first century, having the occasional flight of fantasy about avenging swan maidens and Valkyries, rather than having to avenge anyone or anything yourself.

When we got to the end of the jetty he turned to watch me coming up behind him. Then we stood there together, looking out to sea, with the wind whistling in our ears and the water lapping around us. It made a curious slapping sound as it hit the wooden slats of the jetty.

Neither of us spoke for a moment, and then, slowly, he turned to me, and I found myself looking into his green eyes, fringed with those dark, thick lashes.

He bent closer towards me. I turned my head away from his, but I couldn't seem to move my

165

body with it. I felt his breath on my throat, and my neck began to heat up.

The first thread of her red dress.

The words came into my mind, and they gave me courage. Gwydion is not your client any more, they told me. He's a man, and you're a woman. Don't be a coward. Seize the moment, while you can.

I sense myself already.

I turned my head back towards !

The lagoons were very green, very deep. I wanted to dive into them.

So I did.

It was a long kiss: deep, and warm, and satisfying. There was a bit of fumbling about as well, a hesitant hand up my top, stopping before it got to my breasts, and some pressing together of significant parts of the body; some catching of breath; a closing of eyes; a dizzying of senses; laughter, a strange kind of exultation at the lurch into the hyper-real, the breaking of the rules ... and the surprise, and delight, and discomfort of it all, the crazy jumbling of sensations, his mouth on mine, his tongue inside it, mine inside his, the warmth of his skin, my skin, the skin of his belly, mine, under our hands and, around us, the waves lapping round the jetty, hitting it with that odd slapping noise, and the bitter wind coming in from the sea, making our eyes water and our ears ache. And for me, perhaps for both of us, standing on that rickety wooden structure sticking out into the sea, that sudden sense of the physical world operating by different laws; of somehow walking on water; of falling, falling into a parallel world, where something surreal has happened that you wanted to happen, but never admitted to yourself that you did; and then falling out of it again, and finding yourself back where you started, in the ordinary, the everyday, clinging on to each other, awkwardly, on a half-rotted jetty with grey water all around you, in a chill wind, slightly embarrassed at what you'd done, and wanting to get away from there, get home.

It was the wind, of course, that put paid to any further exploration. Thrilling as the kiss was, neither of us were going to throw off our clothes in the teeth of a howling gale and explore further. It was just too cold even to think about. So we drew apart, and then I said I should be getting home, and we climbed back over the rocks and up the steps, and walked along the cliff top, and through the gate, and across the lawn, not talking, not touching, keeping our distance. We didn't discuss what he'd remembered as a child on the boat. Our bodies in no way acknowledged that we'd kissed. It was as if none of it had ever happened.

When we finally got to the house, to my relief, Arianrhod was nowhere to be seen. So I quickly told Gwydion to say goodbye to her for me, got into my car, and switched on the engine. I couldn't wait to get away.

Before I left, I wound down the window.

'Goodbye, then,' I said. 'Take care. Good luck with ... everything.'

Gwydion rested his arm on the car roof, leaned down, and surreptitiously tried to plant a kiss on my lips, but I swiftly moved my head away.

'Stop that. Someone might see.'

167

He ignored me. 'I'll be in touch.'

I nodded in what I hoped was a none-too-encouraging fashion. 'OK. Take care.'

He tapped lightly on the roof of the car, as though permitting me to leave. I backed the car as he watched me, an amused grin on his face.

I drove off over the gravel towards the gate. On the way out I spotted the peacock strutting through the flowerbed, dragging the long train of his tail behind him, the peahen trotting demurely alongside.

I arrived back at the bungalow in time to eat a late lunch that Bob and Nella had made for us all. I was concerned that they'd have missed me, would be starting to wonder where I'd got to, but my absence, far from upsetting anyone, seemed to have had the reverse effect. Bob appeared relaxed, his cheeks flushed from his exertions in the waves. Rose was her usual cheerful self, and even Nella seemed to have come out of her shell a little. No one asked me where I'd been. So I didn't need to make up any stories, which I was glad about, because lying to people, especially my nearest and dearest, always feels like an imposition to me, a dereliction of my true self.

After we'd eaten we sprawled about in the living room for a while, us with the papers, the girls watching television. When it was time to go, I left them there and went round the house, packing away our belongings. And instead of being irritated by the mess in the kitchen after they'd cooked, and the muddle of clothes and wet towels flung on the floor in the bedrooms, as I usually was, I found myself positively relishing my role in restoring order. For the first time in months, I felt magnanimous towards my family. Generous. Patient. I became intensely aware of how much I loved them all, and I felt how lucky I was to have a family to come home to, and clear up after, and care for; a family that depended on me, for whom I was still essential, and would be for many years to come.

It was only a kiss, I told myself, as I drove back to Cardiff that night. Nothing to get too fussed about. The girls had fallen asleep, curled up in the back under their duvets, and Bob was snoring quietly beside me in the passenger seat. So it was just me, *Late Junction* on the radio, the catseyes, and a long drive home.

The road was dark, and there were no other cars around, so I was able to switch on my headlights full beam. It was raining, and from time to time I saw a frog leap up out of the way, or the white tail of a rabbit scuttle into the hedge. I drove cautiously, aware of the precious cargo sleeping around me, thinking about Gwydion, and the kiss, and Elsa Lindberg, and what I was going to do next.

The kiss, as I said, was no big deal. To be honest, I didn't feel terribly guilty about it. On the contrary, I felt relieved. It had got something out of my system. After Bob had confessed his infidelity, I'd been hurt and angry, and I hadn't found a way to forgive him. Now, I realized, I was beginning to. Despite my protestations to Mari about marriage not being a power game, I'd found she wasn't far wrong. Of course, it was childish and irresponsible to take my revenge on Bob by kissing a good-looking young man, but to be honest, I felt a great deal better for it. At the same time, I knew that I didn't want to risk my marriage by having a full-fledged affair. I didn't really want Gwydion as a lover – he was too young, too needy, too vulnerable. I'd allowed the kiss to happen because I'd been feeling neglected; I'd just wanted some-one, somewhere, to notice me as a woman, and respond to me as such. And now, someone had. So it didn't need to go any further. The kiss had done its job, and that was that.

I drove carefully up the sliproad to the motor-way and checked in the rear-view mirror, acceler-ating as I edged into the traffic and settled into my lane.

No, it wasn't my momentary weakness with Gwydion, but the question of what to do about the whole situation that was troubling me. Ought I not to contact Solveig and tell her what was going on? She'd begged me to help her, to find out what had really happened all those years ago, and now it looked as though we were coming closer to the truth. Yet something told me to wait. Until I gained a clearer picture of the events leading to Elsa's death it wasn't really fair to burden Solveig with each new development. I needed to get the story straight before I went to her.

I leaned forward to turn up the radio as one of my favourite artists, the African kora-player Tou-mani Diabaté, came on. The light flurry of strings made me think of fireflies and humming birds and bats, half-seen creatures that flit about in the dark, and hot African nights with millions of stars up above. Beautiful, mysterious places I'd never seen in my life, and perhaps never would. But I'd made my choices. Here I was in Wales, with the frogs and rabbits, and the fog and rain, and that had its own strange beauty and mystery, too.

Bob stirred next to me. 'OK? Want me to take over?' He sounded half asleep.

'No, I'm fine.'

'Mind if I turn this down a bit?'

'Go ahead.'

He leaned forward, turned the dial and the music quietened. Then he went back to sleep.

I drove on. Although it was late, and the others were sleeping, I felt wide awake, my wits about me. A wind blew up and it began to rain heavily, the cars in front throwing up a fine mist of water in their wake, so that it was hard to see. Inside, our breath began to fog up the windscreen, so I had to keep switching the heating fan on and off to clear it, without getting the car too hot, and I couldn't open the window in case the cold air woke up my sleeping passengers. At times I could feel the wind shake the car, as if it were trying to blow it off the road. All in all it was hard going, but I kept driving, and Bob and the girls kept sleeping, until at last we reached home, safe and sound.

12

On Monday morning I was back in my office, sitting at my desk, relishing the peace and quiet and reading a paper on Recovered Memory. I've got dozens of them on the subject. The central issue – whether a child can be sexually abused or witness a traumatic event, forget about it completely and then remember it, under therapy, as an adult – used to be a hot potato back in the Nineties. But recently the fuss seems to have died down. Not really because any conclusions have been reached, any evidence sifted; sadly, nothing as rational or sensible as that. It's more that everyone seems to have got bored with the whole issue. Psychotherapy, like medicine, has its fads and fashions. Recovered Memory is one of them; and it simply isn't in vogue any more. Satanic Abuse, too, is pretty old hat. Even False Memory Syndrome, the theory countering Recovered Memory, has had its day. And the main reason they've been dropped is that it's all too damn complicated; the whole business of how and why we remember what happened to us as children is so obscure, so fraught with confusion; plus there's so much anger flying around – towards parents, therapists or anyone else who happens to be standing in the firing line – that it's become almost impossible to get at the truth of the matter ... if there is a truth, that is.

Nevertheless, I felt I should go back to my papers on the subject, because now I'd had a client, Gwydion Morgan, with an apparently bona fide Recovered Memory. My first, actually. Of course, I'd had clients come to me before with tales of abuse – some of them with the ring of truth, others quite obviously false. And I'd heard my fair share of stories from my clients, past and present, about traumatic episodes of horrific violence they'd witnessed, or experienced, as children. But I'd never come across an actual death before. Particularly one that had been remembered via a dream. It was a double-whammy. And, I must admit, I couldn't help feeling rather excited about it – if, indeed, the story turned out to be true.

As I went along, I tried to relate what I was reading to Gwydion and his Recovered Memory. And what I read seemed to support what he'd told me. At the age of six he'd have been able to remember what happened on the boat, and report it accurately afterwards; it was also quite possible that he could have repressed the memory of a traumatic episode; and that it could, years later, have been triggered by a dream. What was more, in his case, the facts surrounding the revelation backed up his story.

I began to wonder whether I should go to the police, ask them to look into the matter again, perhaps check the postmortem record. But I decided to wait until I had more evidence; they were hardly going to be in a rush to help – all I had to go on so far was Gwydion's account of the dream.

As I was on the last page of the paper, the

phone rang. I listened as the answerphone came on. Then a voice came through. I recognized it immediately: it was Arianrhod Morgan.

'Dr Mayhew? Are you there?' Pause. She was on a mobile. I could hear the sound of traffic in the street. 'Please, could you pick up? I really need to talk to you. It's an emergency.'

It didn't sound like an emergency, so I didn't pick up.

'I'm outside your office.' Long pause. 'Can you come down and meet me, please. As soon as you can. I'll wait out here.' Then the phone clicked off.

Damn, I thought. For a moment I felt a little panicky. I wondered if there were going to be any more startling revelations about the death of Elsa Lindberg, and, if there were, how I was going to deal with them. And, more trivially, I wondered whether Gwydion had told her of my misdemeanour, that silly kiss on the jetty. He and Arianrhod seemed very close – overly close, perhaps. If he had, it would be embarrassing all round.

And then I thought, come on, Jessica, tough it out. You may be on the trail of a murder here, and if you've got any decency you should stay on it until the whole truth emerges. And this business about the kiss is trivial. Gwydion's not your client any more. You've done nothing terribly wrong. Besides, there's something much more important at stake: the death of a young girl, the necessity, for her grieving mother if no one else, of finding out exactly what happened to her all those years ago; and perhaps, if you're lucky, helping to bring the culprit to justice...

I took my time about going downstairs to meet Arianrhod. As it happened, one of my clients had cancelled that morning, so there was no rush. But I wanted to make a point. I wasn't in the habit of being summoned out of my office to meet people on the street at a moment's notice, and I didn't like it. So before I left I finished the paper I was reading, jotted down a few notes and made sure my desk was neat and tidy. I went over to the hat stand in the corner, put on my coat and hung my bag over my shoulder. Then I stood in front of the mirror for a while, powdered my nose and applied some lipstick. I wanted to look calm and self-possessed for this encounter. Unruffled. But to tell the truth, I was feeling ruffled – very ruffled – and as I walked down the stairs to the front door I could feel my heart thumping in my chest.

When I got to the front door I let myself out. Outside, Arianrhod was waiting for me, sitting on the low wall of the courtyard in front of the building. She got up as I approached, a tense smile on her face.

'Thank you,' she said. She reached forward and clutched my arm, rather dramatically. I noticed she looked pale, drawn. There were dark circles under her eyes.

I drew away as politely as I could. 'I'm afraid I haven't got long.' I glanced back at the building, hoping that no one would see us.

'That's OK. It won't take long. Shall we get a coffee somewhere?' Arianrhod peered vaguely at the buildings lining Cathedral Road. It's one of the main thoroughfares of the city. Where I am, it's mostly private consulting rooms, doctors, dentists, that kind of thing, until you get further down, nearer the centre of town. I realized she hardly knew Cardiff, despite it being the capital of the principality she inhabited.

'No.' There were a few coffee bars we could have gone to in Pontcanna Street nearby, but Cardiff is a small place, and I was bound to bump into someone I knew. 'I haven't really got time. Let's go for a quick walk down by the river, shall we? It's not far.'

It was a bright autumn day, the trees turning to gold beneath a tender blue sky, but there was a sharp nip in the air. We turned into Llandaff Fields, and walked down the side of the sports pavilion onto the high bank that runs alongside the river. There were few people to be seen there at that time of the morning, except for dog walkers and cyclists, none of whom took any notice of us.

Clearly, Arianrhod had something important to say. Otherwise there would have been a bit of small talk as we walked along. Instead, there was silence. I got the impression it was up to me to break it.

'So, how are things?' I tried to sound sympathetic, encouraging, but it was a bit of a struggle. I was still feeling resentful about being called out on this supposed emergency.

She sensed my impatience and immediately looked crushed. 'I'm sorry to disturb you in the middle of your day...'

'Never mind about that.' My resentment began to evaporate. 'Just tell me. What's the problem?'

'It's Gwydion.' She put up her hand to brush a

176

wisp of hair away from her face. I could see that her hand was shaking. I suddenly felt sorry for her and wished that I hadn't been quite so brusque.

We passed a bench on the path. It's one of my favourite spots, high up on the bank, a sheltered place, where you can sit and watch the river run; and, if you're lucky, you'll see herons, and cormorants, and kingfishers darting up and down on the water; and if you're not, you can study the ducks and moorhens in the shallows, and the wind bending the willows, a busy other world of birds and fish and trees, right there in the heart of the city.

'Let's sit down.' I indicated the bench and we went over. It was a good place to be. The metal seat of the bench was warm from the sun. I scanned the river for herons, but I could see none.

Arianrhod sighed. It was a deep, exhausted sigh. Then she began. 'Well, Gwydion's remembered more about the trip on the boat that day. He's told me everything. He didn't just hear what happened. He saw it all, too.' She paused, registering my surprise. 'He says that, when he heard the shouting, he crept up on deck. He put his head out of the hatch for a moment, to see what was going on. Evan and Elsa didn't notice him. They had their backs to him, and they were struggling with each other. Elsa was fighting, screaming, but he wouldn't let go. So she kicked him, hard, in the balls. He was furious, so he came at her. She was sitting on the edge of the boat. She tried to hold on, but he pushed her over the side into the sea.'

Her voice trembled and she came to a halt. I looked down and saw that she was picking at her sleeve, anxiously rubbing and twisting the fabric

177

between her fingers.

'Go on,' I said.

'Just before she fell in, she caught Gwydion's eye and screamed at him for help. Evan looked round, but Gwydion ducked his head down into the hatch again and went straight back to his bunk. He lay down and waited there, his eyes tight shut, until Evan righted the boat and they sailed on.'

'And he didn't tell you anything about it when he got home?'

'No. Not a word. But I noticed...' She paused. 'He was never the same with Evan after that. They'd never been close, but from then on he seemed to be terrified of him.'

I was puzzled. I wondered why Gwydion hadn't told me all this himself.

'So this has all come out in the last few hours, has it? Since I saw you at Creigfa House?'

Arianrhod nodded. 'It's just been such a shock.' She shivered, hugging herself against the cold. 'I can't believe my own husband would...' She didn't finish her sentence, but let it hang there, miserably, in mid-air.

'Of course, I'd never have covered up for him if I'd known,' she went on. 'He told me that he'd taken her out there, and they'd been sailing along, and then she'd just decided, on an impulse, to dive into the water and swim home.'

There was a silence. Eventually I broke it, as tactfully as I could.

'Well, you knew that Evan had taken Elsa out on the boat to seduce her, didn't you? That he'd probably provoked the situation?'

Arianrhod stared out at the river. 'You must

understand ... if you live with that kind of thing, day after day, you learn to ignore it. You have to.'

She put her hand up to her face and covered her eyes. Her gesture reminded me of Gwydion.

'And you knew he was a drunk. And had a foul temper.' I tried to sound as gentle as I could, but facts are facts, and Arianrhod had done her best, for years apparently, to avoid them.

'Of course.' She lowered her head. 'I was on the receiving end of it most of the time. That's another thing you learn to put up with.' She paused. 'But I didn't think he was capable of...'

She stopped short of saying 'murder', but the silence between us spoke volumes.

'Even so, even before you knew, it was wrong to cover up for him, wasn't it? You shouldn't have lied to the police. To the girl's mother.'

She began to sob quietly. I opened my bag, took out a tissue and handed it over. I do it without thinking these days. Every other person I meet seems to burst into tears when they talk to me.

'I know.' Arianrhod's voice was muffled by the tissue. 'I feel terrible about it. But now ... now it's all going to come out.'

'Come out? How d'you mean?'

She wiped her eyes and blew her nose. Then she turned to face me. 'Gwydion's decided to go to the police. He wants to press charges. He's going to tell them that Evan killed Elsa Lindberg.'

It took me a moment to register what she'd said. I knew Gwydion was angry with his father, but I was surprised that he'd decided to take it this far. Surprised, and ... rather proud of him. Gwydion was facing his demons, at last. And he'd

179

done it under his own steam, without any prompting from anyone, as far as I could see.

'Well, good for him,' I said.

Arianrhod didn't seem to be listening. 'It'll completely ruin Evan, of course. When all this gets out. Ruin ... us.' She paused.

I nodded slowly, taking in for the first time what it would mean to her if Gwydion decided to take Evan to court: quite simply, the total destruction of her family, of everything she'd spent her entire adult life protecting. Her husband and only son were about to go to war, in public, over a sordid crime that, whatever the outcome, would rake up a ton of muck and end up humiliating her almost as deeply as it would Evan. How much easier it would be for her, I thought, to kick over the traces, persuade Gwydion not to act.

'But still, it's the right thing to do.' She seemed resigned to her fate. 'And I must support my son.'

'That's very brave of you.'

'The thing is, I'm not sure the police are going to believe him.' Arianrhod lifted her head and gazed out at the river. 'It all happened so long ago. And he's the only witness.'

I followed her gaze. In front of us, a cormorant landed on a small rock jutting out of the middle of the river.

'He was only six years old at the time. Then there's the fact that he'd forgotten it all for so long. And only remembered it now.'

I watched as the cormorant dived into the water for a fish. It came up with its beak empty.

'Of course...' She hesitated for a moment. 'It would help if you could...' She stopped.

'Could what?' I turned to her, puzzled.

She took a deep breath. Then her words came out in a rush. 'Dr Mayhew, I've come to ask if you could act as a witness when it comes to trial. An expert witness.'

I was taken aback. 'Me? But...'

'We'll need you to explain how he came to remember what happened. Through the dream. Under therapy. How you led him to discover...'

'I didn't lead him, he did it for himself.' I thought back. 'We had very few sessions together, in fact.'

'Yes. But you've helped him so much. Been so kind to us. Coming down to visit when he was so ... unwell.'

I was touched at how grateful she seemed. I realized how isolated she must have felt, trying to cope with her errant husband and fragile son.

'Well, I'll do what I can, of course.' I paused. 'I'm happy to report on our sessions, if that's what you want.' I shifted uncomfortably. The metal seat on the bench was beginning to feel hard and cold. 'But I'm not sure it'll be a great help. There really isn't a lot to tell.'

'Thank you.' Arianrhod smiled at me in relief. 'I don't know whether it'll carry any weight, either. It's going to be tough. But it's good to know someone's on our side.'

I smiled back somewhat guardedly. Then I looked at my watch. 'I'm going to have to get back to the office now, I'm afraid.'

'Of course. I'm sorry to have bothered you.'

'Not at all.'

As we got up to leave I looked out at the river

one last time. The cormorant had flown away.

'But next time, Arianrhod,' I said, as we walked off back down the path. 'Do me a favour. Phone up and make an appointment in advance, would you?'

'This doesn't ring true to me, Jess.'

Bob and I were talking over dinner. The children had got up and gone off to watch television, leaving us at the dining table.

I hadn't told him everything about my conversation with Arianrhod. And I'd given him an edited version of the events leading up to it. I hadn't told him about my visits to the Morgan place, or – obviously – what had happened on the jetty with Gwydion last time I was there. And I hadn't told him about my meeting with Solveig Lindberg in Stockholm either, though I had a feeling that, sooner or later, I was going to have to. I'd just outlined the bare bones of the story, told him that an ex-client of mine, Gwydion Morgan, was planning to take his father, Evan, to court for a suspected murder that he'd seen him commit as a child, and that he'd begun to remember under therapy with me. I'd also explained that Arianrhod, Gwydion's mother, had visited me that morning and asked me to be an expert witness when the case came to court, and that I wasn't sure what to do.

'I know Evan quite well. I've worked with him at the Assembly. I just don't believe that he'd commit a murder and then cover it up,' Bob went on. 'It sounds completely out of character...'

I'd never been asked to be an expert witness in

a trial before, and I was beginning to have second thoughts about having agreed, in principle, to help. Bob's a lawyer; he understands this kind of thing, and I don't. Which was why I was asking his advice.

'I mean, everyone knows he drinks too much, that he can be bad-tempered. And he has a colourful love life, of course.' Bob gave a wry smile. 'But he's a decent man at heart. I've always admired him. He's phenomenally cultured. Talented. And generous. He's done a lot for Wales, for the Assembly...'

'Oh, I see.' I could feel my temper rising. 'So just because he's done a lot for the Assembly he can screw every woman in sight and get away with it, can he?'

Bob looked surprised at my outburst. Then he began to realize he was treading on dangerous territory.

'Well, no. Of course not. All I'm saying is that he may have his faults, but I can't believe he's a murderer. Or a liar.'

'So why would his wife say he was, if he wasn't?'

'I don't know. She's a strange woman, by all accounts.' He paused. 'She's probably jealous. She's had a tough time, I should think, and it's taken its toll.'

'And the son? Why would he be gunning for his father as well?'

'Well, perhaps he's taking his mother's side. These things go on in families...'

'Bob, a young girl drowned out at sea,' I cut in. 'She was nineteen. Evan Morgan was trying to seduce her. His son saw the pair of them fighting

183

on a boat shortly before she died.' I gave an exasperated sigh. 'Aren't we owed an explanation? However great a man Evan may be?'

'Yes, of course.' Bob lowered his voice, responding to the frustration in my tone. 'Her death needs to be fully investigated. Evidently, it wasn't at the time.' He paused. 'But I'm just not convinced by this evidence you've come up with. I think we need to hear Evan's side of the story.'

I didn't respond.

'And if I were you,' he went on, 'I wouldn't commit myself to anything.'

'Well, thanks for your advice.' I tried to sound polite. 'But I think I'm going to, all the same.'

Bob finished eating, got up from the table, went over to the sink and rinsed his hands.

'OK. As you wish.' Then he added, as he dried his hands on the towel, 'And I'm going to get in touch with Evan. I'd like to talk this over with him and find out what this is really all about.'

Although his voice remained calm, I sensed he was angry, but I said nothing as he turned and walked out of the kitchen. Just as he did, Nella came in.

She went over to the fridge, opened the door and peered inside. 'There's never anything to eat in this house.'

'Yes there is.' I waved at the fruit bowl on the sideboard.

'Biscuits?'

'We're trying to cut down on them. For Dad. There are some crackers, if you like. Cheese...'

'OK, OK.' She shut the fridge door, went over to the sideboard and picked up a banana.

184

'How's the homework going?'

She shrugged.

'Need any help with anything?'

She shook her head and made for the door. Just before she left she turned and said, 'Oh, by the way, Mum, I'm going to London on Saturday.' Her tone was casual. 'For the audition.'

'Oh yes?' I tried to sound casual, too.

Nella shifted from foot to foot. 'But the thing is, I may have to stay overnight.'

'Why's that?' I kept my voice level.

'The producer guy may not be able to see me till the evening, apparently. He's very busy, but he definitely wants to audition me...'

There was a silence. Then I said what she knew I was going to say.

'I'm sorry, Nella. You can go up to London with Emyr for the day, on the train.' I paused. I hated to spoil her fun, but there was no doubt in my mind. 'If this producer wants to see you so much, he can see you in the daytime.'

'But he can't. It's got to be later on...'

'Well then, Dad will take you up in the car and wait. But you're not staying the night. And that's final.'

Normally Nella would have argued. But she knew that in this case I wasn't going to budge, so she didn't try.

'I'm sorry, darling,' I went on. 'I really am. But it's just not on. You know that.'

She didn't reply. Instead, she threw the banana at the sideboard and flounced out of the door, slamming it behind her.

The banana hit the edge of the sideboard and

landed on the floor beside it. I walked over, picked it up, and for a moment felt like hurling it at the door, after her. But instead I calmly put it back in the fruit bowl, beside the rest of the bunch.

13

It was Saturday and I was shopping in the market. Upstairs, in the pet section, to be precise. Nella had gone to London with Emyr for the day, to audition with the producer. I'd wanted to talk to him in more detail about the arrangements, but Nella had forbidden me to. So instead, I'd given her strict instructions to catch the six o'clock train home, and told her I'd meet her off the train. In the meantime, as the hours ticked by, I was struggling to take my mind off the situation, so I'd taken Rose out to the market. She wanted to buy a rabbit. She'd been pestering me about it for weeks, and I'd finally relented.

It's a funny old place, Cardiff market, a great covered building with wrought-iron doors and a glass ceiling, like a Victorian railway station, and inside, a smell of burned fat, and butchery, and wet fish, and old leather, and cut flowers. Downstairs you'll find the butchers, the pigs' heads arranged in rows like an audience at the theatre, with the prices pinned to their ears, and the fish counter, where along with the scary deep-sea monsters, you can get freshly caught local cockles and crabs and laverbread, that weird, green, salty, slimy seaweed stuff that's supposed to be a delicacy here. There's a haberdasher's, where I often stop to buy buttons, zips and bias binding, that sells the types of fabric you thought went out with the Sixties: yards of nylon lace for net curtains, rolls of brightly patterned Crimplene for dresses, brushed cotton for nighties and pyjamas. There's no concession to the present: the leather-goods stores sell cheap, old-fashioned handbags, suitcases without wheels, straps for watches of the non-digital kind. And upstairs, in the gallery above, it gets even more recherché: there's the ancient second-hand record shop with a life-sized figure of Elvis at the entrance; and beside it, the palm-reader's, where a middle-aged woman with a plastic flower in her dyed black hair flits mysteriously in and out of view, between a pair of purple velvet curtains; and next to that, the greasy spoon, where a selection of hard-bitten men who look like the descendants of Steptoe and Son drink steaming mugs of tea, eat bacon, eggs and beans, and read the racing papers. And opposite that, the pet shop, where Rose and I were standing, looking at the caged songbirds, the newborn kittens, the twitch-nosed rabbits, the crazily coiffeured guinea pigs, the blind baby mice, and the fat white rats with their disturbingly long, pink tails.

'Cruel, isn't it? Keeping them cooped up like that.'

I turned round. The woman who was speaking to me was in her sixties, well dressed, with immaculately cut and coloured hair. She was accompanied by a dapper-looking man, slightly older, and equally well turned out.

It took me a moment to recognize her.

'Jean.' I paused. 'Gosh. You look ... you do look well.'

'Thank you.' Jean smiled. 'This is Windsor.'

I nodded at her companion. He nodded back, but didn't say anything. Instead he went over to one of the cages and looked at the rabbits with Rose.

'That must be your daughter,' Jean said.

'Yes. Rose. My youngest.' I tilted my head towards Windsor. 'Is that...?'

'My new beau. He's moving in with me next month. We're going to live in sin.' Jean giggled.

I was beginning to feel nonplussed. Jean was behaving like a completely different person from the one I'd known. She'd never shown any sign of a sense of humour before. I'd never realized she had one.

I looked over at the rabbits. Windsor had picked up a pellet from the counter displaying the pet foods, and was feeding one to the rabbit, much to Rose's delight.

'Well, that's lovely,' I said. 'I'm pleased for you.'

'Oh yes. It's all turned out very well.' Jean lowered her voice. 'He's very good around the house.'

I nodded, thinking of the curtain rail.

'I'm sorry I haven't been in touch.' Jean waved her hand airily. 'I've been so busy. It's been such a whirlwind.'

I thought for a moment of pointing out that she really should have phoned to cancel the sessions, but decided not to go there, as they say. Instead, a silence fell as we both looked over at Windsor,

Rose and the rabbits.

'Well,' she said eventually. 'Nice to see you again.'

'And you, Jean.' I spoke with sincerity. 'Good luck with everything.'

'Thanks.'

She gave me a little wave, then went over to Windsor and took his arm. As they sauntered off together, I joined Rose at the rabbit cage.

'Who was that lady?' Rose asked.

'Oh, just one of my clients.' I paused, wondering why I didn't feel angry with Jean. She'd quit her sessions without any notice, without a word of thanks. I'd lost fees, wasted time. And yet, seeing her like that had made me feel good. Really good. For a moment I forgot my worries about Nella and remembered why it was that I'd decided, all those years ago, to become a psychotherapist. I'd done it to help people. It was a clichéd phrase, but it was the truth. That had been my aim, and I realized now that sometimes – not often – I managed to achieve it. In Jean's case, I'd only offered a holding operation while she recovered from her grief, but that had, apparently, been all she'd needed to get her back on course.

Rose pointed to a small grey rabbit in the corner, sitting alone. 'That's the one.'

'Are you sure?'

Rose nodded.

'OK, then. Good choice.' I put my arm round her shoulder. 'Shall we celebrate with a bacon sandwich?'

Rose looked up in surprise. 'You mean, over there?' She pointed to the cafe. She knew I didn't like it, that I often complained about the smell of bacon fat that pervaded the market because of it.

I nodded.

She looked pensive. 'Are you happy about something, Mum?'

'Yes, I suppose I am.'

'What?'

'That lady. She used to be sad. And now she's feeling better. That's all.'

'Cool.' Rose paused for a moment. 'Can I have a doughnut as well, then?'

We paid for the rabbit, arranging to collect it later, went over to the cafe and found ourselves a seat at the bar running along the edge of the gallery. I ordered two bacon sandwiches, a cup of tea and a glass of bright green pop that didn't even pretend to bear any resemblance to fruit juice.

As we waited for our food, Rose drank her pop noisily, sucking happily on her straw, gazing dreamily into space. I knew by the look on her face she was thinking about the rabbit.

On the countertop was a copy of that day's *Echo*. The *Echo* is our local newspaper. It normally carries stories of buses failing to run on time, children recovering from suspected meningitis, and baby birds falling out of nests. I glanced casually at the front page, not expecting it to tell me anything more earth-shattering than that a dog had nearly bitten a man, and caught my breath.

In the centre of the page was a headline: EVAN MORGAN CHARGED WITH MURDER. Underneath, there was a picture of him, taken some time ago, and an article that began:

Following sensational revelations received yesterday at the South Wales Echo, *police have charged Evan Morgan with murder. The internationally renowned theatre director spent three hours this morning at Central Police Station being interviewed in connection with the death by drowning, in 1990, of a Swedish au pair employed by the Morgan family. Bob Cadogan, Mr Morgan's lawyer, declined to comment.*

It took me a moment to take in what I'd read: not only that Evan had been charged, but that Bob was representing him. My husband had gone off behind my back and offered his services to Evan Morgan, knowing that I was liable to be an expert witness for the other side. What the hell was he thinking of? Was he trying to make me look a complete idiot? A red fog began to rise up in front of my eyes. I locked my teeth together, in pure fury. I wanted to jump up, then and there, and rush home to confront him. But, for Rose's sake, I stayed where I was.

The bacon sandwiches arrived. Rose opened hers up, smeared tomato sauce over the inside and started to tuck in. I put a squirt of mustard on mine and took a bite. The bacon tasted salty, the bread synthetic. Minutes before, I'd been hungry and would have enjoyed it all the same, but now I'd lost my appetite. Instead I watched Rose eat, trying to be patient as she savoured each bite, laying the sandwich carefully down on her plate each time she took another sip of her drink. Finally, when she'd finished, and was

191

slowly licking the last of the tomato sauce off her fingers, I said, 'Come on, sweet pea. Let's go.'

Rose looked horrified. 'But what about the doughnut?'

'We'll get one for you to eat in the car.'

She began to scowl.

'I'm sorry, Rosie.' I took a tissue out of my pocket and handed it over for her to wipe her fingers. 'We've got to get home.'

'But why?'

'I need to talk to Dad.'

'About what?'

'About something.' I paused, looking for a way to change the subject. 'Now, let's go over and pick up the rabbit. Have you thought of a name yet?'

Rose ignored me.

I persevered. 'I suppose it depends if it's a boy or a girl.'

I got up to go, but Rose didn't budge.

'You said I could have a doughnut here.' Her voice rose indignantly. 'You said.'

I sighed. Rose is a determined child. If she thinks she's being treated unfairly, she digs her heels in. When she does, she's quite immovable. Thankfully her demands are usually reasonable enough, so I try to meet them wherever possible. And, on this occasion, she had a point. I had promised her a doughnut in the cafe. Not in the car, or anywhere else. Besides, there was no real reason to suddenly up sticks and rush off home – other than my mounting anger with Bob, which, to be fair, was nothing to do with her.

'OK, then.' I sat down again, took some money

out of my purse and handed it to her. 'You go up to the counter and order it. But after that, we really will need to get going.'

Rose went off to get the doughnut. Meanwhile, I rolled up the paper and put it into my bag.

When we arrived home, Bob was in the kitchen, drinking coffee and working on his laptop. Rose showed him the rabbit and he took her off to help her install it in the hutch we'd set up in the garden shed. Afterwards they came back in, and there followed a long discussion about nesting, and straw, and litter trays, and pellets, and carrots, and water, and then, finally, once these matters were settled, Rose went upstairs to practise her clarinet.

When she'd gone I produced the newspaper from my bag.

'What's this?' I thrust it under Bob's nose.

'Ah yes.' Bob looked guilty. 'I was going to–'

'How dare you?' My voice was shaking with anger. 'How dare you take this on? Without telling me.'

I threw the paper onto the kitchen table beside his laptop. Then I marched over to the kettle, filled it and switched it on.

'I told you that information in confidence,' I said, as it began to heat up. 'I trusted you. I wanted your advice...'

'Look, Jess.' Bob came up behind me. 'I've done nothing wrong. You know that. I've spoken to Evan, and I'm convinced he's innocent. So I've decided to help him. I've got him out on bail.'

'But why didn't you consult me? You should have asked me first. I could be a witness for the

193

other side. It'll be incredibly awkward–'

Bob interrupted me. 'But you said you hadn't made up your mind yet...'

The kettle began to boil furiously. It's one of those modern ones that heats the water in about fifteen seconds flat, but looks as though it's about to take off when it's doing so.

'No. But you could have talked to me first. Surely this is a decision we should have taken together?'

'Well, yes. But it's so difficult to talk to you at the moment. You're always so distant. So prickly.' Bob's voice rose a fraction. 'Anyway, it's not just about Evan. If I take on this case, it'll be what I need to get my career back on course. We've been talking about this for ages, haven't we? You've always advised me to leave the Assembly and go solo. And now my chance has come up.' He paused. 'This is a real opportunity for me. A chance to break free. I only took the job at the Assembly because I wanted a secure future for you and the children...'

I turned to face him. My whole body was shaking with rage. I was surprised at the intensity of it. And I was surprised at what came out next.

'Don't give me that. You don't care about me. Or the children. The only person you care about, Bob Cadogan, is yourself.' Strangely, I felt as though someone new – me, yes, but not the usual me – was talking. Someone whose voice had been in my head for a long time, but who'd never spoken before, and who was now releasing a huge burden of pent-up anger, to my surprise as much as Bob's. 'All this' – I waved my hand around the room – 'the house, our marriage, the whole thing – is just a bloody sham. A lie.'

Bob's eyes widened. He stepped back in surprise, staggering a little, as though I'd struck him.

'For the last two years, all I've done is listen to you whine on about your career. Then you go off and screw some woman at a conference, just to boost your ego. And now, all of a sudden, you've decided to poke your nose into my business, take advantage of what I've told you, in confidence, about one of my clients. And decide, without consulting me, to defend his lying, cheating bastard of a father, one of your disgusting, lecherous old cronies at the Assembly...' I didn't recognize the words coming out of my mouth. 'Well, I've had enough. It's never going to work between us. Because it's always going to be about you and your ego, isn't it? You're a selfish little shit, and you always will be.'

The kettle reached a climax, then switched itself off. Steam was pouring out of it, misting up the air. I stood by the sink, shaking, looking out of the window, Bob standing behind me.

There was a silence. Then Bob said, in a reasonable tone, 'I'm not little.'

In the past, I might have laughed when he said that, and turned round, and he would have come over and put his arms around me, and we would have kissed and made up. But not this time. This time, he'd gone too far.

'I didn't realize you felt like this about ... about us...' He sounded crestfallen. For a moment I was sorry for him. Sorry, but not repentant, because at last I'd vented the anger that had been bubbling

195

up inside me since I'd learned of his infidelity.

'Well, I do.' I kept my voice low, but it still shook with anger. 'I'm not going to back down about this. I'm going to act as a witness at the trial, whatever you decide to do. Got that?'

I marched past him out into the hall. Just as I reached the front door, Rose came down the stairs.

'What's happening?' She leaned over the banister. She looked anxious.

'Nothing.' The tremor in my voice was unmistakable. 'Nothing, my love. Don't worry. I'm just nipping out for a little while. I'll be back soon.'

But I wasn't back soon. I drove around Cardiff for a while, then found myself taking the road out to Carmarthen, heading down to west Wales. It wasn't that I had a particular destination in mind; I only knew I wanted to get out of the city, drive along a motorway with the radio on, mile upon mile, until I felt calmer, and ready to come back home. So it was odd that, after about an hour, I found myself turning in to a service station, parking the car and phoning Gwydion on my mobile.

The phone rang a few times. I was just composing a message in my head when he picked up.

'Hello. Jessica?' I realized he had my number keyed into his phone.

'Gwydion. It's me,' I said, rather unnecessarily. 'You've seen today's paper, of course?'

'Of course.'

There was a silence.

'How's Arianrhod taking it?'

'Oh, she's pretty philosophical. But all this is

going to be hell for her.' He paused. 'Listen, we need to talk. Where are you?'

'In a service station on the M4. Junction 47.'

'What are you doing there?'

'Oh. Nothing. Just driving around.' I tried to think of a better explanation, but failed.

'Are you all right?'

'Yes. I think so.'

He registered the hesitation in my voice. 'What's happened?'

'Just a bit of a row at home.' It didn't sound so bad when I said it out loud.

'Well, wait there. I'm coming over right now. I'll be there in an hour.'

'OK,' I said. 'I'll wait for you in the coffee bar by the entrance.'

'Keep your phone on.'

He didn't say goodbye, and neither did I.

I got out of the car, locked it and walked over to the service station. It wasn't busy. There were a few teenagers playing on the slot machines in the foyer, and a few more in the burger bar. Other than that, it was pretty much deserted.

I went to the toilets, had a pee, came out and looked at my face in the mirror as I washed my hands. The skin on my face was dull and drawn, and there were bags under my eyes. The damp air had frizzed my hair, so that it looked shapeless and untidy. I scrabbled in my bag, wishing I'd brought some makeup with me, but all I found was a lipsalve and a comb. I did my best with them, but they didn't hide the tired look in my eyes. So in the end I gave up, went out to the coffee shop, ordered myself a double espresso, and sat down to wait.

I usually carry a book in my handbag, and a pencil for making notes in the margin as I go along, just so that I have something to do when I get stuck somewhere, as on occasions like this. They're usually books on psychology, with knotty, technical, words strung into tortuous sentences that force me to concentrate. So, in order to calm myself before my encounter with Gwydion, I brought out my book, furrowed my brow and got down to work.

That week I was reading a biography of my old pal Freud, by his old pal Ernest Jones. Jones was a Welshman, a rather unsavoury one, by all accounts, but it was he who was largely responsible for introducing psychoanalysis to the wider world. The biography was exactly what I needed, a fascinating portrait of a complex man, parts of it crammed with dense terminology, but that day it didn't seem to be drawing me in. Every few minutes my eyes would wander off the page and I'd glance out of the window, checking to see if Gwydion had arrived.

After forty minutes or so, I started to get restless. I thought of phoning him, but I don't like phoning people when they may be driving, in case I cause an accident, and besides, I didn't want to pester him. But somehow, I couldn't sit still and be patient. I was getting more and more nervous. I'd resolved after our last meeting not to see him again, except perhaps in my office for a clear purpose – for example, to discuss my part, if any, in the upcoming trial – yet here I was, once again, straying into his neck of the woods, phoning him on impulse, and doing my best not to ask myself why. I was being childish, I told myself. Time to get a grip. Time to get out, drive home, before any more harm could be done.

I was just getting up to leave when my phone rang. It was Gwydion.

'I'm in the hotel opposite. Can you meet me there?'

I was nonplussed. 'Why all the secrecy?'

He ignored my question. 'I'm in Room 17. On the ground floor.'

'But...'

The phone clicked off. I got up, gathered my belongings and walked out of the coffee bar. The entrance to the hotel was just a few yards away. I came up to it and for a moment had an impulse to walk past it, to the car park beyond, get into my car and drive away. But I didn't. Instead I pushed open the door and headed down the corridor, ignoring the receptionist, who didn't look up as I passed.

I turned the corner, following the signs to Room 17, and stood in front of the door for a moment, glancing quickly up and down the corridor. There was no one around. I knocked.

Gwydion opened the door. He was wearing a tracksuit, as if he'd been out jogging when I called. He looked worried, which didn't surprise me. I went in, and he quickly shut it behind me.

The room was dark, the curtains closed. They were an ugly red and yellow tartan, matching the bedspread. On the walls were the kind of pictures that you buy by the yard for hanging in hotels. To one side of the bed, a door led off to a tiny bathroom. If Gwydion was trying to seduce me, I thought, he'd chosen an odd place to do it.

There was a chair over by the window, so I went and sat on it. Gwydion came over and sat opposite me, on the edge of the bed. My eyes were adjusting to the dark, so I couldn't see the expression on his face, but his gestures were nervous.

'It's good to see you.' He smiled, then gave a deep sigh. 'I've been feeling so stressed what with Evan being arrested. I mean, I utterly despise him, and I know he's guilty, but even so...'

'I can imagine. It must be terrible.'

He reached out and took my hand. I let him hold it. It felt small and childish, innocent and trusting, in his.

'Gwydion, I...' I wasn't sure how to put what I wanted to say. 'I'm not here for...'

'I know.' He let go of my hand. 'I'm sorry about this' – he gestured at the room – 'but I had no choice. I think I'm being followed.'

'Really?' I turned round and pulled the curtain open a crack. I saw that the room overlooked the car park. 'Are they out there now?'

'I think so.' He came over and stood beside me. 'The Peugeot in the corner over there.'

I followed his gaze. I didn't know which car he meant, and I didn't enquire further, but the idea that there was someone out there watching us gave me a strange feeling in the pit of my stomach.

'Who is it?'

'A journalist, I think. And ... well, I don't want them to see us together. Not in the circumstances.'

'I can understand that.'

'I hear your husband's representing Evan.' There was a tone of hurt surprise in his voice.

'Yes.' I paused. 'That's what we had the row about.'

Gwydion put his hand on my shoulder. I could feel that it was trembling slightly.

I didn't want to push it away, so instead I got up, with the intention of finding another place to sit, further away from him. But when I looked around the room there wasn't anywhere else, except the bed. So I sat on that, on the edge, bolt upright.

Gwydion stood by the window and looked down at me. I looked up at him, a safe distance away, my eyes adjusting to the light. He hadn't shaved, and there were dark shadows under his eyes. His lips looked red, as though he'd been biting them. Bruised, even. He had a hunted, haunted look on his face.

I gazed down at the floor. Anything not to look at him standing in front of the window, so close, so real, the light framing his dark head like a halo.

Gwydion responded to my body language, checking himself, as though reminding himself of his manners.

'Can I get you anything?' He gestured at a tray in the corner, with a kettle, two cups, and a neatly arranged array of sachets beside it.

'No, thank you.' I continued to stare at the floor.

He sighed deeply. Then he came and sat down beside me. I froze.

He put his arm around me.

'Jessica. Stop pretending,' he said. 'I know why you're here.'

'I need to talk to you...' I began. 'There are some facts I need to find out more about...'

He didn't contradict me. Instead he put his

201

other arm around me and pulled me gently to him. Then he put his hand under my chin, turned my face towards his, and kissed me on the mouth. And I kissed him back. Hard.

I don't quite understand what happened next. It was sudden, as if a dam had burst and the water had come flooding out. Like a dream, but very real. My tongue was in his mouth, and his in mine, angry, fighting, fierce, like snakes darting between the rocks, looking for a place to hide. The red and yellow checks began to dance in front of my eyes. We rolled over onto the bed, me on top of him, him on top of me. His clothes, my clothes, were pulled away, up, down, around. I can remember body parts coming at me thick and fast, each one a discovery: a belly, a nipple, a thigh; and then they began to come two by two, marching armies of cheeks, lips, ears, armpits, buttocks; and after that the roar of the sea began to throb in my ear, and I closed my eyes, and Gwydion closed his.

And that was when it should have happened. But it didn't. Because, as he reached inside my top, his hand brushed against a tiny button in the centre of my bra and quickly drew back, so that in the midst of it all, I suddenly remembered who he was – a sensitive, traumatized young man, who'd come to me for help. And who I was, a mature, experienced woman who should have known better than to be flailing about with him on the red-and-yellow-checked counterpane of a bed in a Travelodge on the M4, with the curtains drawn against the afternoon light. And a Peugeot parked outside, with a driver inside it who was watching him, and waiting for us to come out.

'I'm sorry, Gwydion,' I said. 'I really don't think we should be doing this.'

'Yes, we should.'

'It's not right.'

'It is. It's exactly right.' His voice was a whisper. I shut my eyes, savouring the moment, then drew gently away.

He looked at me in surprise. 'What? What is it?'

'Look, I don't want to do this.'

'Yes, you do.' There was a pleading look in his eyes. 'I know you do.'

'That's beside the point.' I sat up and began to readjust my clothing. 'Your father's been charged with murder. I might be called in as a witness. It wouldn't do if people knew.'

'We'll meet in secret, then.'

I tried another tack. 'And I used to be your therapist.'

'You're not now.'

'Yes, but it's still not right. And anyway, I'm a married woman. I've got a family to think of. If this came out...'

He looked crestfallen, and I could see why. I'd given him three good reasons why we shouldn't have an affair, but none of them sounded convincing. To either of us. And that was because I wasn't telling the truth. Which was, that between the two of us, it wasn't a level playing field. He was a vulnerable young person, his fragile state of mind sometimes verging on serious mental illness. I was older, supposedly wiser, more stable. I had a responsibility, a duty, to protect him, but instead, here I was, taking advantage of his weakness.

'I wish you'd told me how you felt before ...

before we...'

'I'm sorry.' I didn't explain myself further. I could have told him the truth, but it would have hurt his pride.

Gwydion got up from the bed. He went over to the window, pushed the curtain aside a little way and looked out.

'I think I'd better leave first.' He spoke without looking at me.

'OK.'

I watched him as he zipped up his hoody and ran a hand through his hair, glancing at the mirror on the wall before he left.

'Wait at least half an hour,' he said. 'And if you're tailed on the way home, let me know.'

I nodded.

He picked up the keys to his car, which were lying on the bedside table. Then, as he was leaning over me, he paused.

'It's not...?' he began, then stopped. 'It's not that you don't...?'

There was an anxious look on his face.

I guessed what he was going to say. 'Of course not. I find you very attractive. I'm sure you know that.' I paused. 'It's just that I want to do the right thing. For both of us. That's all.'

The anxious look subsided a little. 'OK. But maybe later, once this is all over.'

'Maybe.' I paused. I wanted to let him down, let myself down, lightly. So I turned my face up to his as he bent over to kiss me.

This time there were no darting snakes. Just a meeting and parting of lips and a soft regret that lingered on for a long time after he was gone.

14

As I was driving back to Cardiff, my phone went off. It plays an annoying little ditty whenever a text message comes in, and I've never worked out how to change it. I glanced at the screen and saw that the message was from Nella, so I picked it up and peered at it, thinking that I really should turn off the motorway and stop, but telling myself that this was important, possibly even an emergency. The screen read: *Staying overnight in London. Back tomoz. Nella.*

I gripped the wheel tighter, and a wave of panic hit me. Not just panic, but guilt. It was entirely irrational to connect the two events – my antics with Gwydion in the Travelodge and Nella's trip to London with Emyr – but I couldn't help it. In my mind, I instantly became an irresponsible mother, disporting herself with her lover in a cheap motorway hotel, all the while allowing her daughter to go up to London with a possible child-molester, a man who preyed on young girls, who had been sacked from his teaching job because of his behaviour. Why had I let her go, I asked myself? What on earth had I been thinking of?

I hadn't expected Nella to openly defy me like this. She'd never done so before, however much she'd argued her corner. I'd been a fool not to realize that Emyr would influence her, that she'd believe his line about making her a star, or whatever it was he'd told her... And who was this producer, anyway? All I had was his name: Tony Andreou. I should have looked him up on the Internet, found out more about him before Nella and Emyr left for London...

As soon as I could, I pulled off the motorway, parked the car and rang Nella back. She didn't answer, so I tapped out a text on the phone. Instead of ordering her to come home, which I felt might fail, I simply wrote: *Please let us know name of hotel and phone number. Reply asap. Mum.* Then I called Bob.

He'd obviously seen from his incoming call list that it was me, because his tone was frosty.

'Listen, Bob, we've got a problem here.' I didn't say 'emergency'. I didn't want to panic him. 'Nella's just texted me to say she's staying overnight in London. With Emyr.'

'But you told her she couldn't, didn't you?'

'Yes.' My voice started to quaver.

'Are you all right?' His tone changed to one of concern. 'Where are you?'

'Oh, just ... driving around. I'm on my way home.'

'Well, get here as soon as you can.' He sounded worried. 'And then we'll decide what to do.'

'Right.' I paused. 'I've texted her to ask where she's staying. I thought if we knew the name of the hotel, that would be something.'

'Why didn't you tell her to get home?' There was a note of panic in his voice. 'I'll phone her now. Give her a bloody good talking-to...'

'No, Bob. She's not picking up. And I don't think that'll work, anyway. Best just to find out

206

what her plans are and then... I don't know. At least we'll have an idea where she is.'

'OK.' He began to sound a little calmer. 'But phone me right away if you hear from her, won't you?'

'Of course.' I paused for a moment. 'And, Bob, I'm sorry.' Tears came to my eyes.

He cleared his throat. 'I'm sorry, too.' His voice sounded strained.

There was a silence. I could tell that, like me, he was feeling frightened and ashamed. We'd done nothing but argue lately. Maybe that was part of the reason that Nella had defied us. And now, if anything happened to her, it would be our fault...

'See you later.' I clicked the phone off, put it down on the passenger seat and leaned forward, my brow against the steering wheel. I felt like banging my head against it in frustration, but instead I began to cry. Just then, the phone piped up with its merry roundelay.

I grabbed it, praying that the text would be from Nella. And to my relief it was. All she had written was the address of a hotel in Paddington, but it was enough.

I immediately called Bob back.

'Listen,' I said, 'I've got the address of the hotel. I'll drive up there.'

'What, now?'

I thought for a minute. It did seem a crazy thing to do, but I was feeling panic-stricken, not only by Nella's message, but by what had been going on in the Travelodge. 'I'll find the hotel and wait for them there. However long it takes. Then I'll bring her home.'

There was a pause. 'D'you want me to come with you?'

I thought for a moment. 'No, you stay there with Rose. I can manage. I'll keep my phone on.'

He gave a deep sigh. 'All right. But take care, won't you. And keep me informed.'

Keep me informed. That was an expression Nella had picked up from her father, I realized. Hearing it, I thought how much I loved her, and him, and Rose, how much I wanted our family to be together, and safe, and happy. And how stupid I'd been to jeopardize that by losing my temper with Bob, and fooling around like an idiot with Gwydion.

'Will do. See you later.' I clicked off the phone and scrabbled for a tissue in my bag. I took one out, wiped my eyes and blew my nose. Then I started the engine, turned the car round and headed up the motorway, this time to London.

When I got there, after an exhausting drive up the M4, I parked the car at the back of Paddington station. The charge per hour was exorbitant, but I told myself this was an emergency. Then I walked down to the hotel. It was a budget bed-and-breakfast in one of those long, white-pillared terraces that border the station, each indistinguishable from the next, although the sign over the front door of this one was somewhat shabbier than most: the sort of place you'd stay in if you didn't know London at all, didn't have much money, and were planning to take a train out the next day. Typical of Emyr's limited imagination, taste and experience of life, I thought, rather snobbishly perhaps, as I went up the front steps.

The lobby inside was a cramped affair, with a reception desk jutting out into the narrow hallway below a staircase leading up to the rooms. There was no one behind the desk, so I pressed the bell. While I waited, I looked around. There was no sitting room, as far as I could see, just a chair jammed into a corner beside a small table with a pile of cards and leaflets on it, most of them advertising minicabs and taxis. If I was going to have to sit it out until Emyr and Nella came back that night, the lobby of the Park Hotel clearly wasn't going to be a very comfortable place to while away the hours.

Eventually a young Asian man appeared behind the desk. He looked tired and pale, with a rash of acne on his upper cheeks. I asked him whether he'd had a booking in the name of Griffiths, Emyr Griffiths, for a double room that night, explaining that I needed to contact him urgently. At first he looked at me blankly, but after a while he agreed to check the bookings, scanning a small computer screen on the desk.

'No Griffiths here. Sorry.'

I spelt out the name, just to be sure, but he was adamant.

'No. Nothing.'

The front door opened and a young woman walked in, dragging a suitcase. She wasn't much older than Nella, and she seemed to be alone. For a moment, before the door swung shut, the roar of traffic filled the lobby, and I felt a wave of panic mounting inside me. Nella had vanished. She could be anywhere in this big city. I'd lost contact with her. She was with a man, a man I didn't trust, and she'd gone missing...

'Excuse me a moment,' I said to the man behind the desk. I was surprised at how calm my voice sounded. 'I just need to make a call.'

I brought out my mobile phone, which I'd taken to clutching in my pocket, and tapped out a text to Nella. *You are not booked in at The Park. I've checked. Where are you staying? You MUST let me know right away. Mum.*

I waited for her to reply, willing the phone to emit its idiotic jingle. But nothing happened. So I took a pen out of my bag, asked for a slip of paper and wrote Nella a note. *Nella, if you get this, please phone me NOW. I'm in London. Will wait until I hear from you. Dad and I are v. worried about you. Mum.*

Then I folded it, wrote her name on it and gave it back to the clerk. He took it, showing no curiosity, and put it beside the computer.

'My daughter is with Mr Griffiths. If they do come back here, will you make sure she gets it? It's important.' A pathetic, pleading note had crept into my voice.

He nodded distractedly, still looking at the screen, so I walked towards the door. Before I opened it, I glanced back at the lobby. The girl was bumping her suitcase up the stairs. As I watched her, I wondered how many stories like mine had taken place at this hotel, imagining all the mothers and fathers who might have come here looking for their sons and daughters, and the children themselves, passing through as they took their first tentative steps into adulthood, arriving at this narrow, stuffy hallway with the traffic thundering by

210

outside, climbing up that staircase, and...

I went out into the road and let the door swing shut behind me.

For an hour or so I wandered around Paddington, stopping once to have a cup of tea in a nondescript cafe near the station – or at least, trying to. Once the tea came, I found I couldn't sit still long enough to drink it, so after a few sips I got up and resumed my aimless walking. I didn't want to phone Bob, not without any news. And I didn't want to leave. I was clinging to the idea that Nella was somewhere in the area, that perhaps I might even bump into her. But as twilight turned into evening, and evening to night, I knew full well that wasn't going to happen.

I began to make my way back towards the car park, not knowing what else to do. I didn't want to drive home yet, but I thought perhaps that sitting in the car, with the familiar paraphernalia of my life around me, would help me to think straight, come up with a plan of action. On the way there I sent Nella another text, this time adding an ultimatum: *Please phone me, Nella. If I don't hear from you, I'm going to call the police.* When I didn't get a message back, I started to feel sick.

As I walked up Praed Street I passed an Internet cafe, and an idea occurred to me. Perhaps I could track down this Tony Andreou, find an address for him and get in touch with Nella that way. I went in. The place seemed to be a meeting point for Arab men, who stood around talking to each other in low voices. They shot me suspicious glances as I walked in, but once I'd found myself a spot, sat down and logged on, they forgot about me and the talking resumed.

There were several Tony Andreous listed, but luckily only one entertainment and events manager of that name, so I went straight to his website. It was a pretty basic affair, just a brightly coloured logo, a small photo of a neatly dressed, middle-aged man with balding dark hair, and a couple of pages advertising dodgy tribute bands, comedians, 'personalities' – none of whom I'd ever heard of – and something called 'Youngster Talent'. Under 'Youngster Talent' there was a phone number to ring for auditions. I rang it, but there was an answerphone message, which didn't surprise me – by now it was coming up to eleven o'clock. I also rang the office number listed on the site, but received the same response. So finally I keyed both numbers into my phone, thinking that I'd try again later, or tomorrow – and was about to get up to leave when I remembered something.

A while back, much to my dismay at the time, a mentally unstable ex-client of mine had got hold of my home address. He'd never come round to the house, only sent me a series of abusive letters, but it had been unnerving, especially as I make sure never to give my home address to any of my clients. I discovered later that he'd tracked me down not by going to my website itself, where only my office address is listed, but by finding out who my website was registered to. As Branwen, the receptionist at work, had explained, this was easy: he'd simply gone onto a search engine, typed in 'whois lookup' and added the name of the site. This had told him that I was the registrant of the domain and given my home address. I'd since had the address removed from the domain information, but had the incident not occurred, I'd never have known that it was listed on the Internet. Maybe Tony Andreou wouldn't know, either.

I duly typed in 'whois lookup' and found Andreou's name as the owner of the website. Under his name, as I'd hoped, was what looked like his home address. It was somewhere in King's Cross. I keyed it into my phone and then went to Google Maps to find out the exact location. After much zooming in and out on the map, I pinpointed it as a block of flats near the main railway lines by the station. I flipped back to the street map, plotted my journey from the car park in Paddington to the block of flats in King's Cross, and printed out the map. Then I got up, paid, and left the cafe.

I walked quickly back to the car park, almost having to stop myself from breaking into a run. There was no rush, I knew. Most likely Tony Andreou would be out for the evening – he was an entertainments manager, after all. But at some stage he'd come back for the night, and I'd be able to collar him, ask him where Emyr Griffiths and my daughter were. That was why I was taking the car rather than a cab – just in case there was a long wait until Andreou came home. I felt keyed up, but now that I had a plan of action, my nervousness was mixed with relief. I had a lead. It was a tentative one, but at least it was something.

Once I got into the car, though, none of it seemed so straightforward. I'm reasonably familiar with the city, having lived there at various times in my life, but the one-way systems had changed and seemed more baffling than ever. I knew exactly where I was, and where I wanted to go, but I had to keep circling around the route so much that I kept getting lost. Eventually I found my way onto the Marylebone Road and stayed on it until I hit King's Cross, only to get lost again once I left the main drag. Finally I found myself in the right street and saw the building, a Victorian mansion block, one of several on a small estate.

I got out of the car, locked it, and crossed the deserted road to the block. I tapped in the number of the flat on the keypad by the entrance, but there was no reply. I tried another number, and then another, and then eventually the buzzer went off and I was able to open the main door. Inside, down a narrow corridor, there was an ancient lift. I pressed the button. The light seemed to be broken, but I could hear the lift coming down towards me. When it got to me the doors opened, emitting a squealing noise and juddering as they did, as if the mechanism was faulty. For a moment I wondered whether it was safe to get in. But the flat, as far as I could work out, was several floors up, so I decided to risk it.

Inside the lift, the light above my head flickered ominously. I pressed the button for the fifth floor and it ground into action. Halfway up it slowed almost to a halt, the light flickering lower and lower until it was almost completely dark. I took out my phone for reassurance, but saw that there was no signal.

The lift juddered to a halt. Then, inch by inch, it rose up the shaft until it was level with the door. I got out, breathing a sigh of relief, and made my way down the corridor to the flat, checking the numbers as I went. By now my heart was thumping in my chest, but I found the courage to ring the bell. Nobody answered. I listened for a moment, and thought I could hear movement inside the flat. There was a spyhole in the door, so I stood to one side of it and pressed the bell again.

This time the door opened, and a young man stood in front of me. He was good-looking, in a bland sort of way, with fair hair cut short and waxed up into a small quiff at the front. He was wearing an oriental-style dressing gown and his feet were bare.

'All right,' he said.

'Hello,' I replied, feeling somewhat foolish because I couldn't bring myself to say 'All right' back. 'I'm looking for Tony Andreou.'

'And who are you?'

'I'm ... well, I'm looking for my daughter, actually, Nella Cadogan. I'm hoping he can help.'

The man looked faintly alarmed, but tried not to show it

'No worries,' he said. 'I'll just go and get him.' He walked off down the hallway, leaving the door open. I peered into the flat and saw that the walls were white, with a white fluffy wall-to-wall carpet on the floor. At the end of the hallway was a peacock wicker chair – the sort a Seventies pimp might lounge about in with several half-naked girls clinging to his legs – and a large urn filled with a potted plant. Just beside the front door was a bentwood hat stand with a straw boater perched on one hook. The whole thing looked like a film set, and a bizarrely anachronistic one at that.

A short, thickset man came up the corridor, followed by two white dogs that barked when they saw me. I recognized him as Tony Andreou, the man in the website photo. He shouted at the young man, who reappeared in the hallway for a moment and shooed the dogs into a back room.

'How can I help?' The man smiled at me politely, but the look in his eyes was wary.

'Mr Andreou. I'm sorry to disturb you like this. I'm looking for my daughter, Nella Cadogan. I believe she may have had an audition with you earlier this evening.'

The man didn't bat an eyelid, but his shoulders stiffened slightly.

'Ah yes. Nella. Lovely girl. And your name is?'

'Jessica Mayhew.'

'Pleased to meet you.' He put out his hand and I shook it. He had a slight accent, and the courteous manner of a foreigner.

'Do come in,' he went on, ushering me into the hallway and closing the door behind me. 'Would you mind taking off your shoes, please.' He paused. 'The carpet.'

'Of course.' I didn't want to take off my shoes, but I couldn't think of an excuse not to, so I bent down and put them beside the door, thinking I could pick them up and run for it, if I needed to make a quick getaway.

'This way, please.' He led me to a door leading off the hall, opened it for me and followed as I walked in. Inside was a white room, with a white grand piano, and more fluffy carpet. The young man was there, and the two dogs leapt up to

216

greet me as I came in.

'Can I get you a drink?' The young man fussed around me. He kept sniffing, I noticed. He couldn't keep still. He was probably coked up, I thought. And Andreou had a weird kind of calm about him, like someone who believes they're on top of their game, but is tranquillized to the nines. 'Tea, perhaps?'

'I'm sorry to rush you, Mr Andreou,' I said. 'But can you tell me where my daughter is? It's rather urgent. She's only sixteen, you see, and–'

'Please.' He held up a hand. 'Don't worry. She's safe and sound. As a matter of fact, she's having a lie-down next door.' He indicated the room opposite the sitting room. 'The audition was a little tiring for her.'

'I'll go and get her up then.' Without asking permission, I turned, walked out into the hallway and knocked on the door.

'Hang on a minute.' A man's voice came from inside. He was half laughing. 'We're busy in here.'

I don't know why I did what I did next. It was hearing that laugh, I think. But without knocking again, I opened the door and walked in.

Nella was on the bed. Her shirt was open, her bra twisted up above her breasts. I was relieved to see that she still had her jeans on. Emyr, for his part, was more or less fully clothed, although I noticed that the top button and the zip of his trousers were undone.

'Fuck,' he said when he saw me, and sprang away from her as if he'd been electrocuted.

I looked at Nella and saw a look of profound relief cross her face, before she turned away from

217

me, covering her eyes with her hands.

'Come on,' I said. I tried to sound as matter of fact as possible. 'Get your clothes on, Nella. We're going home.'

Emyr was zipping up his trousers. 'Look, Dr Mayhew. It's not what you think. I was just...'

'I'll wait outside the door,' I said to Nella, ignoring him.

I shut the door and stood there. Behind me, Tony Andreou and the young man stood watching from the doorway of the sitting room, not daring to speak. After a few minutes Nella emerged, her shirt buttoned, her jacket over her shoulder and her shoes in her hand. She'd bent her head forward so that her hair covered her face. I couldn't see her expression.

'We'll see ourselves out.' I nodded at Tony Andreou and golden boy. Tony gave an embarrassed shrug. As we walked up the corridor the dogs started barking again, so the young man went into the sitting room to see to them. When we got to the front door, I picked up my shoes and put them on. Nella put hers on, too.

Andreou stood at the end of the hallway by the potted plant, watching us. When we were ready to go, he raised his hand.

'About *Jazz Quest*, my dear,' he said to Nella. There was a nasty undertone in his voice. 'You've got a nice voice, very sweet. But you're not quite what we're looking for. We need artists who are' – he glanced at me – 'a little more mature.'

Nella looked wounded, as he'd intended. I resisted the temptation to reply, and we walked out of the flat, slamming the front door behind us.

218

15

I marched Nella down the stairs, out of the building and over the road in silence. But immediately we got into the car and shut the doors, I lost my temper. I reached over, grabbed her by the lapels of her jacket and shook her, my face pressed up close to hers. I don't remember exactly what I said, but I shouted and swore at her. And afterwards I didn't feel the slightest bit ashamed at my lack of self-control; I'd wanted to make her understand exactly what it had been like to wander around London fearing that I'd never find her, so that she'd never do it again. She'd put me through hell, and I needed to pay her back for it.

When I'd finished, I started the car, gripped the steering wheel and headed up the road in the direction of the motorway. I drove slowly and carefully, concentrating on the route, aware that I was in a heightened state of emotion. And after a while, once we were on our way out of the city, I began to calm down.

As we drove along, Nella turned her head away from me, looking out of the window. She didn't speak a word. I could understand why: she was shocked at my reaction, and she felt thoroughly humiliated by the whole episode. So we sat in silence for a long time until, finally, she spoke.

'Sorry, Mum.' There was a tremble in her voice.

'Why did you do that?' My own voice was

shaking. 'You could have just asked...'

'But the audition was in the evening. And I knew you wouldn't let me go.'

'Dad would have driven you up and waited. I told you that.' I gave an exasperated sigh. 'You didn't have to go running off like that, without telling us...'

Nella started to cry.

I wasn't sympathetic. 'Promise me you'll never, ever do anything like this again.'

'I promise.'

She burst into sobs. I leaned over and patted her knee, then gestured at my handbag. She searched through it, found a tissue and went on crying into it.

When the tears had subsided I said, 'Now listen, I want you to tell me exactly what happened with Emyr, from the beginning. I'm not trying to pry, but it's important.'

She sniffed, dabbing at her eyes. 'Well, he came up to me at the concert after school, and said he liked my singing. I could tell he liked me, too.' She paused for a moment, embarrassed. 'And I liked him. But nothing happened before we went to London. When we met up, it was just about recording and stuff.'

There was a silence.

'Go on,' I said.

'After the audition, Tony Andreou took us to a bar, and we all had champagne. Emyr was excited. Happy. And so was I. We got a bit drunk, and then he started kissing me.'

'Did you ask him to stop?'

'No.' She bent her head, so that her hair hung

220

over her face. 'I liked it. I wanted him to.'

'Well, that's nothing to be ashamed of, Nella.' My tone was gentle. I didn't want her to feel too shy to tell me more.

'Then we went back to Tony's flat,' she went on, encouraged. 'He and Sandy, that's his boyfriend, they were taking some kind of drugs, I think...'

'Did you join in?'

'Of course not.' Nella was emphatic in her denial. 'But then it started to get a bit weird, so Emyr told me to come with him into the bedroom. I think he wanted to protect me.' She hesitated. 'He's not a bad guy really, Mum.'

I let that pass.

'Anyway, once we were on the bed, we started kissing again, and then ... well, things got a bit out of hand.'

'Why didn't you try to stop him?'

She looked over at me. I could see, even in the half-darkness, that her eyes had gone round.

'Because I wanted him to. I've got to lose my virginity sometime. I thought maybe this was my chance.' Her voice was serious. 'But when it came down to it, I realized I was scared. I wasn't ready.'

'Did you tell him that?'

'No. I felt I'd gone too far by that time.'

It began to rain. I leaned forward and switched on the windscreen wipers.

'Listen, Nella, it's always your right to say no. At any stage.' I paused. 'And about losing your virginity. Don't leave it up to some man you hardly know. Find someone you care about, someone you can trust. Someone who loves you, or at least respects you. Take it slowly. If he's not experienced,

221

it doesn't matter. You can work it out together.'

Nella looked sceptical. And although I believed what I was saying, I knew perfectly well, from my own experience as a young woman, that sex is rarely as straightforward as that.

For a moment, we both stared out at the road ahead, watching the windscreen wipers batting back and forth, trying to keep the rain at bay.

'OK,' I said, after a while. 'Lecture over. Let's listen to some music. D'you want to plug in your iPod?'

When we got home, in the early hours of the morning, Bob was asleep on the sofa. He'd evidently been waiting up. I shook him awake, gave him a brief account of the story, then went upstairs and sank into bed. He didn't follow me up, and I didn't wait for him to. Once my head hit the pillow, I was asleep.

Next day I got up late. Bob took Rose out in the morning, and Nella slept till lunchtime. I let her take her meal up to her room, and she closeted herself away in her bedroom for the rest of the day. In the evening Bob went up and talked to her. When he came out, I didn't ask him what they'd said. We didn't discuss our argument, either. We'd both apologized on the phone, but now that the drama was over and Nella was safe, it had become clear that neither of us was prepared to give ground. We were still being scrupulously polite to each other in front of the girls, but when we were alone we more or less ignored each other.

First thing on Monday, when I got to my office, I made a phone call to Emyr's place of work, Safe

Trax. I asked to speak to the director, told her what had happened, and threatened to issue a formal complaint. She was horrified – although she didn't sound very surprised – and begged me not to, promising that the matter would be resolved immediately.

After I'd put the phone down I wondered whether I should have gone further and insisted that Emyr should be dismissed from his post; but, on reflection, I realized that he hadn't actually committed any crime. Nella wasn't under-age, and it was quite clear that he'd taken her off to London with her full consent. Whether or not he would have forced her to have sex with him against her will, I couldn't be sure; her own feelings about the encounter also seemed to be ambivalent. Clearly his behaviour had been morally wrong; she was an impressionable teen-ager, and he'd taken advantage of her. But as far as I could see, he'd done nothing strictly illegal.

And, to be honest, I had another reason for hesitating over whether Emyr should be severely punished for his actions. I was uncomfortably aware that, in essence, my lusting after Gwydion hadn't been so very different. Of course, Gwydion was a man in his twenties, not a teenager, but there was still a big age gap between the two of us; and, of course, I was married. What's more, I'd been in a position of authority over him. Gwydion had trusted and respected me; and I'd almost – almost, but not quite – been tempted to abuse that trust. I was ashamed to admit it, but to that degree, my motives hadn't been much more honourable than Emyr's.

As the day wore on, I began to feel more and more exhausted. That morning I had a run of particularly wearing clients. First, there was Harriet, an extremely overweight young woman who seemed unable to hold a serious conversation and had kept up a never-ending stream of brittle banter throughout each session for the past six months; next, Bryn, a middle-aged man with an unrelenting hatred of his controlling mother, which he had transferred to me, lock, stock and barrel, and which showed no signs of abating in the near future; after that, Maria, a severely depressed housewife – 'home-maker' I should say – whose husband had left her, and who sat in silence most of the time, occasionally dissolving into tears when I raised the subject of how she could get help to care for her emotionally neglected children; and finally, Frank, a seventy-five-year-old man with prostate cancer, whose anger and grief at his illness took the form of what he called sex addiction, and what I called staring fixedly at my breasts and making lecherous remarks.

After Frank left, I managed a short lunch break, nipping over to the deli to get a takeaway sandwich and a cup of coffee. It was a bright, sunny day, and I could have gone over to the park to eat, but instead I decided to get back to the office so I could take a nap on the couch. That didn't work out, though. Instead, I had a series of irritating interruptions: Branwen appeared with a card to sign for Meinir, the hypnotherapist upstairs, who was leaving that week; Dougie, the cognitive behavioural therapist, dropped by for some advice on a client; and, to cap it all, a workman started drilling the road outside.

Just as I felt I was going to scream, there was another knock at my door. I glanced at my watch. My first client of the afternoon wasn't due for another hour. And then I remembered that I'd scheduled a meeting with a policewoman about the Morgan case. She'd phoned to ask if I could answer some general questions, even though I hadn't yet agreed to become a witness, and I'd made an appointment with her at the office. I'd meant to think about what I was going to say, but I'd completely forgotten about it. And now she was here.

I took a deep breath, got up and showed the woman in, sitting her down in the armchair I normally use for my clients. I asked if I could get her a tea or coffee, but she refused, so I sat down in the chair opposite and waited while she got out a warrant card and flashed it at me briefly. There was a picture of her on it, looking rather startled by the bright light of the camera, and a name: Detective Sergeant Lauren Bonetti.

'Thanks,' I said and she put it back in her bag. She got out a reporter's notebook and a pencil. I was surprised she wasn't using some kind of electronic gizmo to log her thoughts, instead of such an old-fashioned device. In fact she was rather surprising all round. I'd vaguely imagined an older woman, possibly in uniform, or at least dressed in some kind of dowdy navy-blue outfit, but she wasn't in the least like that. She was about my age, possibly a little younger, with curly brown hair, dark eyes, and freckles, dressed in a rather stylish asymmetric top, shortish skirt, patterned tights and chunky-heeled boots.

'Just a few questions,' she said, flipping over the cover of the notebook. 'I just want to establish a few facts before you decide whether you want to make a statement or not. I'll try not to take up too much of your time.'

There was a pause. I said nothing, waiting for her to continue.

'I need some basic information, that's all. Just to get a picture of how you work.' She hesitated. 'You see, it's rather unusual for us to take this kind of evidence. I haven't had a case like this before.'

I nodded in what I hoped was a non-committal way. I didn't have anything to hide, but I was well aware that this wasn't an informal chat, either. So I was careful not to say anything more than I needed to.

'Now, when was it that Gwydion Morgan first came to you?'

'Back in September. I can tell you the exact date, if you like.'

'That would be useful.'

I got up, went over to my desk and flicked through my appointments diary. 'Here we are.' I read out the date. 'And there were several more sessions after that.' I leafed through the diary, giving her the dates of each one as I found them.

I came back and sat down.

'Thanks. That's great.' She noted something on her page, then looked up at me. 'He didn't stay long, did he?'

'No.' Once again, I didn't elaborate.

'Is that normal? For someone to leave so soon?'

'Yes and no.' I paused. 'Some people stay for just a few sessions, others go on for years. It all depends, really. On what they think they need.'

'I see.' She looked thoughtful. 'So he felt he didn't need more, did he?'

'That's what he said.'

'And what did you think?'

I chose my words carefully. 'He seemed to have found some benefit in the therapy.' I paused. 'But I expect we could have got further, had we carried on.'

She nodded. There was a short silence, and then she said, 'Do you keep files on your patients, by any chance? Case notes, perhaps?'

'Yes. But they're mostly quite brief. These days I tend to rely on this.' I tapped my head.

'No problem.' She gave me an encouraging smile. 'I wonder if you could tell me about those sessions with Mr Morgan. Describe how the dream came out, in your own words.' She paused. 'Don't worry if you get anything muddled up. This is just a preliminary interview. We can take a proper statement later.'

I did my best to run through what had happened in my meetings with Gwydion, starting with the second one, in which he'd mentioned the recurring dream about being locked in a box, and going on to describe, as the sessions progressed, how he'd begun to remember more and more: hearing voices outside the box, realizing that the box was a boat, hearing a scream and a splash as something big, like a body, hit the water. She listened attentively, continuing to make notes, until I came to the end of my story.

227

'Thank you, Dr Mayhew,' she said. 'That's just what I needed.' She paused. 'So this dream went on to trigger Mr Morgan's conscious memory of the events that took place on the boat when he was a child. All those years ago. Is that right?'

'Yes. That's what he told me.'

'Is that a common phenomenon? A dream triggering a childhood memory like that?'

'No. Not common. But it does happen. There are some well-documented studies in the literature.'

'And is the memory of a child as young as six reliable, do you think?'

'I would say so. Theoretically, a child of that age would be quite capable of understanding the significance of a traumatic event and remembering it later.'

She looked satisfied, and I began to congratulate myself on my authoritative tone. But then the conversation took a turn for the worse.

'Now...' She flipped back through her notes. 'There are just a couple more things...'

'Go ahead.' I tried not to sound alarmed.

'Did you have any contact with Gwydion Morgan outside your sessions with him here?'

Now that she'd asked me, I realized this was the question I'd been dreading.

'Yes. As a matter of fact, I did.'

'Would you mind telling me more about that?'

'Not at all.' My neck began to feel hot. 'His mother phoned me after our second session. He was depressed, she said. She was worried that he was suicidal, so I agreed to drive down to the family home to see him.'

'And what happened?'

'Nothing much. It wasn't that serious, he was just feeling rather low. I did my best to talk to him, but he wasn't very communicative. However, he came back for his session the following week.'

I saw no need to mention my other meetings with Gwydion, either at Creigfa Bay or the Travelodge – certainly not the Travelodge – unless she pressed me further, which, to my relief, she didn't.

'Do you usually visit your patients – sorry, I mean, clients – at home?'

'Not as a rule.' I could feel the heat rising up my neck into the back of my head. 'But this seemed to be a genuine emergency.' I hoped it wouldn't spread to my face. 'And I don't like to be too inflexible.'

'Of course.' She paused. 'We've also been in touch with the victim's mother, Solveig Lindberg. It seems you met with her in Stockholm?'

The question hung in the air. There was an awkward silence as I searched for an answer.

'Why did you do that?' She looked up at me quizzically.

'Well...' I wasn't sure what to say. 'I know it sounds odd. But I'd planned a trip around a conference there, and it seemed an opportunity to tie up some ends regarding my client. So just curiosity, I guess.'

There was a brief moment of silence and then she said, 'Goes with the territory, I suppose.' She smiled. 'I'm just the same.'

I smiled back, relieved.

'Well, I think that's about it for today.' She

229

began to gather her things. The notebook and pencil went back into her bag, and she adjusted her top, smoothing down her skirt. 'Thank you so much for your time.'

She put out her hand.

'Not at all.' I shook it, looking her briefly in the eye. I somehow got the impression she trusted me, but I don't know why that was. 'What will happen next?'

'Well, we'll be collecting evidence for the hearing, which will decide whether the case goes to trial.'

'When will that be?'

'A couple of months, I'd say. We've got our work cut out. I'll be in touch again to get a formal statement if we need one.'

'D'you think I'll be called in?'

She paused. 'Yes, I think it's quite likely that you will be.'

'I see.' I couldn't help feeling a little alarmed, but I tried not to show it. 'OK, then. Fine. I'll wait to hear from you.'

I walked her over to the door, opened it and saw her out. I waited as she walked down the corridor. When she got to the top of the stairs she turned, smiled, and gave me a little wave.

I smiled and waved back. Then I went back into my office to wait for my next client.

The following Friday evening, what with the drama with Nella, not to mention my fiasco with Gwydion and the visit from DS Lauren Bonetti, I felt I deserved a break. So after I'd attended to a few household chores, I changed into a black silk tea dress, added a string of pink glass beads, a battered leather jacket, suede ankle boots and my Stockholm beret, and went out.

When I got to the arts centre I found Mari and the usual suspects, Sharon, Polly and Catrin, gathered round a table in the bar. There were a couple of other women there too, who I didn't know so well. I bought a round of drinks, sat down next to Mari, and joined in the conversation. I'd missed the beginning of it, so Mari filled me in.

'You've heard the news?' she said, turning to me.

'No. What news?'

'Our friend Evan Morgan.'

The others stopped talking and looked at me.

'He's not my friend–' I began, but Mari cut in.

'They've fixed the date for the hearing. It was on the six o'clock news this evening. Didn't you see it?'

I shook my head. 'No. I had an evening session.'

There was a silence.

'How come Bob's defending him?'

'I don't know.' I shrugged. 'You'll have to ask him.'

Mari looked sideways at me. 'You know, that business you were asking me about, with the Swedish au pair?' She paused dramatically. 'Apparently Evan took the poor girl out on his boat, tried to rape her and, when she wouldn't have it, chucked her overboard. Left her to drown.'

'Is that what they're saying?'

'More or less. Reading between the lines.'

I knew it was no good getting an accurate picture of exactly what had been reported from

231

Mari. She was incapable of telling a story without exaggerating. So I tried to change the subject.

'Did you get that part in the Bassey film then, Mari?'

She ignored my question, narrowing her eyes, a mischievous smile on her face.

'You know something we don't know about all this, don't you?'

'No, not really.'

She didn't believe me. Neither did the others, who were still looking at me expectantly. I wasn't sure what to say. I didn't want to appear snooty, but neither did I want to involve myself in gossiping about the Morgan family.

'Look, if you must know...' I shot Mari an accusing glance. 'As I've already told Mari, there's a connection between this case and one of my clients. Ex-clients, I should say. I can't really discuss it at the moment. Professional ethics, sort of thing.'

The assembled company nodded gravely. I was pleased to have come up with a credible explanation for my silence on the matter, for the moment at least. But the speculation continued.

'I knew Evan was no angel,' Mari went on, 'but I can't believe this. I mean, rape, murder. I'm lucky to have escaped with my life.'

More grave nodding ensued.

'You know what he's doing now?' Mari's voice assumed a conspiratorial tone, though she was talking at the top of her voice, as she always does. 'He's having it off with that little secretary of his.'

'"PA" they're called these days,' said Sharon, apropos of nothing. 'Not "secretary".'

'PA, whatever. Her name's Rhiannon.'

'Not Rhiannon Jenkins? Bright girl, very pretty. Blonde?' Sharon looked a little anxious as she spoke, I thought.

Mari nodded. 'I don't know her surname, but yes, that's got to be her.'

'I taught her in college a couple of years ago.' Sharon looked mildly shocked. 'She can't be more than about twenty-five or so.'

'Well, there you are. That's Evan for you.' Mari frowned. 'But the weird thing is, so I've heard, that he's serious about this one.' She adopted the conspiratorial tone again. 'Apparently, she's pregnant.'

'Really?' I couldn't hide my curiosity. This was a piece in the jigsaw I hadn't come across before.

'Yup.' Mari looked triumphant as she delivered this choice piece of gossip.

'How do you know?'

'Heard it on the grapevine. It's a small world, the theatre.'

'And...' I tried to sound casual. 'Is she keeping the baby?'

'So it seems. Wants to marry him. Age gap and all.' Mari paused. 'Though this murder charge will put paid to that, I suppose.' She picked up her empty glass. 'Now, who wants another drink? My round, I think.'

I left the arts centre late that night. I wasn't in any hurry to get home. Things were still very tense between me and Bob. We were continuing to avoid contact with each other as much as possible. He'd announced that he was going to visit his mother in the valleys, so he'd taken the girls with him for the weekend. Perhaps, I thought, a little solitude would be good for me. The conflict between the two of us seemed to have escalated rather than decreased after Nella's escapade in London, and I needed some time to take stock.

I didn't notice anything was wrong with the car until I got home. I parked under the street lamp outside the house, in the usual way, got out, locked the door and then I saw it. Spray-painted over the bonnet, in red letters: BITCH.

It was hurriedly done, but the word was un-mistakable. As I looked at it, I felt a current of fear run through me. Emyr, I thought. He must have got the sack, and this was his revenge. Or could it be Evan Morgan, perhaps? To scare me off becoming a witness at the hearing? But he couldn't have known about my visit from DS Lauren Bonetti. And his connection with Bob would surely have prevented him from acting in such a way. It had to be Emyr, I was sure of it.

At that stage I could have panicked, but I didn't. Instead I left the car where it was and walked quickly into the house. Once inside, I bolted the front door, double-locked it and slotted in the chain. I called the police and they said they'd try to send someone round in the morning, but it might have to wait until Monday. I didn't call Bob. I didn't see the point of worrying him while he was away. I made myself a cup of chamomile tea, to help me sleep, and before I went to bed inspected the house, checking and double-checking all the doors and windows to make sure they were secure. Then I climbed the stairs.

Someone out there was trying to frighten me, I

knew. It could be Emyr. Or Evan. Or someone else. But I wasn't going to give them the satisfaction.

I lay in bed for a while with the light on, listening for any sound in the house, in the garden or in the street outside. But all was silent. I listened for the crunch of footsteps on the gravel path outside, the thud of a crowbar forcing a window, the click of a key in a lock, or the squeak of a doorknob turning, but none came. So I switched off the light, turned over, and slept till morning.

The weekend passed uneventfully, but I found it hard to relax. In the morning I waited for a policeman to arrive, but no one came, so at midday I took the car into the garage and was told it had to be resprayed, at vast expense. I left it there, and took a taxi home. I spent the rest of the time tidying up the garden, catching up on the laundry and going over my accounts. During the day, while I was occupied and busy, I felt fine, but it was at night that I began to be afraid. That evening I dutifully toured the house, checking that all the doors and windows were locked, and when I was in bed I froze at the slightest sound in the house or outside. The next morning I felt a profound sense of relief that I'd got through another night without incident. I told myself that the graffiti scrawled on my car was probably the work of a passing vandal, rather than anyone who knew me; that even if it was Emyr who'd done it, the attack would have satisfied the grudge he had against me, and against the world, and he wouldn't be troubling me further. But I didn't quite believe it.

By Sunday afternoon I was thoroughly keyed up, tense and jumpy; so when Bob and the girls came home, I was relieved to see them. I told Bob that someone had vandalized my car and that I'd taken it in to the garage, but I didn't elaborate. After everything that had happened between us, I wasn't about to run to him for help. He didn't seem to notice how edgy I was, and went straight off to his study to work. Nella closeted herself in the bedroom again, so I stayed in the kitchen chatting to Rose. And then, after she'd gone to bed, I went up to see Nella.

I knocked on her door and went in. As usual, she was sitting at her computer, messaging her friends on Facebook. I went over and stood beside her, looking over her shoulder. She immediately clicked off the page, but before it vanished I saw a small photo of Emyr, with some text beside it.

I suppose it was because I was so tense, but without stopping to think, I flew off the handle.

'For God's sake, Nella, what d'you think you're doing?' I was shouting at her. 'How could you?'

'Calm down, Mum.' Nella was taken aback.

I lowered my voice. 'But you promised me you'd have nothing more to do with this man.'

'I'm not doing anything wrong. Emyr's a friend, that's all. He's upset because he's lost his job.' She hesitated. 'I don't suppose that could have anything to do with you, could it?'

I tried to compose myself.

'I did phone them to complain, yes,' I said. 'Because what he did was wrong. He took advantage of you–'

'I'm not seeing him,' Nella interrupted. 'And

236

anyway, even if I was…'

'Nella, look. This isn't funny.' I felt like slapping her, but I willed myself to talk to her in a level voice. 'I wasn't going to tell you this, but someone's vandalized the car. Scrawled something on it.'

'What?' Nella's expression changed from anger to shock.

'You don't need to know what. But I think it may have been Emyr who did it.'

'How can you be sure of that?'

'I can't. I just have my suspicions, that's all.'

'You're paranoid, Mum.' Nella spoke dismissively, but I knew that she'd been rattled by what I'd told her.

'Promise me you won't meet him again. Ever.' Nella looked mutinous, but I carried on. 'And make sure you delete him from your Facebook page.'

There was a silence. I glared at her and she glared at me. Then she backed down.

'Whatever.'

I took that to mean yes.

'I'm sorry I shouted at you,' I said. I spoke gently. I was sorry. Nella's a sensitive person, and I could see that I'd upset her. But I hadn't had much alternative, I felt.

Nella nodded, but she didn't say sorry back.

I walked over to the door. I was upset, and I was trembling slightly, but I tried not to let her see it.

'You know something, Mum,' she said, as I was about to leave. 'You should be more self-aware.' She paused. 'You're getting old, and you're jealous that men find me attractive. More attractive than you. You just can't cope with it, that's all.'

Once again, I felt like slapping her. But the fury she aroused in me made me wonder whether there might be some truth in what she said.

I resisted the temptation to reply 'Whatever', and went out, shutting the door quietly behind me.

16

'Dr Mayhew?'

The voice was one I'd heard before, but I couldn't quite place it.

I hesitated. I always have a momentary impulse, on being addressed as 'Dr Mayhew', to say something pompous like 'The very same', but I managed to resist it.

'Speaking.'

'This is Evan Morgan.'

I was taken aback. Evan Morgan was the last person I'd been expecting to call. All the same, I didn't miss a beat.

'Mr Morgan. How can I help you?'

'We need to meet, right away.'

'And why's that?'

'I have some important information to tell you. Before you give a formal statement to the police.'

'How do you know about my statement?'

'Never mind how I know. I'm just warning you, if you get involved in this, you're going to make a fool of yourself.'

I thought for a moment. 'My husband's put you up to this, hasn't he?'

'Bob? No, of course not. He doesn't even know I'm making this call.'

'Oh. Right.' I tried not to sound sarcastic.

'No, this is entirely off my own bat. You see, there are some crucial facts you don't know about the situation. Gwydion and Arianrhod have been lying to you. Lying all along.'

There was a silence as he waited for my response.

I was courteous, but firm.

'Well, thank you for calling...'

'We must meet and talk. It's for your own good. You'll regret it if you don't...'

'Are you threatening me?'

'No.' The voice on the other end of the line remained low and steady. He didn't sound like the kind of a man who would go out with a can of spray paint and vandalize a car. 'I'm just warning you, you're going to make a fool of yourself if you take the witness stand. Ruin your reputation. You mustn't be taken in.'

'I'm sorry, Mr Morgan, but–'

He didn't let me finish.

'Well, if you change your mind, I'll be in the Smuggler's Rest, Penarth Marina, from eight o'clock. I'll wait for you in the bar.'

'Goodbye,' I said, and put the phone down.

I returned to surfing the Net. Before the phone had rung I'd been trying to find out the current PC thinking about the terms 'obese', 'very over-weight' and 'fat'. The arguments were interesting – some claiming that using the word 'obese' was

239

entirely negative, others that it was a good way to shock people out of denial – but now I couldn't follow them. Rage bubbled up in me again, fury that Bob was once more meddling in my affairs, trying to stop me helping an ex-client.

To clear my head, I got up, went over and looked out of the window. The street was empty, nothing to see but a blank grey sky, and a few dead leaves sailing slowly down from the tree outside to join the ones scattered on the pavement below.

There was a knock at the door and, a few seconds later, my next client of the day, Harriet, waddled in. She was out of breath, and there were beads of sweat on her upper lip. I ushered her over to her chair, taking a seat opposite.

I waited as Harriet struggled into the chair. It's a solidly built armchair, nice and wide, with a tapestry cushion on it. I realized as she lowered herself into it that I'd forgotten to take the cushion off and that she had even less space than usual. I watched her try to sit down, feeling sorry for her. It was embarrassing. I hadn't noticed it when she came in, but she must have put on a few extra pounds since the previous week.

Undeterred, Harriet balanced herself on one armrest and launched into one of her entertaining stories, this one involving her bus journey to the session.

I held up my hand. I spoke in what I hoped was a quiet, encouraging tone. 'Harriet, before we go on, there's something I'd like us to talk about today…'

Harriet ignored me and went on telling her

story. Then the chair began to tip to one side. She shifted position, teetering a little, and continued, but the chair began to tip up again.

It was then that she burst into tears.

I said nothing. Instead, I passed over the tissue box.

I didn't get to the Smuggler's Rest until nine o'clock that evening. Bob was away on a business trip, and I'd had a lot of cooking, taxi-servicing and helping with homework duties to cope with. Besides, I didn't want to appear too eager.

Strange, how quickly one's resolve can weaken. My instinct, when Evan Morgan had called that morning, had been to avoid having anything to do with him; and during the rest of the day I'd been too busy with my clients to give the matter any further thought. But at the end of the day, before I went home, I'd begun to think about what he'd said. So I'd called him back and told him I'd meet him later that evening.

I didn't believe that Arianrhod and Gwydion were lying about what had happened on the yacht, but I still had a nagging sense that I wasn't getting the whole picture. I also knew that Arianrhod was no stranger to deceit; before the whole story came out, she'd told me a number of other lies, in an attempt to cover up. Not only that, but on more than one occasion I'd felt that their behaviour, as mother and son, was odd. I did believe them, but I was acutely aware that in a few days' time, if I went ahead, I'd be making my formal statement to the police. Surely, I thought, it would be wrong to do so without first hearing Evan Morgan's version

241

of events.

The other reason I changed my mind, I have to admit, was curiosity. As DS Lauren Bonetti had pointed out, psychotherapists, like police inspectors, are by nature inquisitive people; it goes with the territory. And it's nothing to be ashamed of; if you weren't a nosy parker, you wouldn't be able to do your job properly.

Yet, as I parked the car outside the pub, I began to feel nervous. I was about to meet a man who'd been accused of murder. A man who might very well take a dislike to me, who might want to stop me making my statement to the police, or persuade me to change what I had to say. Of course, it was highly unlikely that Evan Morgan would harm me in any way – abducting me at this stage of the game would hardly help his cause – but even so, I couldn't help being a little afraid.

The Smuggler's Rest isn't the kind of place where you'd be likely to bump into any of your friends, which is probably why Evan Morgan had chosen it. It's not that it's a dive; far from it. It's one of those modern pubs that proudly displays its gleaming olde-worlde tropes everywhere you look. There's an unconvincing ship's wheel over the bar, and festoons of fishing nets hang from the ceiling, hosting an alarming array of lobster pots, starfish and coloured glass bottles. A generic, wipe-clean menu, offering generic, child-friendly food, graces each highly varnished table. It's the kind of place where you don't feel comfortable. It's too clean, too modern, and pretending too hard not to be.

The room was fairly empty as I walked in, with

only one or two people at the bar, and a few small groups sitting at the tables. I saw Evan Morgan at the bar with a drink. His back was bent, and his chin was propped up on his hand. I couldn't help registering that he was a startlingly handsome man. Not just for his age, either. One of those rare beings who seem to acquire gravitas with their greying hair, and an authoritative presence, rather than fading slowly into insignificance, as most of us do.

He didn't see me as I approached, but then he looked up, and his expression changed.

'Dr Mayhew. Thank you for coming.' He smiled, put out his hand, and I shook it briefly.

'Not at all.' I was about to apologize for being late, but decided against it.

'What can I get you?'

'A whisky, please. Just a small one.' I felt in need of something strong, to steady my nerves. But I told myself I'd stick to one drink only, because I was driving.

'Ice?'

'No, thank you.'

He waved at a table by the window. 'Let's go and sit over there, shall we? We'll be more comfortable.'

'Fine.'

I walked over to the table, sat down and looked out of the window. The pub overlooked the marina. Outside there were yachts lined up on the dockside. Of course, that's why he'd selected this place. I could just hear their masts clinking in the wind over the low canned music of the pub.

Evan came over with the drinks, put them on

the table and sat down opposite.

'I won't keep you long. I know you're a busy woman.' He took a sip of his drink, which looked like a gin and tonic.

'Thanks. I'd appreciate that.' I took a sip of mine. It was a good-quality whisky, smooth and warming, and a rather larger shot than I'd ordered.

'I'll come directly to the point then.'

He paused and glanced quickly around him. There was no one nearby, except for a couple of middle-aged women talking animatedly to each other as they ate their fish supper.

'To be quite frank,' Evan continued, 'I'm not blameless in this story.' He frowned, as though mulling over how best to begin. 'But one thing is certain. I didn't kill Elsa Lindberg. That is a complete fabrication, on the part of my wife.' He hesitated. 'And son.'

I thought I detected genuine emotion in that moment of hesitation, almost as if he couldn't bear the thought that his son had turned against him; but then I remembered that Evan had been an actor, as well as a theatre director. It was his job to make me believe in the tale he was telling me, and he was evidently pretty good at it.

'I did take Elsa out that day on the yacht,' he went on. 'She was Gwydion's nanny, she went with him everywhere, so that was normal enough. But – I won't lie – I also wanted her to come because I found her very attractive. And ... at the time, things weren't going well between me and Arianrhod.' He hesitated again, but this time there seemed to be no regret, no sadness in his face.

I nodded, then checked myself. I wasn't on

244

duty now. This wasn't a therapy session, though it was beginning to sound like one.

'Anyway,' he continued, 'it was a beautiful day. Bright sunshine, sea as calm as a millpond. No real sailing to do, so I was drinking. Quite heavily.' He paused and looked up at me. Those eyes, I thought. The irises were just as deep, as green, as Gwydion's, though the whites had coloured with age. 'I'm an alcoholic, you know that, of course. Recovering now.' He gave a wry smile. 'If you ever recover.'

I didn't smile back.

'Elsa was drinking, too. Not much, she was a sensible girl. Just to keep me company.' He sighed. 'I got on well with her. She was so bright, such fun.' The sadness came into his voice again. 'We talked about Strindberg, I remember. She was studying him at university. Then... I don't know ... one thing led to another...' Once again, he looked me in the eye. 'I don't deny it. She was a beautiful girl, and I wanted her. She wanted me, too. That was very clear.' He looked away.

'Where was Gwydion while all this was going on?' I tried not to sound judgemental as I spoke.

'Oh, he didn't see anything. He was in the cabin below, lying down. He always got seasick on the yacht. I was trying to train him out of it, help him find his sea legs.'

'Not the best way to do it,' I ventured. 'Seducing the au pair while you were out on the trip.'

'What can I say?' Evan shrugged. 'I was very self-involved at the time. Still am. I was in an un-happy marriage, and I took my pleasures where I could find them. Gave them, too, I might add. No, I

245

don't regret any of that, not one bit.' He paused.

There was a short silence.

'So why did Elsa jump off the boat? Why would she do that?' I asked.

'Well, as I said, the sea was very calm that day. We weren't far out, and Elsa decided to swim back into the bay on her own. She was an exceptional swimmer, so it seemed completely safe. I watched her swim away. She moved beautifully in the water, like a seal...' He broke off. 'Anyway, I certainly didn't fight with her, push her overboard or anything like that. She jumped off the side of that boat of her own accord. It was entirely her decision. And it was so calm, such a lovely day, that I decided to sail on for a little while before coming in behind her. The weather was glorious. That's why I couldn't believe ... I simply couldn't believe...'

He shook his head. He seemed genuinely distressed at the memory. 'I really just can't explain how she drowned. When she didn't come back, I was panic-stricken. We searched everywhere. I wanted to go to the police. But Arianrhod...'

I waited. This was the side of the story that I'd come to hear.

'To my eternal shame, Arianrhod persuaded me not to. Said my reputation would be ruined. That I'd be accused of murdering Elsa in a drunken rage, or some such nonsense. I was scared...'

For a moment I saw the fear in his eyes that I'd seen so often in Gwydion's, and I realized that, under the gravitas, his air of being a man of the world, there was a part of him that was as insecure as his son.

'And she can be a very dominating woman...'

That didn't tally with my impression of Arianrhod, but I let it pass.

'So I did as she ordered. Tried to cover the whole thing up. Lied to the police. Even lied to Elsa's mother when she came over.' He frowned. 'That was strange. She looked so like her daughter. It was uncanny.'

I had an impulse to confront him about his attempt to seduce Solveig, too, but thought better of it.

Evan picked up his drink and took a large swig. There wasn't the faintest whiff of alcohol coming off it, and I realized that it was just fizzy water.

'Of course, it all had to come out sooner or later. And in a way I'm glad it has. It's been on my conscience all these years, covering up the truth like that.' He gave a deep sigh, then looked me straight in the eye again. 'But I'm not a murderer. Gwydion is lying – I didn't fight with Elsa, or push her over the side of the boat.'

'Why on earth would he lie about it then?' I took a sip of my drink. 'To me? To the police?'

'I can tell you exactly why. His mother's putting him up to this. It's as simple as that.'

'But why would she make a false charge against you? If you're found guilty, she stands to lose a lot too, doesn't she?'

For a moment, I thought I could detect a flicker of guilt steal over his face, but if I did, it was soon gone.

'Because she hates me. My wife absolutely loathes me. Wants to see me go down.'

'Why, though?'

'It's obvious. Hell hath no fury, et cetera.'

I took another sip of my drink. I wasn't sure what to make of Evan's tale. At certain moments, I was convinced that he was lying; at others, his words rang true. And it wasn't just his words. I've become pretty adept at studying my clients' body language, their gestures, their expressions, noticing the gap between what they say and how they behave. Evan's gave me the feeling that he was, for the most part, genuine; but there were also moments when it seemed he might still be hiding the truth. It was unlikely that he'd spray-painted my car, I reflected; but perhaps not altogether impossible.

'Well, Mr Morgan...'

'Call me Evan.'

I nodded, but I didn't take him up on his offer. 'Thank you for filling me in.' I glanced at my watch. 'But I think I'd better be heading off now.'

He looked taken aback. 'Don't you have anything to say about all this?'

'I'm not in a position to comment.' I looked out of the window at the yachts. 'But I'll certainly think about what you've told me. Take it into account.'

Evan followed my gaze. 'That's mine out there. The one with the pale yellow hull. *Miss Julie.*'

'Is it the one ... the same one?'

'The one I took Elsa out on? Yes, as a matter of fact, it is. Would you like me to show you round it?'

'Sorry, I'm a bit pushed for time.' I finished my drink and put the empty glass down on the table.

Evan looked downcast. 'Well, look, if you feel

like coming back, I'm free tomorrow...' There was an air of quiet desperation in his tone, but he did his best to hide it. 'I'm living on the yacht at the moment, just for the time being, until...' His voice faded away mid-sentence, as if he couldn't quite believe that he was soon to be tried in court for murder.

'Thank you.' I was polite enough, but I hoped to convey that I had no intention whatsoever of visiting him again.

'And you've got my number, haven't you, if you need it?' The desperation rose to the surface. 'On your office phone.'

'That's right.' I picked up my bag, which was open on the chair beside me. As I did so, Evan glanced at it and noticed the paperback poking out of the top.

'Oh,' he said, leaning forward to read the title. His tone of voice changed. 'The Jones biography of Freud. Are you enjoying it?'

'Yes.' I wondered whether he was trying to ingratiate himself to me, but there seemed to be genuine interest in his enquiry. 'Very much, on the whole. The schisms later on get a bit tedious.'

'If you think that's bad, try the three-volume version.' He paused. 'But what an incredibly gifted man Jones was.' He spoke with enthusiasm. 'As a writer, a thinker ... quite apart from his brilliance as a doctor.'

I couldn't help catching his enthusiasm. 'All those languages, too...'

'Introduced psychoanalysis to the English-speaking world. Wrote books on all kinds of subjects, from nightmares to vampires to figure-skating. Saved Freud from the Nazis.' He paused. 'Not bad for a colliery boy from Swansea.'

I nodded. 'It's surprising he's not more famous.'

'He would be, if there weren't so many skeletons in his cupboard.' Evan grinned. 'I've often thought of making a film about his life. It's got everything – intrigue, adventure...'

I nodded again. I found myself wanting to continue the conversation but, instead, I let a silence fall. Then I got up to go.

Evan got up too and put his hand out.

I shook it. He held on to it briefly, pressing it a little, before I drew it away.

'Goodbye,' he said. 'Until we meet again.'

'Goodbye,' I replied.

Then I turned and walked out of the pub, aware that his eyes were following me as I went.

When I got home, Bob was back, sitting at the kitchen table with his laptop. He didn't look up when I came in. I hadn't told him about my meeting with Evan Morgan, and I wasn't about to. The only matters we discussed with each other these days were our domestic arrangements, mostly to do with the girls. And even those had become fraught with tension.

I went over to the kettle.

'D'you want a cup of tea before I go up to bed?'

'No, thanks.'

'Are the girls asleep?'

'Rose is. I don't know about Nella.' He looked up for a moment. 'A boy came over to see her this evening. With a guitar.'

'Oh yes?' I was intrigued. 'What's he like?'

'Seems pleasant enough. Polite.' He frowned. 'But when I went into her room to look for the phone, I found them kissing on the bed.'

'Did you knock first?' I asked, busying myself with the tea.

'No. But...'

I turned to face him. 'Well, you should have, Bob. That's her private space.'

'Don't be ridiculous. I'll do what I want in my own house.' I was surprised at his tone. This was new to me, Bob acting the authoritarian pater-familias. 'And I won't have her taking boys up to her room. After what happened in London...'

'She's sixteen, for heaven's sake.' I tried not to raise my voice, but I did, a fraction. 'She's going to kiss boys, and if she wants to do it in the privacy of her bedroom, I can't see why she shouldn't. I'm certainly not going to try and stop her.' I paused. I thought of telling him about my conversations alone with Nella, and asking him about his. But we didn't seem to have that level of intimacy any more. 'I think we should be pleased about this. A boyfriend of her own age–'

'All right, *I'll* have to do it then,' Bob cut in. 'I'll tell her if he comes round, she can entertain him downstairs in the sitting room. I don't want her ending up pregnant.'

'Bob, you're overreacting.' I spoke more gently. 'Nella's growing up. It's not easy to take in, is it?' I wished I could have found a tactful way to add, 'And the fact that you're not having sex with your wife isn't helping, either', but I couldn't. He was too angry, and although I was trying to keep calm, his uncharacteristically macho behaviour

251

had riled me, too.

'Oh, give me a break.' Bob got up and walked swiftly to the door. 'You're not on duty now, Dr Mayhew.'

He walked out, slamming it behind him. Great, I thought. A night on the sofa.

That evening I crept into the sitting room with a duvet and pillow after everyone had gone to bed. I programmed an alarm call on my mobile so I'd wake at six-thirty in the morning, before they got up. I didn't want the girls to know that I was sleeping on my own downstairs. I tried to make myself comfortable, but I slept fitfully: the sofa was too short, and I kept waking up during the night with a crick in my neck. At 4 a.m., just when I'd managed to settle into sleep, the phone rang.

'Hello?' I picked it up, disoriented.

There was no reply, just a low, slow breathing, in and out, in and out.

'Who is this?'

The breathing continued, getting louder and louder.

I clicked off the phone angrily. The screen showed 'Number withheld'. I put the phone back on the coffee table, turned over, and tried to get back to sleep.

A couple of minutes later, it rang again. This time I picked it up and switched it off. Then I lay awake, staring up at the ceiling, until it was time to get up.

17

When I got to my office the next day, I had a surprise waiting for me. Arianrhod was sitting on the wall outside.

The moment I saw her, I panicked. What if she knew about my meeting with Evan and had come to bawl me out? What if a shouting match ensued, right here, out in the street, in front of the building? I'd assumed that she and Evan were incommunicado, now that he was living on the boat, but the Morgan-family dynamic, as I've said, was so tangled and twisted that I'd begun to feel I was always one step behind. It wasn't a feeling I liked.

I resisted the temptation to pretend I hadn't seen her, turn down the nearest side street and run away. Instead I walked straight up to her.

'Arianrhod. What are you doing here?' After meeting Evan, I couldn't help viewing her in a slightly different light. She seemed so timid in her demeanour, yet he'd described her as cruel and vindictive. However unfair his judgement might have been, I found myself beginning to wonder whether there was any truth in it.

She was immediately apologetic. 'It won't take a minute, I promise. It's about Gwydion.'

So she didn't know about my rendezvous with Evan.

I gave a sigh of relief. 'You'd better come up,' I said. 'But I've got a client coming in half an hour,

253

so it'll have to be quick.'

Arianrhod nodded. She looked tired, I noticed. There were dark circles under her eyes and her skin had a waxy texture to it.

We went into the building. Branwen looked up as we passed, puzzled. She knew my first client wasn't due in until nine. I shot her a glance that said, don't worry about it, and she returned to her computer screen.

Arianrhod and I went upstairs to my office. She waited as I unlocked the door and ushered her in.

'Please.' I indicated the chair opposite my desk. Then I went round to the other side, sat down, switched on my computer, and waited until it stopped emitting its various bleeps. 'Won't be a minute.'

By switching it on, I wanted to make it clear to her that I didn't have unlimited time to talk. And that these unscheduled visits to my place of work were extremely unwelcome.

'Right. Now, how can I help you?' My tone was more impatient than I'd intended. I was curiously discomfited at having someone in my office before I'd had a chance to prepare myself. It was something that hardly ever happened and, when it did, I felt more than a little undermined.

Arianrhod took the hint and came directly to the point. 'Gwydion's gone into The Grange,' she said.

I immediately regretted my brusqueness. The Grange is a private clinic situated in the Vale of Glamorgan, just outside Cardiff. The place where the rich go to do battle with the occupational hazards of privilege: alcoholism, eating disorders, that kind of thing.

'Just for a short while,' she added. 'I'm hoping he'll be out soon.'

There was a tremble in her voice as she spoke. I glanced down and noticed that she was twisting the fabric of her coat sleeve.

'I'm sorry to hear that,' I said. 'Very sorry indeed.'

'I wondered...' She went on twisting. 'I think it would help if you could visit him there.'

I shifted uncomfortably on my chair. I wondered how much Arianrhod knew about my dealings with Gwydion. She and her son were on very intimate terms, I knew that much. Would Gwydion have told her that he'd met me on several occasions outside the sessions, that there'd been a sexual connection, albeit a limited one, between us?

'Arianrhod, I should explain...' I hesitated. 'It's not really very good practice for a therapist to resume contact with a client, once the client has decided to terminate the therapy.'

She gave me a reproachful look. I realized the jargon had offended her. So I tried switching to plainer language.

'It's just not done, really, to see former clients.' I paused. 'It can lead to problems ... of attachment ... on both sides.'

I'd come as close as I could to explaining the reasons for my reluctance to visit Gwydion. I wasn't inclined to go further.

'I take your point. But it's just that he's so distressed. And he seems to trust you.'

I changed the subject. 'Why's he been admitted?'

255

'Well, he was becoming very unbalanced. Paranoid, convinced people were following him.' She sighed. 'But there are other things, too ... well, you know what he's like. Better than me, probably.'

Was there a hint of sarcasm in her voice? If so, I ignored it.

'It's the stress of the hearing coming up,' she went on. 'It's all been too much for him.'

'I can imagine.' For a moment, I felt a wave of sympathy for Gwydion, but then I checked myself. 'But I'm sure he's in good hands at The Grange.'

Several of my clients had come to me from a sojourn there, as it happened. Gwydion was the only one of them to make the trip the other way round. 'The staff there are very experienced, very skilled.' I paused. 'I expect he'll be out before long.'

'That's what I'm worried about, though. He might not be out in time.' She stopped.

'For the rehearsals?'

'Yes. And...'

'The hearing?'

So that's what all this is about, I realized. Arianrhod's main worry was not her son's distressed condition, or the damage to his career prospects, but that he might not be able to give evidence against Evan at the upcoming hearing. In fact, it struck me that she had changed since our last meeting; she was no longer upset by the prospect of the hearing, but seemed to be positively relishing it. Perhaps, after all, there was something in what Evan Morgan had said about her.

Arianrhod started to rub at her sleeve again. This time I didn't feel so sympathetic.

'Well, thank you for letting me know where he is.' I glanced at my watch. 'But I'm going to have to get on, I'm afraid...'

'So you'll go and see him there?' She affected not to notice my efforts to close the conversation. 'Try and get him back on the straight and narrow?'

The straight and narrow. I thought that was an odd expression to use, in the circumstances, but I let it pass.

'I'll certainly think about it.' I stood up. 'Now, if you'll excuse me...'

This time, Arianrhod got up to go. Together we walked over to the door.

'Please.' She stopped at the door and clutched my arm. 'Do go and see my son, Dr Mayhew. It's our last chance.'

Our last chance. That was another strange thing to say, I thought.

'Goodbye, Arianrhod.' I drew my arm gently away. 'And do remember to telephone next time, won't you?'

She nodded obediently, almost like a small child. But I noticed that she didn't say yes.

I opened the door, waited till she'd walked through and shut it firmly behind her. Then I went back to my desk and began to sift through my emails.

I didn't go to see Gwydion that day. I was busy at work, and at home. Nowadays Bob seemed to be out most of the time. I couldn't blame him – the tension between us had been running high, and it was a relief to be away from each other – but it

257

meant that I was doing more than my fair share of looking after the girls. The other reason I didn't rush was that I had doubts about whether it was a good idea to resume contact with my former client. I didn't want to encourage him in his misguided attachment to me; of course, that might have passed by now, but I couldn't be sure. At the same time I needed to find out more from him about the accident. I mistrusted Evan, but since my discussion with him I had also begun to doubt Arianrhod's story. I was hoping that Gwydion, despite his fragile state, might possibly help to shed more light on the whole issue, so that I could make up my mind about whether to stand as a witness or not.

Next morning, when I drove over to The Grange, it was raining. Not raining properly, just drizzling unenthusiastically, as though the weather itself had given up making an effort. One of those days when the cold and damp seep into your bones, you look up at a colourless sky and find it hard to imagine that you've ever seen a patch of blue up there. I'm not normally given to gloom, but when I got out of the car and surveyed the ugly sub-Deco pile, it was hard not to feel downcast. On a fine day the building might have been imposing, even rather grand; in the dank air of a wet Welsh morning it was, at best, discouraging, at worst somewhat menacing – as though, in this building, sheer unadulterated dreariness had distilled into its essence, gathered strength, threatening to overcome all who entered its dismal portals.

As I walked up to the doorway an elderly man appeared. He was clean and tidy, carefully dressed, but there was a wild look in his eye. I nodded politely, hoping to avoid further contact, but as I passed, he put out his arm to stop me.

'I'm broken,' he said. 'I'm broken and I can't be mended.'

Alzheimer's, probably, I thought. I felt sad for him, so I stopped for a moment.

'Yes.' He frowned. 'I'm lost, you see. I need to report myself as a missing person.'

Just then a nurse appeared in the doorway. 'I'm so sorry,' she said, in a heavy Eastern European accent, and led the man away.

I followed the two of them into the hallway. Inside, on a highly polished side table, there was a huge floral display of madonna lilies in a blue and white Chinese vase. They gave off a sweet, sickly scent that almost, but not quite, masked the smell of institutional food and stale urine that wafted down the corridor. The hall was newly decorated in a tasteful Farrow & Ball-style paint combo, and portraits of ancient worthies in heavy gilt frames hung on the walls. They nearly, but not quite, dispelled the impression that this was a hospital: a private, high-end one, but a hospital all the same.

I asked for Gwydion, and a nurse ushered me up to his room. He was sitting by the window, gazing out at the view. When we came in, he turned to greet us, a beaming smile on his face.

'Jessica. How wonderful to see you.'

The nurse shot me a warning glance and left.

I sat down in the chair opposite his. 'How are you, Gwydion?'

His face was flushed, as though he'd been running.

'Great. Never better, actually.'

He grinned at me. I recognized that type of smile. It was manic, possibly seriously so. I wondered what medication he was on.

'I'm going to be leaving here soon,' he continued. 'I'm being let off. Because I've stopped myself dreaming the dream. And I've buttoned up all the buttons.'

When you go into a mental hospital – psychiatric healthcare facility, I should say – you often seem to be entering another dimension. People speak a different language – not just the patients, but the doctors too. But the strange thing is, the patients speak a kind of sense, tell a kind of truth, that the sane never do. The man I'd met at the doorway, with Alzheimer's, evidently was broken, couldn't be mended; and he was, in an all-too-real sense, a missing person. In Freudian terms, the disturbed mind expresses itself in codes that can be cracked, sometimes easily, sometimes with difficulty. Gwydion, too, had begun to speak in these codes. I could see that he'd deteriorated since I'd last seen him, and was beginning to lose his grip on reality; but it was my job to listen, and try to make sense of what he said, rather than to intervene.

His smile widened. 'They'll never come undone again.'

I nodded. I was feeling guilty, wondering whether my rejection of him in the Travelodge had perhaps contributed to his breakdown.

'You see,' he went on, 'sometimes she wanted them done up. And sometimes she wanted them undone. I couldn't always remember which. I was such a scatterbrain.' He ran a hand through

260

his hair. 'So I used to be scared of them. But I'm not any more. Look.'

He pulled up the bottom of his sweater. Underneath I saw that he was wearing a blue cotton shirt with buttons down the front. 'I can wear them, touch them, and everything. They've taught me how to do that here. So it's all sorted now, and when I get out I won't need to worry about the rehearsals.'

'That's great, Gwydion. Well done.' I didn't know what else to say.

'The thing is, I've got to give evidence soon. About Elsa.' He began to look anxious. 'I've got to tell them about the dream.' He paused. 'I should be able to remember that, don't you think?'

I nodded vaguely. I wasn't quite sure where this was heading.

'I mean, it can't be all that difficult. They were fighting on the boat, I know that. I heard them, the two of them.' Gwydion's voice took on a childlike tone. 'I saw them. They were sitting by the wheel, kissing. It made me feel sick, so I went down into the cabin. And later, when I came up, I saw them fighting.' He paused. 'I was sad about Elsa. She was so nice. I thought she was for me. But she wasn't. She was for Evan.'

There's no way he's going to be able to give evidence, I thought. No way.

'Evan unbuttoned her mouth. I saw him, lots of times. And then, when we went out on the boat, he pushed her into the water. That's right, isn't it, Jessica?'

'I don't know.' I looked Gwydion in the eye. 'Is that what you saw?'

There was a long silence.

'Yes, it is.' He returned my gaze, quite steadily. His voice returned to its normal, adult cadence. 'Evan pushed her overboard, into the sea.'

'You're sure?'

'I am.'

Perhaps he might be able to give evidence after all, I thought.

We stopped talking for a moment and looked out at the view from the window. The building was surrounded by a large garden, separated from the fields beyond by a ha-ha. There were sheep grazing in the fields, and in the far distance you could see the sea. I wondered whether the ha-ha was there to stop the sheep getting into the garden or the patients from getting out of it. Probably both, with the emphasis on the patients.

Gwydion broke the silence.

'You're looking nice today.' He was staring at me as though he'd seen me for the first time.

'Thank you.'

I was wearing a plum-coloured woollen dress and black patent Mary-Jane shoes that fastened with a buckle at the side. I'd taken the precaution of leaving my coat, with its buttons, in the car.

'Maybe when I get out of here, we could meet up for a drink.'

'I don't think so, Gwydion.'

I looked down and noticed that he had put his hand under his jumper and was absent-mindedly stroking the buttons on the front of his shirt.

I felt it was time to leave. I could see Gwydion was manic, perhaps hypomanic, and I knew that people suffering from the condition sometimes experience intense, and usually inappropriate, sexual urges.

'Will you come back and see me?'

'I'll try to.'

I gave him what I hoped was an encouraging smile, and got up to go.

In an instant, his mood changed. He turned away from me and went back to staring out of the window.

'Take care, won't you,' I added. I felt sad to be leaving him there, all on his own, sitting looking out at the view like an old man living out his last years in a nursing home.

But he didn't reply. As far as he was concerned, I'd already left the room.

Back in my office, I went straight to my couch and lay staring up at the ceiling, watching the leaves of the trees throwing their shadows on it, and trying to make sense of what Gwydion had said to me. I replayed our conversation in my mind, paying attention to the exact words that he'd used. It's a tip I learned from the master, and from Lacan: that the mind plays with words, conflates and confuses them, tries to give the speaker, and the listener, the slip; but I also know that, if you do your best to follow the trail closely, it can sometimes, with luck, lead you to the truth.

I've stopped myself dreaming the dream, Gwydion had told me. Well, that was pretty straightforward. He was telling me that his recurring dream was now over, that he was relieved of it. Strangely, though, he'd spoken as if he'd ordered his unconscious to dispel it, and had somehow managed, against the odds, to succeed. There was a sense of pride in the way he'd announced the news, like a small child who has managed to carry out a difficult task. And his next words had also confirmed that impression: *I've buttoned up all the buttons. They'll never come undone again.*

That was Gwydion the child speaking, of course, and the child who went on, *You see, sometimes she wanted them done up. And sometimes she wanted them undone.* You didn't have to be much of a therapist to work out who 'she' might be, or an avid Freudian to suspect that there was a strong sexual aspect to all this. Evidently, 'she' was Arianrhod, the mother, who had frightened Gwydion, the child, with her conflicting demands, to button and unbutton as she commanded.

But how did this connect to the dream? Could it be that Gwydion had been ordered, by Arianrhod, to 'button up' or 'unbutton' about the dream? Such an interpretation made a kind of sense. If Gwydion had had the dream as a child, in the days when Arianrhod was still trying to keep her marriage intact, and had told his mother about it, she might well have instructed him to keep quiet about it. But now, he was being asked to tell all, not only to Arianrhod, but to a judge and jury, in order to put his father behind bars. Such a conflict of interests, it was plain to see, might well lead a young man, still very attached to his mother and with hostile feelings towards his father, into deep mental torment.

I cast my mind back to my first session with Gwydion. He'd come to me with the button phobia, and that had now, apparently, been cured.

264

But what if the cure had plunged him further into mental illness? What if the button phobia had been his bulwark, his attempt to create a symbolic, almost talismanic, protection for himself, against the reality of his situation: that he was still at the beck and call of his mother, that she called the shots, told him when to button his lip, when to unbutton it. And what if he continued to do her bidding because of his strong, perhaps still-sexualized, attachment to her, and his hatred of his father?

I thought of the phrase Gwydion had used about Evan kissing Elsa, a child's phrase: *Evan unbuttoned her mouth.* That would have provided a further cause for hatred of his father: Evan, the errant husband, was free to do all the buttoning and unbuttoning he pleased, in contrast to Gwydion, the little boy, who had no control over the women that he loved: his ever-changing roster of au pairs, and his timid, neurotic mother.

The Oedipus complex, as I'm only too aware, is one of Freud's more unpopular theories. It's difficult to stomach, the idea that an adored child might harbour sexual designs on his mother and want to kill his father. The Victorians were horrified by it, and over a hundred years later so are we. It flies against our basic experience of parental and filial love; and on top of that, there are all the ramifications about the female child, the Electra complex, penis envy, and so on, which are far from convincing. But in my view, broadly speaking, it doesn't seem to stretch credibility to an absurd degree to suggest that a boy might want to keep his mother to himself – after all, in most cases, she's his first source of food, of warmth, of care, of love – and wish his father would, if not perish at said infant's hand, at least disappear off the radar for a while. Sophocles was onto something when he wrote *Oedipus Rex*, and so was Freud when he dreamed up the Oedipus complex. That's why those ideas have lasted: because they tell us a story about ourselves, a story we don't want to hear, but feel compelled to listen to, despite ourselves.

A car went past the window outside, throwing a shaft of light through the shadows on the ceiling, moving the leaves in mysterious, circular patterns. It was only four o'clock, yet already the nights were drawing in. The window rattled as the car went by, and I felt a draught blow in. A sense of dread ran through me, briefly but deeply. Or perhaps it was an uncomfortable sense that I was beginning to find out more than I wanted to about the Morgan family, more than I'd bargained for when I first took on Gwydion and his button phobia; and that, now I'd set out on the trail, I'd let myself become bound to follow it, wherever it might end.

18

On Thursday evening, towards the end of another exhausting week, I went late-night shopping with Mari in town. On the whole I'm not much of a one for retail therapy. The sight of the high-street shops disgorging a never-ending stream of badly made, ill-fitting clothing no doubt stitched together by half-starved children on the Pacific Rim never fails to depress me. However, Catrin's boutique in the Arcades, along with a few other independently run ventures in the same area, was a haven of taste and sanity. We stopped off there for an extended trying-on session. Catrin had saved me a couple of outfits in my size, and collected together some vintage costume jewellery for Mari to view. I bought a pair of navy-blue capri pants with a zip up the side, and a cropped cream sweater to go with them. Mari chose a Sixties rhinestone brooch that she immediately clipped to her jacket lapel, though it was totally unsuitable for daytime wear. Then, armed with our booty, we went for a drink at the cafe opposite the shop.

We took a table by the steamy window that fronted onto the street, and looked out as the sky began to darken over the town. Mari ordered a red wine, and I had a coffee. When it came, it was hot and sweet. As she chatted, I took a swig, warming my fingers on the cup, and for the first time in days felt myself begin to relax.

'Any more news about the Morgan case?' Mari tilted her head on one side and looked at me quizzically.

'Not really.'

I didn't want to discuss the subject. As I've mentioned, discretion is not one of Mari's virtues. I didn't want her spreading a lot of rumours about the case and, more particularly, my part in it, so I didn't elaborate.

'Will you be giving evidence? For ... your client?'

Mari's tone told me that she was desperate to know who the client was, but I ignored it.

'They want a statement from me, yes.'

'Have you made it yet?'

'Not formally, no. I'm still thinking about it.'

'Oh?'

'There are one or two things I'm not sure of. Small details.' I didn't want to give too much away. But on the other hand I knew that, as an ex-girlfriend of Evan's, Mari might well be a useful source of information. And, to be honest, I'd grown rather curious about Evan himself since I'd met him.

'Tell me, Mari,' I said, trying not to sound too interested. 'Did you ever go sailing on Evan's yacht?'

'Of course.' She paused. 'I think he took all his paramours out on it – a rite of passage, as you might say. There's something very sexy about being seduced on a yacht. I suppose that's why rich men have them.' She gave a short laugh, then checked herself, remembering what had happened to Elsa Lindberg.

'Did you go often?'

'Three or four times at most. As I said, we weren't together long. But it was a lot of fun.' She sighed. 'Looking back on it, I suppose it wasn't very safe. We often got quite drunk out there. I remember one time, a storm blew up. Evan crashed around the boat, mucking about with the sails, reeling them in, reefing them up, or whatever you do, and I had to hold on to the tiller.' She smiled at the memory. 'I know nothing about sailing, yet there I was, trying to steer this bloody great boat, with him yelling instructions at me. Of course, the wind was so strong, I couldn't hear a thing. And the tiller was so heavy, I could hardly budge it anyway. In the end we almost capsized.' She took a sip of her wine. 'Madness, really.'

'Weren't you scared?'

'No, not particularly. In those days everything seemed fun.' There was a hint of sadness in her voice, as though she wished those days could have gone on longer, forever perhaps. 'It's strange, isn't it,' she continued. 'I wouldn't have thought Evan capable of ... of this. Rape. Murder.'

'No?'

'Not at all. He could be bad-tempered at times. He's got a very short fuse. But I never saw him hurt anyone. I never felt physically threatened by him.' She frowned, as if she was trying to puzzle something out. 'You think you know people. But you don't, do you?'

'Yes and no.'

It was a feeble response to her question, especially for someone who's supposed to be a psychotherapist. But to be honest, that's been my experience. In most cases you can make some headway with people you encounter as you go through life – get to understand them, earn their trust, begin to trust them. But there's always the odd one that remains unknowable, that blind-sides you, shakes your faith in human nature. The type you simply can't fathom, whose inner life is a complete mystery. I haven't come across many like that, but there have been a few. Evan Morgan might be in that category, for all I knew.

We stopped talking about Evan, and Mari

turned her attention to the subject of the up-coming Bassey biopic. She'd got a call-back for the part of Bassey's mother, Eliza Jane, by all accounts an extraordinary character. Normally, I'd have been fascinated by what Mari had to say, but I realized as she chatted on that I couldn't concentrate. And, what with my heavy roster of patients, I'd had enough of bizarre personalities and aberrant human behaviour, however amus-ing, for one day. So, after listening politely for a while, I made my excuses, pecked Mari on the cheek, and left.

Outside, it was a beautiful clear night, a full moon and a dazzling array of stars shining like diamonds on the velvet of a jeweller's window. I drove home slowly, savouring the eerie light, glad to be away from the babble of human voices. Then, as I pulled away onto the main road out of town, I began to think about what Mari had said. Something about her story had struck me, at the time, as odd, but it was only now that I was on my own that I realized what it was. She'd spoken of steering the yacht with a tiller. Gwydion, on the other hand, had mentioned that, when he'd seen them, Evan and Elsa had been sitting at the wheel of the boat. It was the same yacht, I'd established that; so one or other of them had been wrong about the steering mechanism of the boat. I wondered which one it was.

I cast my mind back to my meeting with Evan. He'd pointed out the yacht when we were sitting by the window in the pub. Did it have a wheel or a tiller, I wondered. I really couldn't remember. I wasn't even sure if, from that distance, I'd have been able to see.

I glanced at the clock on the dashboard. It was coming up to eight. Under cover of darkness, I thought, I could make a quick detour to the marina, take a look at the yacht, and drive on, without anyone noticing. Evan might be on board, of course, but if I was outside, in the car, just driving by, he'd never notice.

When I got to the marina, all was quiet. It's not a busy spot at the best of times, and that evening it was deserted. I drove past the pub, glancing anxiously in at the window as I did. I half expected to see Evan looking straight out at me, but all I could make out was that the lights were on, and there were a few people inside. Then I saw that the main part of the quay, where the yacht was moored, was inaccessible to traffic. I hadn't noticed before, but there was a row of bollards in front of it. I'd have to park the car nearby and walk the short distance over to the quay.

I parked the car in a deserted spot by the harbour, cut the lights and got out, as quietly and unobtrusively as possible. I shivered as the chill night air hit my chest and tried to zip up my jacket, but my hands were trembling, so instead I hugged it around me.

It was a windless night, with only a subdued clinking coming from the masts of the boats. I walked along the silent quayside until I came to Evan's yacht, still tied up at its usual mooring. I peered in at it. It was immediately obvious that it had no wheel at the back end, like some of the larger, more modern boats. Instead it had a long, elegant wooden tiller.

271

I gave a sigh of relief and satisfaction. That was all I needed to know. I was just about to turn and leave when a light went on, the door of the cabin opened and Evan Morgan walked out.

'Dr Mayhew. What are you doing here?'

Damn, I thought. I had no reply. So I did what I usually do in such situations, where there's no other way out. I came clean.

'Sorry to disturb you, Mr Morgan.' I wondered whether that sounded ridiculous, whether I should be calling him Evan. 'I just wanted to check a detail on your boat, that's all. For my statement. To the police.'

For a moment he seemed alarmed. But then he recovered himself.

'Well, you'd better come on board and take a look around.' He stepped forward, offering me his hand so that I could jump onto the boat with him.

It was curiosity, I suppose, that made me take his hand, hop onto the cockpit of the boat and follow him down into the cabin. I wanted to see the inside of the cabin, be in the box that Gwydion had told me about in his dream. Experience it for myself. I wanted to know whether what Gwydion had told me was true; not that I thought he'd lied to me, but I know all too well what strange tricks memory, and the mind in general, can play on us. And I'd seen for myself that he'd definitely been mistaken about the wheel; there was no wheel on Evan's yacht. What else had he mis-remembered? Perhaps the interior of the cabin would tell me more.

'I was just passing by,' I said as I went in behind

him. 'I can't stay long.'

'Drink?' he asked, ignoring me.

I looked around. The cabin was neat and tidy, the polished wood gleaming. To one side there was a small table, with a seat behind it, built into the woodwork. To the other, a galley kitchen, and beyond that, in the prow of the boat, a bed, nestled in a V-shaped frame.

'Well, if you're having one.'

'I'm not. As I told you, I don't drink any more.' He indicated the glass of sparkling water on the table, beside a laptop and a pile of papers.

He went over to the kitchen, took out a bottle of whisky from a cupboard, a glass from another, and poured me a drink.

'No ice. That's right, isn't it?' He brought over the drink. I noticed his hand was shaking slightly.

I took a large gulp, and then another one. The alcohol immediately went to my head.

'What was it you wanted to check on the boat?'

'Oh, nothing much, really.' The whisky burned in my throat, but it gave me courage. 'I just wondered ... was the tiller always there?'

'The tiller?' The cabin was cramped, so we were close up against each other. I couldn't help looking into his eyes. 'Of course.'

'You haven't changed it, have you?'

'How d'you mean?' He looked straight back into mine.

I breathed in the smell of him. The pheromones. I wondered if they were genetic.

'I mean...' I seemed to be losing track of what I was saying. 'Was there a wheel there before?'

'A wheel?' His brow furrowed. He seemed

genuinely puzzled. 'Why would there be a wheel?'

I shrugged and looked away. 'Just wondering, that's all.'

There was an awkward silence, and then he went over to the table, sat down, and waved me over.

I sat down opposite him. I tried to stop my legs from touching his under the table, but it was awkward because the space beneath was so small.

'It must be difficult for you, this situation. What with Bob defending me, and so on.'

'Not really,' I lied. 'We don't talk to each other much about work.' Or about anything else at the moment, I could have added, but I didn't.

He could see that I wanted to change the subject, so he obliged.

'You remember we talked about Ernest Jones last time we met?'

I nodded.

'Well, I was intrigued by our brief chat. You inspired me to find out more. Take a look at this.'

He pushed the laptop over towards me. I twisted my legs to one side, rather awkwardly, and peered at the screen. On it was a sepia-toned picture of a young woman with soft brown eyes and full lips, standing by a tree. She was wearing some kind of loose white garment, and her long, dark hair hung in a dishevelled plait over her shoulder, tied with a drooping bow. I wondered who she was.

'Morfydd Owen,' Evan said, as if reading my thoughts. 'Ernest Jones's first wife. They were only married a year. She died tragically young.'

'She's beautiful,' I said.

'She was one of the few female composers of the time,' he went on. 'A singer, as well. Really gifted.'

274

He leaned over, closed the screen, and brought up another image, of a brown-eyed man with carefully parted hair and a large moustache, wearing a stiff white collar and a spotted tie.

'Here he is. Ernest Jones. Freud's Mister Fix-It.'

The man had bright eyes and, underneath the moustache, a small mouth with moist, shiny lips. He wasn't bad-looking, but there was something curiously unprepossessing about him.

Evan leaned back from the laptop. 'You know, the more I find out about him, the more fascinated I am.'

I nodded, remembering what he'd said at our first meeting. 'Are you serious about making a film of his life story?'

'I don't know. I still have to find the right angle on it. But it's certainly a possibility. I've got access to funding, at any rate...'

His enthusiasm was infectious. I thought momentarily of Bob's admiration for him and wondered whether he might perhaps be right after all. And then I thought of the way he had treated his wife, and felt a familiar anger bubble up inside me.

'I mean, once all this fuss is out of the way,' he went on. He swallowed nervously, picked up his glass and took a sip. As he set it down, I noticed his hand was still shaking.

But anger for who, I asked myself, as I began to calm down again. Was I angry on Arianrhod's behalf, or was I perhaps projecting my anger with Bob onto Evan?

'Of course, I've got a lot of other stuff on the go at the moment,' Evan said, flipping the image off the screen and closing the laptop.

It would have been a good opportunity to quiz him about Bob's role in defending him, but I decided not to take it. I was still hoping that Bob would decide to back down, in deference to me, and that we'd have a chance to resolve the situation between the two of us, without any interference from outside.

'What I really need is someone who could research this for me,' he went on. 'Take the idea a little further. Someone with some specialist knowledge of the subject.' He hesitated. 'You wouldn't be interested, would you?'

I was taken aback. 'Me? No, no. I'm not a film researcher. I've never done anything like that in my life. Besides, I've got a busy practice to run. I wouldn't have time...'

I was giving him all the negatives, but even as I spoke, I couldn't help feeling pleased that he'd asked me. And excited at the idea of such an unexpected, albeit unrealistic, prospect.

'You'd be well paid, of course. Enough to take a sabbatical.' He paused. 'It'd involve some travel. To the places Jones visited during his life. Toronto. Vienna. New York. Paris. London. And west Wales, of course.'

I didn't reply, but I felt a thrill of excitement run through me.

'I don't think so.' I glanced away.

'Give it some thought, at least.' He leaned towards me. 'I'd like to work with you. You're smart. And...'

He let the sentence trail off. I should have left it there, but something stopped me. I wanted to know what he was going to say next. I wanted to be flattered.

'And what?'

'Well, you've got both, haven't you – the brains and the looks.' He paused. 'You could do anything you wanted, you know you could.'

I took another sip of my drink. I had to admit, I was intrigued by his proposition. And by his evident attraction towards me. Whatever his faults, there was no denying that he was a dynamic person, wholly engaged in – and engaging about – his work. There was a generosity about his enthusiasm that was thoroughly invigorating. I hadn't really factored that in before. And, unlike my relationship to his son, ours was one of grown-ups, of equals. I wondered what it would be like to work with him. If he was proved innocent of the murder, as I was beginning to suspect he would be, who could tell what might happen between us in the future... And yet, with his reputation...

I stopped myself short. There was something destructive in my attraction towards him, I knew that. An impulse to break Bob's trust, to betray him, in the way he had betrayed me. With Evan Morgan, too, a man he liked and admired. Whatever was impelling me, it was like looking over the edge of a cliff and feeling the urge to jump.

'I really ought to be getting home now.' I glanced down at my watch.

'Listen,' he said, taking no notice of my attempt to leave. 'Why don't I take you out to lunch next week? We can go somewhere quiet and talk more about all this.'

I thought once more of raising the question of

Bob, and the hearing, and his defence, but once more I couldn't find the words.

'I'm not sure. I'll phone you.' I got up, took my bag and began to look for my car keys.

He got up too, and stood beside me, watching me.

'This doesn't change anything, you know,' I said as I turned to go. 'I'm still thinking of making that statement.'

'Of course.' A troubled look came over his face. He seemed, for a moment, to be considering saying more, but then thought better of it.

'Goodbye. I hope we'll meet again. Soon.'

'Goodbye.'

I turned, walked over to the door and let myself out. The last I saw of him, he was standing in the cabin, under the light, gazing after me.

I walked quickly down the quay, back to the car. The only sounds were the quiet lapping of the water and the tinkling of the boat masts. As I reached the spot by the harbour where I'd parked the car, the moon went behind a cloud. I shivered as I put my key in the lock and opened the door. Then I heard a voice behind me.

'Don't move.'

A pair of arms reached around my body from behind, pinning me down. I looked down and saw a hand holding a gun, its snout pointing towards my chin.

For a moment I thought I was going to faint. Then my stomach seemed to turn over and I could feel the length of my gut constrict inside my belly, as if it was being squeezed, and opening again, in a painful spasm.

'Get inside the car.' It was a man's voice, low and guttural.

I did as I was told. Keep calm, I told myself, as I opened the door and sat down in the driver's seat. I was tensing my whole body and willing myself not to let go. For some reason, losing control of my bowels seemed more terrifying to me, at that point, than being abducted by a stranger.

The man slammed the door and walked round to the other side of the car. I still had no idea who it was. I could only see his torso in front of the windscreen. I fumbled with my key, aware that if I was quick, I could put it into the ignition and take off before he had time to get into the passenger seat. But my fingers seemed to have turned to jelly, and I dropped the key into my lap.

The passenger door opened and the man got in beside me. As he bent his head to enter, I realized with a shock who it was: Emyr Griffiths.

'You fucking bitch,' he said. He grabbed me by my jacket and twisted it up to my chin, pulling my hair. 'Scared, are you?'

I nodded vigorously, clenching my buttocks. I was shaking with fear, yet determined not to respond to the contractions pulsing in my lower belly.

'Good.' He laughed, then let go of me, pushing me onto the steering wheel, which dug into my ribs.

'Drive,' he said.

Somehow I managed to get the key into the ignition, turn on the lights and start the car. I didn't dare look directly at him, but as I glanced in the rear-view mirror to back the car, I saw that his

279

hair was unkempt and that he was unshaven. There was a smell of stale sweat coming from him, and I also caught a whiff of alcohol on his breath.

As we drove away from the harbour, past the pub, I wondered whether I could somehow stop the car, raise the alarm, get help. Evan Morgan was still on his boat, I knew. If only I could wind down the window, call out to him. But Emyr was holding the gun in his lap. It was large and black, with some kind of sighting device attached to it, such as you'd use for hunting. Outdoorsy, Boy Scout-type that he was, I imagined he'd know very well how to use it.

We drove in silence, up the road leading away from the marina. Then he told me to take a right turning off it, into a narrow lane that led into a cul-de-sac. As we drove slowly up the bumpy strip of tarmac, the streetlights grew sparser, until they disappeared altogether. At the end of the lane we reached a row of lock-ups, sur-rounded by empty scrubland.

'Get out,' he said. 'Don't try anything.'

I eyed my bag, on the floor by his feet. It had my mobile phone in it. I wished I'd kept it in my pocket.

I did as he asked, switching off the engine and the lights. But instead of taking the key out of the ignition, I left it in. He didn't notice.

He got out of the car, came round to my side, and pulled me out roughly. Then he marched me towards one of the lockups, pointing the gun into the small of my back. I didn't resist. With one hand he took out a bunch of keys from his pocket, unlocked the metal door and opened it.

280

He pulled it up, pushed me through and pulled it back down again. It clanged shut with a bang.

Inside, he switched on the light, and I saw a small, cramped room stuffed with musical equipment of various kinds – amplifiers, keyboard racks, microphone stands held together with gaffer tape. In one corner was a mixing desk, with a large pair of speakers hung above it, and a mass of wires emanating from the back of it. A nasty smell of mould pervaded the air.

'D'you want to hear the track I recorded with Nella?' he asked, walking over to the mixing desk. He was still holding the gun, but he'd stopped pointing it at me.

'Yes, of course.' I dreaded hearing the sound of her voice in this cold, claustrophobic little room, but I was frightened to demur.

He switched on the mixing desk, booted up a computer screen, fiddled with a few knobs, and her voice came over the speakers, loud and clear.

'Please. Turn it off.' I tried to stop myself from speaking, but I couldn't help it.

Emyr came towards me. A sheen of sweat coated his forehead.

'You see what you've done?' He was close up to me, breathing in my face. The smell of his breath was sour, acrid. 'You've ruined my life. Lost me my job. This...' He waved the gun at the mixing desk. 'This was my last hope...'

'I'm sorry, Emyr.' I tried to keep the quaver out of my voice. 'I didn't mean to...'

'Yes, you did.' He began to shout. '*Jazz Quest* was my big break. Nella's big break. You turned her against me...'

'You must understand, I have nothing personal against you.' I was surprised at how calm I sounded. 'But I needed to keep my daughter safe. I'm her mother–'

'That's enough!' He shouted me down, but I knew that something in what I said had struck a chord with him. 'She was safe with me. Perfectly safe. I was like a father to her...'

This time, I said nothing. I simply looked him in the eye.

'Stop staring at me!' he screamed. He pointed the gun at my head. I forced myself not to turn away, keeping my gaze steady.

I watched from the corner of my eye as he lowered the gun. Then, to my alarm, he turned it on himself.

The gun went off, and I jumped. I felt something warm and wet slide out of my body. Then, nothing. No blood. No screams of agony. Nothing. Emyr'd shot himself and nothing had happened.

I walked towards him, gently took the gun from his hand and put my arm around his shoulder.

'It's all right, Emyr. It's all over now...'

He began to cry, shaking with sobs, his whole frame slumped against me. I glanced down at the gun, turning it in my hand. On the side of it, in small letters, was printed: *Excel X83 .68-Caliber Paintball Pistol.* Since he'd shot himself at close range and there was no sign of bruising on his neck, I realized that he hadn't even loaded it with a marker.

I heaved a sigh of relief, which came out as a groan. Then I put the gun in my jacket pocket. Nella's voice was still coming out of the mixing desk, so I walked over and turned it off.

'Stay here,' I said. 'I'm going to get help.'

I turned, pulled up the door of the lock-up and went out to the car. I opened the door, reached inside for my bag on the floor, got out my phone and punched in a number that was on my contacts list.

'Hello? Barbara, it's me, Jessica Mayhew. I'm sorry to trouble you. I've got an emergency here.' Inside my trousers, the liquid was spreading down my legs, but I ignored it. I'd deal with it later, when I got home.

'An ex-client,' I went on. 'He's not very well, I'm afraid. Could you send someone down here, please? Yes, police officer and social worker. Right away.'

19

The next day, and over the weekend, I got as much rest as I could, but by the time I returned to work I found myself unable to concentrate. The aftershocks of my encounter with Emyr Griffiths were still with me, but I was relieved that the situation had been resolved.

He had been duly sectioned, and was now safely ensconced in Whitchurch Hospital, under the expert care of my colleague Barbara Brown. I'd decided not to press charges. I'd briefly explained to Bob and Nella what had happened, giving only the barest of details, but I hadn't seen any reason to tell them just how traumatic the experience had been for me. I was still angry with Bob, too proud to let him into my emotional life; and Nella, I felt, had already learned her lesson. I was hopeful that, eventually, Emyr could begin to piece his life together again, and I felt reasonably confident that he wouldn't be troubling us in the future. No, it wasn't the issue of Emyr that was bothering me, but the continuing question of whether I should agree to give evidence on Gwydion's behalf at the hearing, which had been scheduled for just under a month's time.

The worst of it was, I had no time to think. The usual stream of clients was passing through my consulting rooms, along with some new recruits, each of them with their own tale to tell and their own complex set of emotional demands. But I was unable to give them my full attention. Instead, to my shame, I simply watched them impassively, wishing they'd go to hell and leave me in peace. I found myself impatient with Harriet's angst-ridden laments about her failure to stick to a diet, even though only a short while ago I'd been thrilled that she'd at last broached the subject of her weight during the session. I felt like telling her to exercise some self-control for once, stop being such a slob, and cease looking to me for sympathy. Bryn's furious tirades against me filled me with anger; I wanted to yell at him to grow up, stop blaming his mother – and me – for his own failures, and get a life. Maria the housewife's un-abating misery also failed to move me; when she began to sob silently, instead of feeling sympathy, I thought of her children, and felt sorry for them for having such a useless mother. And when Frank started to complain about his sex addiction and stare at my breasts, I had to muster all my self-control not to get up, take him by the lapels and frogmarch him out of the room.

When Frank left, I closed the door behind him, leaned back in my chair, stretched my arms, wriggled my aching shoulders and gave a sigh of relief. At last I had a moment to myself. I looked out of the window, watching the last of the yellow leaves fluttering down from the tree outside, and found myself able to think once more.

The question that was uppermost in my mind was whether Gwydion had been lying to me, albeit unwittingly, about his experience on the yacht all those years ago. He'd described seeing Evan and Elsa sitting together by the wheel of the boat – yet there was no wheel. The yacht was steered by a tiller, not a wheel – I'd seen it with my own eyes. It was only a tiny detail, and by itself insignificant, but it was enough to make me doubt the accuracy of his story entirely. Gwydion had reported a memory, apparently in good faith, but it seemed possible that he could be mistaken. Evan's fate didn't hang on my testimony alone – there would be plenty of evidence from others, of course, such as Gwydion, Arianrhod and Solveig – but since I had a supporting role to play, it was important that I should be entirely sure of my facts before I offered to make a statement. If Evan was innocent, I didn't want to add my voice to those who wanted to see him go down for murder; neither did I want to make a fool of myself and damage my reputation.

I got up from my chair, went over to the bookcase at the back of the room, took down a file, and leafed through it until I found what I was looking for. It was an article entitled 'The Formation of False Memories' by the American psychologist Elizabeth Loftus.

I remembered it now. This was her controversial 'Shopping Mall' study about implanting false memories. She was arguing that, in many cases, our memory of an event is not reliable, but is distorted by what has happened before and after it. To try to prove this, she arranged an experiment in which subjects were repeatedly told by family members that they had been lost in a shopping mall as young children, even though no such event had ever taken place. The subjects later reported that they remembered this event clearly, even supplying details of the location, the person who had rescued them, and so on.

I read on, fascinated by her description of the cut-and-paste technique that our brains engage in, using snippets from actual events, to produce a nicely formed, meaningful memory of an event that is largely fictitious, yet believed by the subject with absolute certainty. She concluded:

People can be led to remember their past in different ways, and they can be led to remember entire events that never actually happened to them. When these sorts of distortions occur, people are sometimes confident in their distorted or false memories, and go on to describe pseudo-memories in substantial detail. These findings shed light on cases in which false memories are fervently held. The findings do not, however, give us the

286

ability to reliably distinguish between real and false memories, for without independent corroboration, such distinctions are generally not possible.

I thought about how all this applied to Gwydion. Clearly his recovered memory, triggered by his recurring dream, could be false, even if he himself believed it to be true. He could easily have taken details from real trips on real boats and, quite unconsciously, cut and pasted them into this particular childhood memory of the trip on the yacht with Evan and Elsa. That explanation seemed to fit with my experience of him; I had sensed that he was telling me the truth about what he remembered, even though it was causing him a great deal of anguish. But if he was mistaken, and the memory was false, that still left the question: who had implanted it in him? And why?

I cast my mind back to my last encounter with Gwydion. What was it that he'd said about the buttons? *Sometimes she wanted them done up. And sometimes she wanted them undone.* It had struck me at the time as Oedipal, as quite clearly related to his disturbed relationship with his mother, Arianrhod.

What if it was Arianrhod who had implanted the memory in Gwydion? Not just instructed him to lie to me, but repeatedly and consistently, over a period of time – perhaps from childhood – got him to believe it himself? Told him the story of how his father had taken him out on the boat with Elsa, and how he'd witnessed the accident, or murder, as a result of one of his father's drunken rages? And then told him, perhaps, that it was a secret?

Sometimes she wanted them done up. Only now, it wasn't. Now, she wanted him to go to court and tell all. *And sometimes she wanted them undone.*

I finished reading the paper, closed the file and put it back on the shelf. As I reached up, I felt momentarily dizzy, as if I was going to faint. I leaned against the bookcase for a few seconds, closed my eyes and waited for the sensation to pass. I wasn't too worried. After a long day of seeing clients, one after the other, I often find myself a little woozy, as though I have run too far and too fast, or downed a glass of wine too quickly. It was simply the effort of concentrating for an entire day, closeted in this one room with a succession of clients and the pressing throng of 'the neuroses', as Freud called them. He used to go walking in the Alps to get away from them. Not being a Victorian paterfamilias, I didn't have that option. The girls would be at home now, I knew, waiting for their tea, needing me to check their homework, drive them to ballet class, band practice, or whatever it was that evening; or simply to be there, sitting next to them, with a cup of tea and the newspaper, as they watched television.

I went over to the hat stand, got my jacket and looked in the mirror. The bags under my eyes were back, along with a fetching pair of semicircular bluish shadows. My face was slightly flushed, my cheeks a little blotchy. My hair wasn't looking its best, either. When I'm tired, it has a habit of re-arranging itself to look untidy, with strands that stick out, however much I try to smooth them down. Yet, strangely, although I looked exhausted and a little dishevelled, there was something unusual in my face that day, I thought; a sparkle in my eye, a glimmer of curiosity, of liveliness, playing around my features. Perhaps it was that Evan's interest in me had made me feel more attractive; or, more importantly, that I was beginning to get closer to solving the mystery of the girl's death. Whichever it was, and it could have been a little of both, as I tugged at my hair, trying to make it look respectable, I couldn't stop a smile coming to my lips. I felt alive again, alert and, despite my fatigue, ready for action.

People are sometimes confident in their distorted or false memories, and go on to describe pseudo-memories in substantial detail. A wheel or a tiller? That one small anomaly in Gwydion's account of what had happened on the boat could perhaps lead me to the truth. But to find out, I'd have to go back to The Grange and talk to him again.

When I got home, Nella was in the front room watching television with her new boyfriend. I saw them through the window as I came up the path, one dark head, one fair, sitting on the sofa together holding hands. Rose wasn't with them; she'd stayed in school to rehearse for a concert that was being held at the church in a few days' time. I'd forgotten, which made me feel a little guilty.

I went into the kitchen, made a pot of tea, put a few biscuits on a plate and took it in to them on a tray. When I walked in, knocking briefly before I entered, the boy got up and cleared some space on the coffee table so that I could put the tray down.

'Mum, this is Gareth.' Nella stayed sitting on

the sofa, staring at the screen, more out of embarrassment than rudeness, I felt.

'Hello. Good to meet you, Gareth.'

'And you, Mrs...'

'Jessica.'

He nodded, smiling at me. He was small and slim with soft brown eyes and a nose-piercing that did little to dispel the general impression of innocence about him.

He took the tray from me and laid it carefully down on the coffee table. Nella leaned forward and took a biscuit.

'Thanks, Mum,' she said. There was a pause. Then she added, 'Did you have a good day?'

'Not bad.' I was touched by her enquiry. Since the episode with Emyr she'd been uncharacteristically solicitous.

I looked over at the television. 'What are you watching?'

'*Come Dine with Me.*' Gareth sat down again. 'It's rubbish, but we're addicted.'

I smiled, feeling a sense of relief. Nella had found a boyfriend, a confident, engaging young man who was not too shy to talk to her mother.

'Actually, we've got some recording to do,' he went on. 'I've brought my recording desk over and we're going to set up in Nella's room. I hope that's OK with you.'

'Fine. No problem.'

'We just need to make a few rough demos,' Gareth went on. 'Then we're going to go over to a studio that belongs to my cousin, in Newport, and record the songs properly.'

'Gareth says the tracks I did with Emyr were

290

really lame,' Nella added. 'I'm going to bin them and start again.'

I felt like going up to Gareth, throwing my arms around him and kissing him. But instead I said, 'Well, that sounds great.'

Gareth had started to pour out the tea. 'Would you like a cup before you go?' he asked, turning to me.

'No, thanks,' I said. 'I've got to go out again now. Just one more appointment and then I'm done. See you later, perhaps.' I smiled at Gareth, trying not to beam. 'And good luck with the recording.'

It's not very far from my house to The Grange. A few wet country lanes, edged on either side by dripping hedges; a dreary stretch of B-road with nothing much to recommend it except a clear view of a featureless expanse of sky; a dip down into a neat, prosperous commuter village, full of lawyers and media folk; a patched tarmac path up to a large, white-painted institution built in the Twenties, and you're there.

I got out of the car, locked it and walked over to the entrance of the house. Under the darkening sky the place looked uglier than ever. I pressed the bell and stood waiting until a nurse appeared. Like the one I'd seen on my last visit, she spoke English in a heavy Eastern European accent and seemed quite happy to let me go upstairs to see Gwydion, even though I hadn't made an appointment. This time, I found my way to his room by myself, since I now knew where it was. I walked along the corridor, the creaking floorboards announcing my arrival, and knocked tentatively at the half-open door of his room.

There was no reply, so I put my head round the door. I saw Gwydion seated at the window. The room was dark. The curtains were open and he was looking out at the view.

'It's me, Jessica. Can I come in?'

He didn't turn his head, so I walked over to him and gently touched him on the shoulder. He glanced at me briefly, and then went back to looking out of the window again.

'Shall I sit here?'

He nodded.

I sat down quietly in the chair beside him, and looked out, too. Outside, I could just about make out the ha-ha at the end of the garden, and the glimmering white backs of the sheep in the fields beyond. In the distance you could see the lights of the power station by the coast, and nearby those of the local airport. It wasn't exactly a beautiful sight, but in its own way it was striking. There was something unnatural and otherworldly and rather theatrical about it, like a Gustave Doré etching, or the animation for a sword-and-sorcery video game.

I glanced over at Gwydion, trying to gauge his mood. He looked gaunt, his cheekbones jutting out from the side of his face, but it could have been just that the shadows in the half-light of the room emphasized the angularity of his features.

'How are you getting on?'

He shrugged. I could see that he was depressed, but I persevered all the same. I was even mildly encouraged by his demeanour; at least he was less manic than when I'd seen him previously.

'Feeling any better?'

He shrugged again, still gazing out of the window.

There seemed nothing to be gained by drawing out our exchange, so I came quickly to the point.

'Gwydion, I want to talk to you about what happened on the boat. If you don't mind.'

I could see him stiffen slightly, but I went on.

'You see, I need to get the story clear before I can make my statement to the police.'

I paused to see if he'd react, but he didn't, so I continued, 'There are some little details that make me wonder...'

This time, he turned his head. His eyes looked larger than ever, great green pools glittering in their sockets.

'What little details?'

'Well, for instance...'

'Are you saying you don't believe me?'

He spoke more in surprise than anger, as if I'd wounded him, turned on him suddenly.

'No.' I understood that he was hurt by my questions, but I wasn't going to let him off the hook. 'I just need you to explain what happened to me more clearly. I mean, just to take a small point, you say there was a wheel on the yacht, yet there wasn't. The boat has a tiller. I've seen it. So...'

'What does that matter?'

I tried to be tactful. 'Well, it makes me begin to wonder...'

'If I'm lying?'

'If you've remembered right.' I hesitated. I didn't want to upset him, but there was no alternative. 'It was a long time ago, Gwydion. And you were a

293

young child. It's possible you could be wrong, isn't it? Anyone can make a mistake–'

'I'm getting a bit sick of this, you know,' he interrupted. 'People poking their noses into my life, trying to make me say what they want me to say, about an event I can hardly remember. No wonder I've been ... ill. I wish you'd all just get off my back, and leave me in peace.'

'Look.' I spoke as gently as I could. 'I'm sorry. I know this is hard for you. But I have to decide whether to make a statement to the police. And, before I do, you've got to tell me the truth. For your father's sake. And for your own.'

There was a silence, and then he turned away from me, gazing out of the window. I could sense that he was wondering what to say, so I kept quiet. Then he began to speak.

'It did happen.' He still didn't look at me. 'I was on that yacht with Evan and Elsa, and I saw him push her overboard. It's my earliest memory. I can remember it clear as day. I've always known that he killed her. I've had to keep it a secret all this time and now I'm expected to–'

He broke off suddenly. Once again I waited until he resumed.

'Arianrhod swore me to secrecy. She told me that if I ever told anyone, Evan would have to go to prison. And it would all be my fault.' He paused. 'I accepted the situation, the way you do when you're a kid. It was our secret, hers and mine. I never questioned that keeping quiet about it was the right thing to do.'

I followed his gaze, looking out of the window as the sky on the horizon darkened.

294

'Of course,' Gwydion went on, his voice low, 'the secret cast a huge shadow over my childhood. It gave me some huge hang-ups, like the button phobia. Undermined my confidence. Made me terrified of Evan. Ruined our relationship, really. I mean, although he was always domineering towards me, he could be very affectionate, too – but I rejected him completely after that. And over the years, although I was pretty fragile some of the time, I got used to the situation. Then...'

He stopped, turned to look at me as if to re-assure himself I was listening and, when I nodded, looked away again.

'Ari changed her mind about going to the police. After all this time, she suddenly decided that we should tell them everything. I suppose things had got to an all-time low between her and Evan.' He began to rub at his neck distractedly. 'I mean, the pair of them have always fought like cat and dog, but since Evan got this new... I don't know what you'd call her ... girlfriend. Mistress. Whatever. She's younger than me, anyway.' He paused. 'I think when he took up with her, Ari finally realized that she couldn't go on, that the marriage was over. So...'

He came to a halt. I realized that I was sitting on the edge of my chair and leaned back, trying to appear relaxed.

'...she decided to shop him,' he went on. 'And she came up with a story to explain why she hadn't gone to the police before. We'd pretend that I'd had a recurring dream about the murder, that it had thrown up a recovered memory. That was where you came in.'

He glanced at me again for reassurance, but this time I found it hard to give him any.

'We found you on the Internet. Under the UK Association of something or other. You were listed as one of the therapists in Cardiff. You were the first name. So we ... I ... phoned you. And then I came to see you.'

There were stars in the sky now, tiny points of light, which seemed to have appeared suddenly, as if by magic. Although we'd been looking steadily at the horizon, we hadn't seen them come out.

'I wanted to make my visit seem plausible, so I started with some real problems. The button phobia, and my insomnia. But then I went on to the dream, which I made up. And...' He paused, registering my puzzled expression. 'I'm sorry, Jessica. I did lie to you. I never had a recurring dream. Or a recovered memory. But I did see the murder. I know I did. That much is true.'

'So, let me get this straight,' I said. I was having trouble taking in what he'd told me. 'Your mother tells you to go to a psychotherapist, pretend you've had a recurring dream and that, in the process, you've recovered a memory. Of your father killing a young girl on a boat twenty years ago. That way, Arianrhod can explain why she never reported Evan to the police at the time of the incident. Is that what you're saying?'

Gwydion nodded. He looked relieved that I wasn't angry. Strangely, I wasn't. I was more surprised than anything else.

'The thing was,' he said, 'I couldn't really keep up the pretence. You were so kind, so understanding...' He looked down. 'I felt terrible lying to you.

That was why I left that first time. I couldn't go on deceiving you. And then when I came back, I began to realize you could help me sort out my real problems, so I stayed. I really felt we were getting somewhere. But Ari started pushing me to finish the sessions, tell you the final part of the dream, where I heard the splash in the water, so that she could put her plan into action. That's why, I left so abruptly.'

'I see.' I felt hurt, but I didn't say anything. Instead, we both continued to look out at the sky. The stars got brighter, and more appeared, as we looked.

'And on top of that...' He stopped.

'What?'

He stared ahead, unable to meet my gaze.

'I found you – find you – very attractive. Even though you're so much older than me. And not the glamorous kind I usually go for.'

Thanks very much, I thought.

'So I started lying to Ari about us.' He began to rub at his neck again. 'About ... you know ... our near-affair...'

Our near-affair. That was a succinct way of putting it, I reflected.

'And in the end, I suppose, all the layers of lying got too much. I got confused.' He took a deep breath, held it for a moment and let it out slowly. 'So here I am.'

There was a silence. We both looked out of the window and watched as, in the distance, a plane took off from the airport, its blue and red lights winking in the darkness. Seeing it rise into the sky like that, too far away to hear any sound, or

297

to make out the shape of it, was curiously re-assuring. For a moment I wished I was on that plane myself, in limbo up there, bound for a new, unknown destination, far away from this earth-bound tangle of history and emotion. And I sensed that perhaps Gwydion did, too.

'I'm glad you told me the truth,' I said. 'I think you'll feel better for it.'

He nodded.

'It's usually best to be honest, even if it hurts,' I went on. 'It's too much of a strain on our minds if we don't.'

'You think so?'

I nodded.

'Well then, I might as well also tell you...'

I wondered what was coming next.

'I think I'm in love with you, Jessica.' He turned to look at me. The pupils of his eyes had widened, so that they looked darker, softer.

Transference, I thought. Same old, same old. And then I remembered kissing him on the jetty at Creigfa Bay, and rolling around on the bed with him in the Travelodge, and felt ashamed that I'd encouraged him in his fantasy. I'd been in lust with him, not in love. I'd used him, for my own selfish reasons.

'I don't think you are, really, Gwydion.' I spoke gently. 'It's quite common for clients to attach themselves in this way to their psychotherapist...'

'And you? What about you? Do you normally respond in that way?'

'No, of course not.' It was my turn to feel ashamed now. 'I'm very sorry about that. I got carried away.'

'So you do feel something for me?' He was looking at me intently. 'Tell the truth. Go on. If you're so keen on all this honesty.'

'Gwydion,' I said. I was flustered, but trying not to show it. 'You're a very attractive man. You must know that. I couldn't help responding to that...'

He frowned. 'So what you're saying is, you just wanted a quick fling? And that's all.'

'No.' I could feel my cheeks flushing, and I knew that, as I spoke, I was lying. Now that he'd raised the issue, I realized that was probably what I'd wanted from Gwydion. But there was no way I was going to tell him that. Sometimes the truth hurts, and it's better not to tell it.

He was looking at me questioningly, as if expecting me to explain myself further.

'I'm a married woman, Gwydion.' I paused. 'You know that, don't you? And you are – you were – my client. It wouldn't have been right to pursue the relationship, and that's why I stopped it.'

That was true, too, of course. Sometimes there are many truths, and you don't have to tell them all.

'And I don't think you really are in love with me,' I went on. 'I think you're hurt and confused and you're looking for a mother figure.'

'Maybe. But what's so wrong with that?'

He had a point. You don't have to be a card-carrying Freudian to agree that it's perfectly normal, commonplace even, to look for a distant echo of a parent in a romantic partner.

I shook my head. 'It's just not on, Gwydion. Sorry.'

Gwydion sighed, but it wasn't a very deep sigh,

I noticed. I sensed that his fantasy of being in love with me was a fragile one, more a type of daydream than a deep, painful attachment, and that, in time, it would pass as he became stronger and more able to cope with the world. But even so, I could see that it was going to be difficult for him to let it go, in the short term anyway.

He began to stare out of the window again. I sat with him in silence for a few minutes. Part of me wanted to raise the subject of the hearing, and how what he'd told me about lying to me in the sessions would affect that, but I sensed this wasn't the time or place.

Eventually I said, 'I really must be going now. Good luck with everything.'

'Thanks.' He paused. 'There's a chance I'll be out of here in time for the rehearsals, I think. I feel pretty down, but I'm sleeping better. And the button problem seems to have resolved. For the moment, anyway.'

'That's good.' I got up, went over to his chair and patted him on the shoulder. To my surprise, he grasped my hand.

'Thanks, Jessica. Thanks for everything.'

'D'you want me to come over and see you again?'

'No.' He squeezed my hand. 'I'm going to have to do this on my own. But I know I can. I'll be out of here soon. I think I'm going to be all right.'

'I think you are, too.' I squeezed it back.

He bent his head and pressed his cheek against my hand. It was a touching gesture, like that of a little boy.

I leaned down and brushed my lips against the

top of his head. 'Goodnight,' I said.

We both knew that goodbye was what we meant, but we didn't say it. Somehow the word would have been too harsh.

'Take care driving home,' he said. 'It's dark out there.'

'I will.'

He got up, walked me over to the door, and closed it behind me. I went downstairs and out of the front door. When I arrived at the car, I looked up at his window and saw him standing there, looking down at me. He waved, and I waved back.

Sometimes there's no need to tell the truth because it's already been told.

20

The next day I cancelled all my appointments with my clients and drove down to see Arianrhod at Creigfa House. That's not something I do at the drop of a hat; letting my clients down at short notice, quite understandably, provokes distrust and endless recrimination. But I was furious. Furious with Arianrhod for duping me, of course, but even more furious with her for using Gwydion to get at his father, out of sheer spite. I knew that she had every reason to hate Evan; she'd been serially betrayed and humiliated by him over many, many years; but nothing could possibly justify the way she'd gone about taking her revenge. I was going to confront her with what she'd done, make sure she retracted the entire story before any more harm was done.

I didn't tell Bob where I was going. I didn't want to involve him at this stage of the proceedings. We were still on bad terms and, to be honest, I felt extremely foolish about my credulity in the whole Morgan affair. I was in no rush to tell him what an idiot I'd been – particularly as I was beginning to suspect that my willingness to believe Gwydion's story had been motivated, to some degree at least, by my own disgust at Bob's infidelity. Projection, it's called. It's pretty obvious when you see it in others, but in this case I'd been completely blind to it in my own behaviour.

So my plan – if I had a clear plan that day, which I'm not sure, in retrospect, I did – was to talk to Arianrhod, get her to go to the police, admit that she'd been lying, and take it from there. Presumably the case against Evan, who was currently the only suspect, would quickly collapse; Bob would no longer be needed to defend him, at least in the short term; I could step down as a witness, hopefully with some dignity intact; and then – perhaps – we could begin to put this behind us. Of course, the debacle would be a blow to Solveig, and we would be no nearer to finding out exactly what had happened to Elsa. But if there was a case to be made against Evan – and I was by no means sure, now, that there was – it would have to be built up again, from scratch. That was the only way forward. Clearly the truth would have to be told, whatever the consequences.

It was a cold late autumn day, the last of the leaves putting on a final show of colour as I drove west to Pembrokeshire. They lined the motorway like faded dancing girls at the Folies-Bergères, their tattered petticoats of red, yellow and gold fluttering in the wind. To begin with, I hardly registered their presence, preoccupied as I was with my thoughts. But after a while the sheer beauty of the landscape got to me, and I began to feel fresher, lighter. I could handle this situation, I told myself. Arianrhod was evidently much more vindictive and manipulative than I'd realized; but at the end of the day she was just an unhappily married woman, searching for a way out of the mess she'd made of her life. I, on the other hand, was an experienced psychotherapist, who'd be able to understand her machinations, try to help her let go of them, play it straight for once. It was me who had the upper hand here. Whatever transpired, I'd be one step ahead of her, and I would do well to remember that.

But when I turned off the motorway onto the road that led to Creigfa House, the trees grew denser, clustering around the road, their branches bare against the sky. Drifts of dry leaves fluttered in front of the windscreen, blown this way and that by the movement of the car. As I drove through the whirling flurries, I began to feel less sure of myself.

I reached the house with its great iron gate. Today there was no need to press the buzzer. The gate was open. That struck me as ominous, though I wasn't sure why. For a moment I wondered whether to turn the car round and head home. I couldn't help wishing that I'd thought this whole plan through a little more carefully, before steaming down the motorway to confront Arianrhod. I'd been angry, yes; and curious to find out more. But I hadn't really put my mind to the fact that Arianrhod's behaviour was deeply disturbing: she'd used her vulnerable son to get at her errant husband; tried to use me, as well, forcing Gwydion to tell me a pack of lies about his recurring dream, so that I could appear as an expert witness in court; and generally twisted the facts, so as to make Evan look guilty of a murder she couldn't be sure he'd committed. What sort of a mother would do that to her child? To her husband, however much she hated him? What kind of woman was Arianrhod?

I started as I heard the cry of a peacock. It was a shrill scream, as if the bird was in pain. But there was also something angry about it, something aggressive, menacing. I realized, when I heard it, that I'd made a mistake coming here. Whatever business I had with Arianrhod could have been conducted with her on the phone, or at my consulting rooms in Cardiff. I shouldn't have visited her at home. It was inappropriate. Not to say extremely unwise.

I was just about to turn the car round and drive off when I saw a tall, dark figure walking down the gravel path towards me. As it got closer, I saw it was Arianrhod. She was waving at me to bring the car in.

It was too late to change my mind. Besides, as she neared the car I realized that she didn't look in the slightest bit menacing or sinister. In fact, she was the same as ever, dressed in her dark blue sweater, her jeans and her battered brown loafers.

Her hair might have been a little wilder than when I'd seen her before, the grey beginning to encroach on the dark a little more. And when she stood by the gate, waving me in, it could have been that her face was a little more lined, more careworn, than when I'd last seen her. But she didn't look threatening, not in the least. She looked like what I knew her to be: a woman who'd once been beautiful, once been desired, but who, like so many beautiful, desired women, had never quite found her place in life; and who now, in her waning years, had found herself defeated by a series of battles in a long, bitter war of a marriage. Someone to be pitied, perhaps. Or, rather, to feel empathy for. There but for the grace, et cetera, et cetera. But not someone to be afraid of.

I drove through the gate and up the gravel drive to the house, scaring the screaming peacock as I went. It scuttled into a hedge, and when I got out of the car it was nowhere to be seen. Neither were any of its brothers and sisters. Except for Arianrhod, the place seemed to be deserted. There was a rather forlorn air about it that I hadn't noticed previously: unswept leaves covered the lawn, the paint on the latticed windows was peeling, and brown mould spotted the stone swags festooning the doorway. I remembered that Arianrhod was living here on her own now, Gwydion in the clinic, Evan on his yacht at the marina. It must be lonely for her, I thought. Lonely and depressing, with the family finally gone, split apart, leaving her on her own to defend the mansion and its grounds against the damp, and the cold, and the salt wind blowing in from

Creigfa Bay.

Arianrhod ushered me into the house. She was polite, I noticed, but not as friendly as she'd been in the past. I put that down to the fact that she'd evidently been living alone for some time, pre-occupied with her own thoughts. You can some-times tell when a person has spent too long without the company of other human beings: they lose track of the social cues we usually take for granted, chattering too much, or alternatively lapsing into a brooding silence. So it was with Arianrhod. After she'd led me into the kitchen, sat me down and got me a cup of tea – forgetting to ask whether I'd prefer coffee, or something else – she made no effort to engage in conversation, but instead busied herself with rolling a cigarette.

I looked around the kitchen. It was cluttered with newspapers, half-empty packets of biscuits and smoking paraphernalia. There were stacks of dirty cups and saucers by the sink, along with DIY equipment – a screwdriver, nails, a can of spray paint. The air was sour with the smell of stale nico-tine. Arianrhod had evidently holed herself up in here, drinking tea and eating biscuits and reading the paper and smoking. There didn't seem to be evidence of anyone else using the place, except the cats, whose feeding bowls were lined up by the back door, emitting a smell of rancid meat. One of the cats was asleep on a chair beside the Aga.

I waited as Arianrhod lit her cigarette, inhaling deeply. She didn't ask me, as she had done before, whether I minded if she smoked. It was as if she no longer had any use for such social niceties.

I decided to break the silence. 'Do you know

why I'm here?' I spoke in a quiet, level voice.

She exhaled, waving away the pall of smoke that hung around her. Funny how I'd found it beautiful before, her dark head surrounded by all that curling blue smoke. This time it just seemed depressing, an ageing woman smoking herself to death in her messy kitchen, with only her cats for company.

'No idea.' It wasn't hostile, the way she said it, but it wasn't exactly warm, either.

'Have you spoken to Gwydion recently?'

'No. He doesn't seem keen to talk to me at the moment. Says he has to get ready for the trial. Needs "space", as he calls it.' She grimaced.

I sympathized with her, to a degree. I'm not keen on 'space', either. In fact I'm not keen on any of that smug psycho-babble people throw around these days, whether the negative buzzwords, like 'co-dependent', 'in denial', or – even worse – the positive ones, like 'empowerment', 'being grounded', and so on. Whenever someone starts to talk like that, I instinctively mistrust them. But in this instance I could see what Gwydion had been getting at. He did need space, away from his mother, and the more of it, the better.

'Well, then...' I hesitated. I wasn't quite sure how best to put what I had to say. 'I went to see him yesterday. He's been very distressed by all this.'

'Oh?' Arianrhod didn't seem particularly concerned.

'Yes. Very.'

Arianrhod gave a deep sigh. 'I'm sorry to hear that.' She didn't sound very sorry. 'But I don't really think I need to know all this. I've done my best to help...'

'No, you haven't.' I tried to remain calm, but her blasé attitude was beginning to anger me. 'In fact, your son's mental state is partly your fault, as far as I can see.'

Psychotherapists don't like using the word 'fault'. It's not one of the approved buzzwords. But in this case, I felt it was fair enough.

'What on earth do you mean?'

'You told Gwydion to come and see me. Told him to tell me a pack of lies about a recurring dream he'd been having. A dream in which he witnessed his father pushing Elsa Lindberg overboard on the yacht.'

'Is that what he said?'

'Yes. And I believe him.'

Arianrhod looked down at her cigarette, tapping the ash off it into the ashtray.

'He faked the whole thing at your behest,' I went on. 'He came to me with this story of a recurring dream, and then pretended to have a recovered memory about the murder. He did it so you could explain why you hadn't been to the police before about Evan, and to dupe me into being a witness. Am I right?'

Arianrhod took another drag of her cigarette, held the smoke in her lungs for a couple of seconds, and then let it out.

'And it was you who sent me that photograph of Evan with blacked-out eyes, wasn't it? To kick-start the whole process?'

There was a silence, and then she nodded assent.

'Well, aren't you going to say sorry, at least?'

'Sorry.'

Her voice was flat. She sounded like a sulky child being made to apologize for a minor misdemeanour. I wanted to slap her.

'It's bad enough lying to me, using me for your own ends,' I continued, 'but what I really can't understand is how you could have done this to Gwydion. You can see how vulnerable he is.'

Arianrhod didn't reply.

'In fact, I actually hold you responsible for Gwydion's breakdown.' I was in full flow now. 'You've manipulated him, lied to me, and all to get at Evan.' I paused. 'But what I don't understand is why.' After my conversation with Gwydion I knew why, of course. But I wanted to hear her explanation. 'If you were so keen to put Evan behind bars, why didn't you inform the police twenty years ago? Why wait until now?'

'I'll tell you why.' Arianrhod spoke slowly and firmly. She seemed entirely unrepentant about what she'd done. 'Because recently I found out something about Evan. You know about this knighthood he was up for?'

I nodded.

'Well, I heard him talking about it on the phone to Rhiannon, his so-called PA. He didn't know I was listening. He told her he was planning to wait it out on the yacht until he got the knighthood, then divorce me. Set up home with her. Marry her. The day after the knighthood was going to come through, he'd begin proceedings.' She paused. 'I couldn't believe it. Cradle-snatcher. Bastard.' She seemed almost to be talking to herself. 'He's nearly old enough to be her grandfather. It's disgusting.'

She took another drag of her cigarette and looked at me, as if remembering that I was still there. 'This was the final straw, as far as I was concerned. Evan's always had his women, but the fact that he was going to set up home with this one ... she's pregnant, so I've heard. Doesn't know what she's letting herself in for, the little fool.'

She stopped for a moment, and a look of anguish suddenly came over her face, before vanishing just as suddenly.

'Anyway,' she went on, 'I'd always defended him before, tried to keep the marriage going. But there was no point any more. So I decided, at last, to spoil his plans. Do what I should have done many years ago, and report his crime to the police, instead of going on covering up for him.'

'But why didn't you just pick up the phone and report him? Why did you have to involve Gwydion in all this?'

'I needed to explain why I hadn't gone to the police before. Getting Gwydion to come to you and say that he had recovered a memory of the incident seemed more believable. Especially if you could act as an expert witness at the trial.' She lowered her voice, as if talking to herself. 'It was a good plan. If Gwydion hadn't screwed it up, it would have worked. But now...' Her voice trailed off.

My anger subsided a little. Arianrhod had used me, used Gwydion, to further her own ends, but I couldn't help sympathizing with her to some degree. Evan was a man apparently without shame or guilt – I knew that from personal experience. He took what he wanted, when he wanted. And now, as he was moving into his old age, he'd decided to set up house with a younger woman. Leave the wife he'd mistreated for so many years, the wife who had faithfully supported him through thick and thin, put up with his womanizing, covered up the scandal about Elsa Lindberg. It wasn't surprising that when he'd finally betrayed Arianrhod completely, she'd decided to take her revenge, put her husband in the dock, as a last act of defiance.

'Tell me, Arianrhod,' I said. 'What really happened to Elsa? What do you know? What does Gwydion know?'

Arianrhod laid her cigarette carefully in the ashtray, and began her story. I sensed she was choosing her words carefully.

'I remember it well. It was a beautiful day for sailing, but I didn't want Evan to take Gwydion out on the boat. He was only six, and he couldn't swim. It wasn't safe, and he hated going. But Evan insisted. I went out for the day, to take my mind off it, and when I got home that afternoon I found Gwydion alone in the house. Elsa wasn't there, and nor was Evan. Gwydion was in his room, lying on the bed, crying. Something had traumatized him, and I got him to tell me what it was. He said he'd seen his father kissing Elsa on deck, and then he'd felt seasick, so he'd gone to the cabin to lie down. While he was there he'd heard them fighting, so he'd come up and seen Evan pushing Elsa off the side of the boat. I managed to calm him down, and when Evan got home, later that evening, I asked him about it. He told me that Gwydion was lying, that there hadn't

311

been a fight. Elsa had just decided, of her own accord, to swim back to shore from the boat.'

She paused, as if casting her mind back, and then went on. 'Elsa didn't come home that night. When her body turned up on the beach the next day, Evan told me it was an accident, that she must have drowned as she tried to swim into the bay. He was distraught, or pretended to be. Then he admitted that the previous day he'd been trying to seduce her. Told me that if it was discovered that she'd been on the boat with him, his career would be ruined. Begged me to help him.' She sighed. 'So I did as he said, and when the police came, I backed up his story.'

'So it was Gwydion who told you that he'd seen Evan push Elsa in the water?'

'Yes.'

'You had no other evidence.'

'No.' Arianrhod looked puzzled. I could see she was wondering what I was getting at.

'He was only six. Didn't it ever occur to you that he'd made up the story? Out of anger towards his father, perhaps?'

'Children don't make up things like that.'

I tried a different tack. 'The thing is, I noticed, when Gwydion told me the story, he got one little detail wrong. He said that when he saw Evan and Elsa kissing, they were sitting by the wheel of the yacht.' I paused. 'I actually went down to Penarth and checked Evan's yacht, and I saw that it has a tiller, not a wheel.'

Arianrhod looked nonplussed for a moment. Then she recovered herself. 'Maybe he had it changed.'

'Why would he do that?'

'Oh, how should I know. I don't know anything about boats. I can't stand them.' She was irritated now. She picked up her cigarette and tried to take a drag, but it had gone out, so she put it back in the ashtray.

'And another thing. Elsa was a good swimmer.' I didn't say how I knew that. I didn't want to give away too much information. 'And it wasn't far into shore. How would she have drowned on the way back?'

Arianrhod shrugged. 'The currents out there are treacherous. And the tide has a way of coming in very fast in the bay. Once it's in, you can't get a foothold on the rocks. You're out of your depth.'

'Yes, but she could have climbed in on the jetty.'

'That can be difficult, too.' She paused for a moment. I could see she was thinking about something. Something she wasn't telling me.

She got up, as if having made a sudden decision.

'Come on,' she said. 'I'll take you down there and show you, if you like.'

21

Outside, a wind was blowing up. There was a faint rustling of trees as we walked over the lawns behind the house and into Arianrhod's seaside garden, bounded by its high walls. With winter coming on, it didn't look as pretty as it had done last time I'd visited. As we passed by, I noticed that she'd been neglecting it. She hadn't been deadheading the roses, the flowerbeds were full of dry brown stalks, and the vegetable patch had been left to moulder, untouched.

She opened the small wooden door set into the wall and led me out onto the clifftop path outside. We made our way carefully along the track, trying to avoid the mud, and stopped for a moment at the top of the steps to look at the view. There wasn't much to see that day. A thick mist had descended over the brown water, and the sky above was a leaden grey.

I peered down the slippery steps cut into the rock that led to the beach below. The tide was in, right up to the foot of the cliffs. I hadn't seen the bay like this before, the water completely covering the flat expanse of volcanic rock beneath. I shivered involuntarily, remembering the first time I'd come here and stood looking out to sea on the cliff edge, with Arianrhod; and the second, when I'd gone down the steps with Gwydion, to the beach far below.

Arianrhod noticed me eyeing the steps nervously.

'Come on. I'll lead.'

She began to walk down the steps, turning to wave me down after her. She didn't hold on to the handrail, balancing herself by holding her arms out on either side of her. I was more cautious. I grasped the rail, manoeuvred myself onto the steps, and then slowly, carefully, took each one, feeling its bumps and cracks with my foot before putting my full weight on it.

Arianrhod looked back and grinned. 'See you at the bottom.'

She walked, practically skipped, down the steps ahead of me. She seemed suddenly energized, carefree almost. I hadn't seen her move like that before. I wondered, fleetingly, whether it was the danger, the possibility of falling, that had excited her. But mostly I concentrated on my own slow progress down the steps, praying that I wouldn't trip and hurt myself. I'm not a daredevil, never have been; I know some people get a kick out of taking risks, but I don't – not the physical kind, anyway.

When I finally reached the bottom of the steps and walked out onto the jetty, Arianrhod was standing looking out to sea. She didn't turn round as I came level with her.

'It's quite deep out here, isn't it?' I said. 'When the tide comes in like this.'

'Mmm.' Arianrhod wasn't listening. She seemed distracted. 'Let's walk out to the end,' she said, still gazing out at the horizon. 'That's where Elsa would have swum in. I'll show you.'

I looked down at the boards on the jetty beneath my feet. I hadn't noticed it before, but some of them were missing. Others were soft with seawater.

'Is it safe? I mean, in all this wind?'

Arianrhod turned to look at me. I saw a glimmer of amusement in her eye that struck me as curious, in the circumstances.

She nodded, took my arm, and led me down to the end of the jetty. We stood there for a moment, the wind blowing in our faces, the water all around, making a peculiar slapping noise as it hit the wooden boards beneath our feet. I thought of the time Gwydion and I had kissed there. The sound of the sea hitting the decking had excited me then; now it just made me feel afraid.

I wished she would let go of my arm. I didn't feel comfortable with her holding it, but I felt it would be rude to withdraw it.

'Why wouldn't Elsa have been able to climb up here?' I said as we stood there, looking out to sea. I was almost speaking to myself. 'It would have been easy enough, wouldn't it? Unless...'

I felt Arianrhod's grip on my arm tighten.

'Unless there'd been someone standing here. Someone stopping her from–'

I don't know exactly what happened next. My arm was squeezed tight, and I felt a shock as a sudden jolt came from behind. Shock, and confusion.

'What...' I struggled to get away, but I'd been taken by surprise. Arianrhod was pushing me, pushing me hard, over the edge of the jetty.

I teetered for a moment, staring down at the thick brown water below. There was another jolt, this one harder, and then she let go of me. I felt myself falling, and as I hit the icy water a stinging pain rushed through my belly, my arms, my shoulders, my head, my back, my whole body.

My head went under and I found myself gasping for breath. When I came up again, I was only inches from the jetty, so I instinctively put out my hand and grasped on to one of the wooden boards, holding on to it for dear life.

Arianrhod was standing above me. The expression on her face had darkened to one of pure rage. It was only at that moment that I realized she was intent on stopping me from getting out.

I tried to grasp the jetty with my other hand and scramble onto it, but she stepped forward, lifted her foot and, quite deliberately, brought it down hard on my fingers.

I cried out in pain and let go. A wave came in, slapping me over the head, filling my mouth with water. As the water crashed over my head, I began to choke. There was an agonizing pain in my hand. But the wave passed, and I came up, so, once again, I swam towards the jetty.

When I reached it, I moved to put my hand out to grasp it, but hesitated. Instead, I stayed beside it, treading water, looking up at Arianrhod.

She bent down. For a split second I thought she was going to change her mind and pull me out, but instead she grinned at me.

'Now you know,' she said, raising her voice against the wind. 'That's what happened to Elsa. She drowned. And you're going to drown, too.'

I found it hard to believe what she was saying, but the look on her face terrified me.

'Please...' I whispered, but my voice was carried away by the wind. 'Let me...'

I edged my fingers onto the jetty.

She stood up, ready to bring her foot down on my fingers again. 'That'll teach you to screw my husband. You. Elsa. And all the others.'

I drew my hand away.

'But I didn't... I haven't...'

'Oh, maybe you haven't. Not yet. But you will sooner or later, won't you?' Her voice took on a

317

sneering tone. 'What line did he spin you, then? Don't tell me, he said he'd put you in a film. You're a bit old for that, I'd have thought.'

It was a shot in the dark, I felt sure. Arianrhod couldn't possibly have known about my meetings with Evan. Even if she had somehow got wind of them, I hadn't done what she was accusing me of. I started to protest, but then I realized, with a growing sense of shock, that even though she was clearly guessing, she wasn't far off the truth. I'd fallen for Evan's chat-up line – flattering my intelligence, as well as my looks – just like all the others. I'd behaved like a silly young girl, no different from poor Elsa with the Strindberg line. And about to meet the same fate.

Another wave hit my head and I went under again. This time it turned me over, so I was upside-down under the water. Or, rather, I didn't know which way up I was.

I told myself not to panic. Instead I held my breath, keeping my mouth closed, waiting until the wave had passed and I could right myself, come up for air. I could hear a voice in my head, my own voice. *This is ridiculous*, it was saying. *This can't be the way you're going to die. This is just water, cold water. You can swim out of it, climb up onto that jetty. You can't let some madwoman stop you.*

As the water swirled around my head, I could feel tiny stones and pebbles in it, filling my nose, my ears, my hair.

I kept holding my breath.

Then I heard another voice, this time a voice I didn't know, running through my head. *Yes, this is ridiculous*, it said. *But didn't you know? Death is ridiculous. Everybody's death.*

I began to flail about. I needed air. I needed to come up, but I didn't know which way was up.

This is your death, Jessica Mayhew. And it's going to be ridiculous. Utterly ridiculous, like everyone else's.

Nella, I thought. Rose. Bob.

Another wave hit me, and I felt my body crash into something hard. This is it, I realized.

I can't die now. They need me.

I put out my hands. It was a pole. An iron pole. The pole of the jetty. If I could just find the end of it...

My lungs were bursting. I felt my way up the pole, hoping it was the right way, but I didn't come any closer to the surface. It was no use, I realized. Sooner or later, water or no water, I was going to have to take a breath.

I was just about to take in a lungful of water when my head popped out of the sea.

I began to cry with relief, gasping for air. There was hope, after all. I was still in the sea, with no way out, but at least, for the moment, I could breathe...

I looked up at the jetty. My vision was blurred. Initially I thought I saw that it was empty, that there was no one there. But then I made out the figure of Arianrhod still standing there, towering above me.

I clung on to the pole of the jetty, determined not to let go.

She came towards me, ready to push me away from it. Under the water I wrapped my legs around the pole and let my body float away from it, so that she couldn't reach me. As she bent over, I saw the fury in her face.

I used my free arms to splash her with water as she leaned down. It was a feeble gesture on my part, but it enraged her.

'You've only got yourself to blame.' She hissed the words, brushing the water from her eyes. 'You knew perfectly well what you were up to. You'd no right to mess around with people like that. Flaunt yourself, take whatever you wanted, whenever you wanted. It just wasn't fair...'

She was looking at me as she spoke, but she seemed almost to be talking to herself, reciting an ancient litany of resentment.

'I'm only doing what I have to do,' she muttered under her breath. 'You bloody well deserved it. Sitting there with that nice, kind smile on your face, as if butter wouldn't melt.' Her voice began to rise. 'Silly little bitch. This is your own stupid fault, not mine...'

She sat down on the edge of the jetty and began to use her legs to kick me off the pole. As she did, one of her shoes dropped into the water beside me.

I picked it up and hurled it at her head. She ducked, and it missed. Once again, it was a feeble attempt at defiance, but it served to infuriate her further.

She took off her other shoe and threw it at me. It caught me full in the face and I felt a sharp pain across my forehead. I gasped, my mouth filled with water, and my legs uncurled from the pole. Another wave hit me, but this time, when my head went under, I managed to remain upright.

When the water cleared, I peeled off my jacket,

320

which was heavy with water, and looked up at the jetty. Somehow I kept hoping, each time I went down, that I'd come up and realize this was just a bad dream. But each time, Arianrhod was still there, her dark head outlined against the sky.

'Please, God,' I whispered to myself, 'help me.'

I could no longer feel my toes or my hands, and the aching cold was spreading from my head into my torso and limbs. If I didn't get out of the water soon, I knew, it would freeze me to death. It was only a matter of time.

I swam up to the jetty again, as close as I dared.

'You can't do this, you know,' I shouted. 'You'll go to prison...'

She wasn't listening. She probably couldn't hear, with the wind whistling in our ears. But I persevered all the same.

'I can explain what happened with Evan. Just let me come in. We can talk...'

She gazed out to sea, ignoring me.

I stayed out there, a safe distance away from the jetty, treading water, for what seemed like hours. I felt the cold begin to freeze my body, first my feet, then my legs, then my hands and arms.

It's just a matter of time, I told myself. But time was on her side, not mine.

It was then that I looked up, into the distance, and saw a tiny figure standing at the top of the steps of the cliff. I looked away. What if I'd imagined it, like some parched traveller dreaming up a mirage in the desert? But when I looked again, the figure was coming down the steps, towards the jetty. From the way it moved, it looked like a man.

I didn't cry out. The man was too far away to

hear me. And I didn't want to alert Arianrhod. I didn't know who it was, or whether he had come to help me, but I knew that, whatever happened, when he reached the jetty there was a chance I could scramble out and survive. Time was on my side once more.

So I stayed where I was, treading water. Three times the waves hit me, submerging me. Each time I came up, I feared that the man would be gone. But each time he was still there, coming nearer and nearer, until at last he was on the jetty.

I saw Arianrhod turn in surprise.

It was Gwydion.

When I saw him, my heart leapt. How or why, I wasn't sure, but I knew that he'd come to save me.

Before he reached the end of the jetty, Arianrhod ran towards him. I couldn't see clearly, but she seemed to fall into his arms. They seemed to be embracing. A sudden panic ran through me as I wondered whether I'd been wrong. Perhaps Gwydion hadn't come to my rescue after all. Perhaps he and Arianrhod were in this together. Perhaps he'd come to help her drown me. Or to gloat.

I began to cry. Not proper tears, but the kind of theatrical whine a child makes when it doesn't get what it wants. This was too much, I told myself. First, the promise of hope. And now...

I watched as the embrace turned to a struggle. I heard snatches of shouting, carried on the wind. Then Gwydion ran forward. He came to the end of the jetty and bent down, holding out his hand towards me.

I swam forward. By now my legs were completely numb. So I pulled my body along using my arms, until I reached the edge of the jetty.

As I did, Arianrhod came up behind Gwydion. She was screaming at him, pulling at his shoulder. But he ignored her cries, pushing her away.

I reached out my hand and caught his. I saw his look of shock as he registered the cut on my face.

'Leave her there, the whore.' Arianrhod was beside herself now, shrieking in his ear. 'She's been sniffing round your father, the bitch, like all the rest of them.'

I felt Gwydion start as she spoke the words. He looked straight into my eyes, and I looked back into his. He didn't ask me anything, and I didn't say anything, but I knew he knew that there was some truth in what she'd said.

He hesitated for a moment, but his grip on my hand didn't loosen.

If I'd had the presence of mind, I would have lied. Told him I'd never been anywhere near his father, anything to get out of that icy water. But I didn't. Instead, I cried out, 'Help me, Gwydion. Please, help me.'

He reached out his other hand towards me. I grasped it and, in one swift move, he pulled me out of the water.

Once he'd got me out on the jetty, he carried me in his arms, staggering slightly, and laid me down gently on the boards. My body felt like a dead weight. Water was streaming from my clothes. My head was spinning, and I wondered for a moment whether it was too late, whether I was now going to die.

Gwydion bent over me, holding me by the shoulders as I began to retch, dredging up the seawater from my lungs.

I hung my head, clutching it with my hands, hoping that the spinning would stop. But it went on. Then I started to shiver violently.

'We're going to have to get her back up to the house.' He spoke sharply to Arianrhod. 'Come on, give me a hand here.'

Arianrhod didn't reply.

Gwydion tried to pick me up, but I signalled to him to wait. I was feeling too sick to be moved. So instead, he took off his jacket and wrapped it around me.

I heard him get out his mobile phone and dial a number.

'Yes, and police,' he said, in response to someone on the other end of the line. Then he began to give them directions as to where we were.

I don't know what happened next. I seemed to drift in and out of consciousness, seeing nothing in front of my eyes but water, and rocks, and sea, and sky. I felt so sick and aching that I wanted to die, wanted to slip peacefully away into the blackness that was waiting to claim me.

Then I heard a distant roaring sound. I looked up, barely able to raise my head, and saw a great fat insect buzzing in the sky. It was still far away, but it was bearing down on us. As it came nearer, I realized, dimly, that it was a helicopter. And that it was coming to help us.

That was when I heard a cry, and then a splash. I looked over my shoulder and saw that Arianrhod had dived off the end of the jetty, and was swimming out to sea.

'Gwydion,' I said. My voice seemed to have disappeared somewhere into my chest, and all that came out was a croak. 'Do something.'

But Gwydion didn't move. Instead, he stayed beside me, shielding me from the wind, as the blades of the helicopter whirred above us, coming closer and closer down to land.

22

It doesn't take long to get used to being in hospital. I'd only been there a week, but already I was looking forward to my mid-morning cup of tea, fretting about what to tick on the menu for lunch, and being nosy about the other patients' visitors. I was becoming institutionalized, I realized. It was time I got out. There wasn't much wrong with me, and my lungs had cleared, but they weren't letting me go till I got my strength back. I was fine in bed, but when I got up, I was weak and shaky on my legs. And I was sleeping through large chunks of the day – though I could have done that better at home, I reflected, what with all the noise, and comings and goings, and constant interruptions of hospital life.

A nurse approached my bed. I closed my eyes, pretending to be asleep. I didn't want any more medication. I was getting fed up with going through the day, and the night, in a fog.

'Someone to see you,' she said. I assumed it

would be Bob, who'd been visiting me every day, usually with the girls in tow, but when I opened them, I saw Mari standing at the end of the bed.

'Hi,' I said. I waved towards a chair beside the bed. 'Take a pew.'

Mari came over and enveloped me in a hug.

'How are you, *cariad*? I wanted to come in before, but Bob said you weren't up to it.' She looked slightly put out.

'He's just fussing. I'm fine, really. I'll be out of here soon, I think.'

She sat down on the chair, fished in her bag and brought out a small box of chocolates, wrapped up in gold paper and yellow ribbon, with a yellow paper flower on the top.

'Oh.' I reached over and took the box. 'Thanks.'

'Artisan, darling,' she said, a note of self-mockery in her voice. 'Arm and a leg.'

I slipped the ribbon off the box, opened it, and took a chocolate. I couldn't be bothered to choose which one. Then I handed it to her.

She studied the guide carefully and chose her chocolate. It was a white one, with a tiny frosted rose on the top.

We sat in silence for a moment, sucking our chocolates. I was enjoying mine, although it was making me feel slightly queasy.

'So.' She tilted her head on one side as she spoke. I realized that, for once, she was choosing her words carefully, trying her best to be tactful. 'You've been in the wars, then, I hear.'

'Mmm.'

'Want to talk about it?'

'I suppose so.' I swallowed the last of my chocolate. 'I've been a bit of an idiot, to tell the truth. I didn't know Arianrhod Morgan was such a...' I hesitated for a moment, realizing that I didn't actually want to discuss all this. It brought back frightening memories, memories that gave me crazy dreams at night, nightmares about being blind and deaf and dumb, and floating upside-down in water, and watching my fingers falling off my hands, and being unable to breathe...

I stopped for a moment, unwilling to pursue the conversation. Mari offered me another chocolate, but I refused.

'What happened to her, anyway?' she asked, taking another one herself.

'She drowned. The police found...' I paused, unable to continue.

'The body?' Mari spoke in a low tone, registering my hesitation.

'It was washed up on the beach, the next cove round from the bay.' I paused. 'She couldn't have swum around there, the police said. It was too far. And the water was so cold, she'd probably have ... succumbed ... quite quickly.'

For some reason, I couldn't say the word 'died'. 'Succumbed' wasn't a bad alternative, though. Ernest Jones used it whenever one of his patients kicked the bucket as a result of his ministrations. One of Freud's friends 'succumbed' when he recommended extra-large doses of cocaine to buck him up. I'd never heard it used to describe drowning, but it was a useful euphemism in general, I thought. I might employ it more in future.

Mari sucked her chocolate pensively, drawing

in her cheeks. 'Well, thank God for that,' she said. 'Bloody psychopath. She could have...' She was about to say more, but checked herself, noticing the look on my face.

There was a short silence, and then she asked, 'What happens now?'

'Well, it's a question of picking up the pieces, I suppose.' I paused. 'All the charges against Evan Morgan have been dropped. And Bob's been in touch with the girl's mother, Solveig Lindberg, to tell her what happened. You see, when...' I petered out again, lost for words. 'When I was at the jetty with Arianrhod, she told me that she'd... Well, she confessed that Elsa's death was her fault.'

My voice shook a little as I spoke. Mari noticed and controlled her curiosity, sensing that I wasn't ready to go into details.

'How did the girl's mother take the news?' she asked, changing the subject.

'Solveig? She was very emotional, apparently. But it's laid the whole thing to rest for her. After all these years.'

'Have you spoken to her?'

'Not yet. I will do, though. And Bob says she's going to come over and visit when I get out.'

Mari reached over and squeezed my hand.

'Well, at least something good has come out of all this, then,' she said. 'And Gwydion? Bob said he'd come to your rescue at the beach.'

I hesitated a moment. 'Yes. He must have known I'd go down to see Arianrhod, after what he'd told me. And that she wouldn't ... respond very well. He was devoted to her, but I suppose he realized there are limits.' I paused. 'He'd grown quite attached to me, you see.'

There was a short silence, and I wondered whether Mari had guessed there'd been something between us.

'How's he coping now?' she said, eventually.

I didn't know a great deal about Gwydion's state of mind. For obvious reasons, I'd avoided bringing up the subject with Bob. I'd also avoided the subject of Evan, for similar reasons. But Bob was helping Evan in the aftermath of the case, and had reported that Evan had been very attentive towards Gwydion after his mother's death. As a result, Gwydion was making a remarkable recovery.

'Pretty well, I think, considering,' I replied. 'He's out of The Grange, so I hear. And Evan's been coaching him for a new TV part he's got coming up. There's been a bit of a rapprochement there, I think.'

I smiled, and Mari smiled back. Then I sighed and laid my head back on the pillow, suddenly tired.

'There are so many bits to this puzzle,' I said. 'The trouble is, I can't think straight at the moment.'

'You don't need to, Jess.' Mari's voice was unusually gentle. 'Everything's fine. Just concentrate on getting well.'

There was another lull in the conversation. I was having trouble keeping my eyes open, but I did my best to hide it. 'Another chocolate?'

Mari must have noticed my fatigue. 'No, no. They're for you. And anyway, I'd better be going.' She got up. 'We can talk more another time.'

I would have liked her to stay longer, but I felt

too weak to argue. So she kissed me goodbye, and I watched as she walked out of the room, giving me an airy wave as she left.

It was nice of her to stop by, I thought. I closed my eyes and began to drift into sleep.

Moments later, I opened them to find Bob standing over me.

I glanced at the clock. Two hours had passed. This was always happening, it seemed. I had no recollection of being asleep, of dreaming, of time going by. Great chunks of the day went missing, got lost. It was getting better, day by day – but it was a slow process. I was impatient to get back my strength, and beginning to wonder if I ever would.

He leaned down and kissed me on the cheek. Then he sat down on the bed.

'You'd better not let the nurses see you doing that,' I said.

'Why not?'

'Germs.'

'Oh, for God's sake.' He reached over and took my hand. 'You're my wife, aren't you. I can do what I like with you.'

I laughed, and so did he.

We'd made up our quarrel, more or less. We hadn't discussed the details – that was still to come – but he'd said that once I got out of hospital he wanted us to start afresh. The whole episode had made him realize how much he loved me, how much he wanted our marriage to work. To be honest, I wasn't altogether sure that I felt the same, though I didn't say so; I was waiting until my brain began to function more normally before making any decisions.

In actual fact I was feeling somewhat stunned at the repercussions of Bob's brief fling a while back. Because I'd unconsciously projected my anger at Bob onto Evan, as the cheating husband, I'd failed to pick up on the fact that Arianrhod was trying to frame Evan for murder, let alone that she was the murderer herself. As a result, I'd very nearly lost my life. I'd also come close to playing a part in a potential miscarriage of justice, by giving evidence at Evan Morgan's hearing. And all because I'd taken my eye off the ball, let Bob's passing indiscretion cloud my judgement.

I'm not a moralist where marital infidelity is concerned. I've heard enough lurid stories about it in my consulting rooms to understand that human beings are not very good at monogamy, and mostly struggle to abide by what some would see as an oppressive cultural norm. I'm generally sympathetic, not only to those who are cheated, but to those who do the cheating, too; how people manage, or fail to manage, their sexual drives is a subject of enormous complexity and contradiction, as Freud pointed out all those years ago; and nothing much has changed since his day. Indeed, I'm always puzzled by my younger clients, who may talk about sex in an offhand, vulgar way, yet are often very judgemental when it comes to the issue of infidelity in a long-term relationship.

So it was all the more surprising that, when the problem came into my own life, I should have reacted the way I did. And, worse, been so blind to what I was doing. I should, at least, have talked the situation over with a colleague, contacted my supervisor, got some perspective on what I was doing. Instead, I carried on regardless, thinking I was managing my feelings of jealousy and anger in an admirably calm, sensible manner. Sometimes I think psychotherapists have less, rather than more, insight into their own behaviour than other people; we get cocky, we think we're one step ahead, that we know our own weaknesses, and can manage them; and that's fatal. That's the biggest self-delusion of all. I'd learned something from my ordeal, the hard way. In future, I'd have to be more careful. More humble...

Which still didn't answer the question: what about me and Bob? His brief fling had been far from 'insignificant', as he'd described it. It had shaken up both our lives, in ways that neither of us could have foreseen. Did it matter now? Well, I'd got my own back, or at least had the chance to, with Gwydion. If Mari's view of marriage as a power struggle was right – and, after witnessing what had happened in the Morgan family I was beginning to agree with her assessment – some equilibrium had been achieved. But did I trust Bob now? Yes, more or less. His instincts about Evan had been right, mine had been wrong. I still respected him, admired him. Loved him. But not, perhaps, in the simple, unquestioning way that I used to...

'Jess, are you OK?' Bob was speaking to me.

I realized I'd drifted off again, lost in my own thoughts.

'How are the girls?' I said, making an effort to connect with him again.

'Fine. They made you some choc-chip cookies. Here.' Bob waved towards a plastic container by the television table.

'How sweet of them. I'll have one later, with my tea.' I paused. 'What about what's his name?'

Bob looked puzzled.

'You know. Nella's boyfriend.'

'Oh, Gareth. Well, he appeared again today. They seem to be spending a lot of time together. Playing the guitar and singing and stuff.' He paused. 'He seems like a decent enough chap.'

He shrugged, and I realized he'd come round to Nella's new suitor.

'And Rose? What's she up to?'

'She's fine. She's decided she wants a companion for Miffy.'

'Who?'

'The rabbit.'

'Oh.'

I felt distressed that I'd forgotten the name of the rabbit, as well as Nella's boyfriend.

'Don't worry,' he said, as if reading my thoughts. 'We're all managing fine for the time being. But we need you back soon, Jess. I need you.' A look of anguish came over his face. 'I never realized how much, until now.'

I reached out and took his hand, surprised. Bob's not usually a one for passionate declarations. He seemed surprised too, and a little embarrassed.

'Oh,' he said, letting go of my hand. 'I nearly forgot. Something came for you today, in the post.'

He brought out a small package and handed it over. I looked at the printed label on the front. It had come from an Internet site selling antique jewellery, direct to my address. It was carefully

333

wrapped, so it took a while to open. In fact half-way through I gave up, and Bob had to finish the job for me.

'Look,' he said, handing me a small box. There was no greeting card with it. I lifted the lid and inside, nestled in tissue paper, was a necklace. I held it up.

It was a slim silver chain dotted with tiny grey gemstones. On the end of it was an antique pendant made of mother-of-pearl. The pendant was round and exquisitely carved, with the scene of an old-fashioned ship on a wavy sea, each billowing sail, the crest of each wave, intricately worked into the smooth shell.

I looked more closely, holding the pendant up to the light. The mother-of-pearl was streaked and translucent, like fog bathing the ship in an eerie glow, but in the middle of it, over the mast, the sun shone from behind a carved cloud, through four tiny holes.

It was then I realized what it was.

I leaned my head forward and Bob put the pendant around my neck.

'It's pretty,' he said. 'Who's it from?'

'Oh. Just an ex-client of mine,' I replied. I looked down and saw the little ship gleam in the light. 'A man who used to be scared of buttons.'

This Large Print Book for the partially sighted, who cannot read normal print, is published under the auspices of

THE ULVERSCROFT FOUNDATION

THE ULVERSCROFT FOUNDATION

... we hope that you have enjoyed this Large Print Book. Please think for a moment about those people who have worse eyesight problems than you ... and are unable to even read or enjoy Large Print, without great difficulty.

You can help them by sending a donation, large or small to:

**The Ulverscroft Foundation,
1, The Green, Bradgate Road,
Anstey, Leicestershire, LE7 7FU,
England.**
or request a copy of our brochure for more details.

The Foundation will use all your help to assist those people who are handicapped by various sight problems and need special attention.

Thank you very much for your help.